CRITICS PRAISE MELANIE JACKSON!

"Melanie Jackson is an author to watch!"
—Compuserve Romance Reviews

"An unusual romance for those with a yen for something different."
—*Romantic Times* on *Dominion*

"I recommend this as a very strong romance, with time travel, history and magic."
—*All About Romance* on *Night Visitor*

"Intriguing . . . Ms. Jackson's descriptions of the Cornish countryside were downright seductive."
—*The Romance Reader* on *Amarantha*

"Melanie Jackson paints a well-defined picture of 18th-century England. . . . *Manon* is an intriguing and pleasant tale."
—*Romantic Times*

A NIGHT VISITOR

The ancient door's bolts were rusted; it took a bit of effort to unlatch and open, so she had a moment to take in her visitor through the growing crack before he strode over the sill on long, lithe legs, a fair stretch of which showed beneath his rumpled kilt.

"*De tha thu 'deanamh?*" the man demanded of her, his bottomless brown eyes framed in the longest, silkiest lashes she had ever seen.

"What?"

"Ye'd be one of the sassanach women then," he said, his deep voice shifting into heavily accented English that resembled the local Scots' dialect. He stared at her palm for several seconds, clearly debating whether to take it.

"Aye, yer the one. There's nae point in denyin' it. I'll dae my duty by ye, lass, and lay wi' ye if that's what ye wish. But I want my skin back first."

THE
SELKIE

MELANIE JACKSON

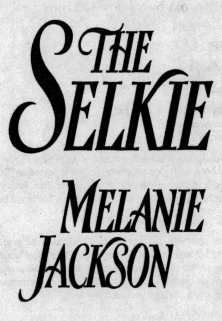

LOVE SPELL NEW YORK CITY

For the scribblus romanticus:
Lynsay and Susan and Lisa and Susan and Christine and Susan.

LOVE SPELL®

February 2003

Published by

Dorchester Publishing Co., Inc.
276 Fifth Avenue
New York, NY 10001

ISBN 0-505-52531-3

The name "Love Spell" and its logo are trademarks of Dorchester Publishing Co., Inc.

Printed in the United States of America.

"O, cradle row, and cradle go,
and sleep well, my bairn within;
I ken not who thy father is,
nor yet the land he dwells within."

And up then spake the gray selkie
when he woke her from her sleep,
"I'll tell ye where thy bairn's father is:
he's sittin' close by thy bed feet."

"I pray, come tell to me thy name,
Oh, tell me where does thy dwelling be?"
My name it is good, Sule Skerry,
And I earn my living on the sea.

"For I am a man upon the land;
but I am a selkie on the sea,
and when I'm far frae ev'ry strand,
my home is in Sule Skerry.

"Now foster well my wee young son,
aye for a twelve-month and a day,
and when that twelve-month's fairly gone,
I'll come and pay the nurse's fee."

And with that weary twelve-month gone,
he's come tae pay the nurse's fee;
he had a coffer fu' o' gold,
and another fu' o' the white money.

"And now thou will pay a hunter good,
and a right fine hunter I'm sure he'll be;
and the first shot that e'er he shoots
will kill both my young son and me."
—from *The Great Selkie of Sule Skerry*

Prologue

The water was cold and choppy, with a heavy tide starting to run. The sea had her moods, so she did, but they were no worry to a man who understood them. Ian wasn't concerned with the thick dark or the strong tide. He had a deep keel on his boat, and a good sail as well as oars. It would take a full gale, or a whale, to overturn him.

He helped himself to another modest dram of whiskey, shuddering with pleasure as it went down. The fiery peat always tasted best when drunk at sea on a cold wintry day. Or night. He'd probably had a bit more of the drink than he should have, but it was difficult to maintain a rosy glow on a windy night in the northern isles. And he needed to stop the violent shivering or he couldn't man the oars, could he? And he needed the bloody oars to hold his place in the water.

At last! Something was glimmering down there in the inky sea. Ian quickly shipped the oars and leaned over the gunwale, hand extended.

The first time he'd seen her he'd thought she was a giant seaworm come to attack him. But he couldn't have been more wrong. Her name was Syr. She was a finwoman and she was unbelievably bonnie. Her name was a bit heathenish, but after they were married he'd call her Sarah after his grandmother. His father would like that.

Ian smiled his welcome with blue-tinged lips and plunged his hand into the sea. But the face that rose out of the water was not his beloved's. It was dark and saturnine, and half-hidden in a tangle of wild black hair. It also had something very wrong with its mouth and jaws, which seemed to have splinters of jagged bone embedded therein.

Finman!

Ian jerked back and gave a small gasp, which turned into a yell as the black thing crawled into the boat after him. It knelt over Ian's prone and paralyzed body, and with what might have been a laugh it grabbed the gunwales with impossibly long arms and tipped them both into the sea.

The one sometimes called Ruairidh O'Uruisg came up onto the land and clambered up on the stone above the tide's highest reach. It was the ninth day, so he could easily leave his sub-aqueous home and walk upon the land as a man with no fear of lunar interference. He could remain here for a year and a day, or for however long he did not eat of land salt or run afoul of the tidal moon.

He did not plan on this being a long visit, though his extended pilgrimage ashore would come on May Day, as it traditionally did for his people; after Beltane, when the door to their oceanic abode would be opened to the world and the young men of his kind would go forth to find mates. His father said that he and his brother were ready to travel far inland and begin this most important of searches now, but Ruairidh preferred to honor tradition and wait. Anyway, being on land was uncomfortable for him. He would begin the annual search for a mate next Beltane eve, just as he had always done. It didn't seem wise to break with tradition in a time when the People were disappearing.

For they *were* disappearing. One clan at a time, they were dying out; first the women, then the men. The People of Avocamor would emerge after the Season in Inundation, and word would come that another clan was gone. It was not surprising; with no females of their own they were left with problematic unions with human women, which were unproductive as often as not. And those human females that had babes had to have their children taken from them and brought to the sea or else they would die when the change came upon them.

Carefully, Ruairidh blew a straight line in his fur from chest to navel and then slipped out of his skin. He laid it carefully aside and then, opening a bladder bag, took up the somewhat wet clothing he had brought with him and set about shaking it out. The dripping plaid was not a garment he cared for; it smelled of sheep instead of proper fur, and it was confoundedly heavy when wet. Which was often, as it always seemed to rain when he was ashore. Still, he could not walk the land of men naked in the light of day, so the covering was necessary.

He was bound for the home of one John of Taigh an Crot Callow. The old man had apparently forgotten his ancestor's blood vow, taken after a father and two sons were spared drowning one stormy night when their boat overturned in the firth. The vow was that the fisherman, and all of his children and the children's children who would live because of this act of mercy, would each swear on their eleventh birthday that they would forever refrain from hunting the People, or making a living from trading in their skins.

4

For four hundred seasons, a hundred years, the pact had held.

But now something had happened. Though he had sworn the oath himself, John had attempted to kidnap a selkie pup the week before, possibly to hold it for ransom, or mayhap so that he could steal its skin. The young male had been injured almost unto death before he escaped.

The People had striven to be sympathetic and resisted acting in haste. The poor man had gone quite mad with the recent death of his son, often standing at the sea's edge, calling for the People to let his son's soul free that it might go on to heaven. But, of course, that was impossible; the People did not have the boy's soul.

Perhaps they had erred in returning John's son's body to land after the storm had taken him. It had seemed a kindness at the time; but many humans still believed that a drowned man who died with a red nose was the victim of water spirits, like the sorcerous finmen of the north, who were supposed to be able to suck a soul out of a man's body and then keep it forever in a state of torment under an inverted urn inside a secret undersea cave.

It was rather annoying when humans confused the People with Others and their legends became mixed. Selkies had never taken a man's soul. They would not know how. They were not

5

nixies or kelpies or even of the Tylwyth Teg. They were simply the People of the Firth. And their only tie to the finmen was their dependence on the sea.

Of course, the selkies' only link to humankind was the land pilgrimage to find mates. This annual event was necessary for survival, for the People had no daughters, no women of their own now. That was the fault of the humans who, fearing to lose the daughters and sisters, hid the blessed women—the *NicnanRon*—or killed them outright, claiming they were vessels for demons.

Once they had had them. But no more. They were not even able to replenish their own women. Daughters born of MacNicol females bred true *NicnanRon,* females of the selkie kind who could live in the sea. But there had not been a MacNicol birth for more than a century. Not since the time the People had saved the fishermen of Taigh an Crot Callow. The clan of MacNicol was extinct in this territory, and other human women of childbearing years had likewise grown scarce. Selkie births were fewer every decade, though the recent human war might have made more willing women available through widowhood.

Some of the People believed that the recent scarcity of females was a judgment against them because they had interfered in the affairs of hu-

6

mankind and allowed the fisherman and his sons to live. Their act had proven the selkies' existence, and not being able to stay silent on the miracle of their deliverance, the human fisherman had told others, and the selkie persecution had begun—the hunting of seals in other places and the hiding away of the women.

Ruairidh shook his head, trying to clear his thoughts of this recurring concern. Being on land was always difficult at first. He felt disoriented and ungainly, and wished he could spare himself a day to practice walking and speaking the difficult human speech.

However, there was no time for him to acclimatize. He was an emissary and soldier from Avocamor. Whatever the old man's intentions—kidnapping or murder—old John had to be reasoned with before he did irreparable harm and broke the truce. Man and Selkie had lived in harmony for a hundred years on this small stretch of coast. The People did not want to fracture the peace, but they would not tolerate a human making war upon their precious young, for it amounted to genocide.

Ruairidh's task was to stop this—in whatever manner and by whatever means were necessary.

Chapter One

Scotland 1929

It was spring. In London the park benches were all occupied by lovers, holding hands and gazing into each other's eyes or at the glorious moon. Those that were temporarily without mates wandered the well-groomed paths, staring wistfully at the soft and fragrant flowers. Or they went for rides in the country in their motorcars. Or they meandered down glittering night streets, thronged with well-heeled theatergoers. But they all looked at the moon.

Hexy Garrow had known that world, once upon a romantic time. . . .

8

A single tear traced down her cheek and splashed the stone upon which she sat.

But where was *she* this year during the season of lovers? Sitting all alone on a cold rock in an unelectrified part of Scotland, staring at a sullen sea as the sun set into it. The only thing vaguely romantic about the scene was the distant and haunting tune someone was playing on a pennywhistle.

If her brother could see her now, he would grin and tease: *no successful siren she* . . .

Of course, Rory Patrick was gone now, lost somewhere in the very sea she was looking at while questing after legends he hoped would bring great innovations of treatment to medical science. He would never say anything to her again, not even if she could somehow swim down to where his bones lay. . . .

She had half an urge to do that. As children she and Rory Patrick had been drawn to the sea with an almost unnatural attraction. They had wanted to wade right out into the waves and see what treasures were beneath them: sunken ships, lost cities, pirates' gold. She'd had no fear of sea beasts or tides then, and neither had he.

But that had changed. Now she was afraid. And alone.

Hexy shook herself, refusing to give in completely to melancholy. She might have what her

brother called *allergies,* a sort of catarrhal afflic-
tion that made her eyes tear against her will,
but she would not weep real tears for things
past. So her family was gone—many in Europe
were in the same situation. War did that to people. And perhaps the loss was worth it, if they
were right and this had been truly "the war to
end all wars."

The fact was, she should not be sitting anywhere. She had been sent down by Jillian Foxworthy to find the misplaced fur coat of the
woman who insisted it was necessary for her
comfort even though she was headed for Italy,
where it would be too warm for sable. Jillian was
a kind enough employer, but flighty, and sometimes irrational and demanding enough to
make Hexy wish for escape. This was one of
those times. Scotland always irritated Jillian's
nerves and made her pettish and superstitious.
She strove mightily to remain sensitive to the
feeling of those around her, but it went against
her nature when she was in the north, and she
lost the battle of manners more often than not.
Jillian's shrill voice could drill holes in steel.

Hexy sighed and sank a pretty chin onto her
fist. A second irritating tear fell from her reddened eyes and her nose began to itch, tickled
by phantom smells. Her allergies were annoying, but she was not yet ready to abandon her
melancholy thoughts and return to Fintry. The

loss of another beau deserved at least an hour of mourning.

One had to be reasonable and not exaggerate the attachment, she told herself. London was not just the home of poets and courtly lovers; it had its share of romantic pretenders who looked lovely but were secretly full of selfish evasions and cynical practicality. When reality came up against romanticism, those poseurs were willing to choose an attractive bank account over an attractive face. The criterion of wealth was one of three impediments that James Wentworthy IV had held against her.

Her American citizenship was another. So the U.S. Senate had refused to ratify the Versailles Peace Treaty, and America had failed to join the League of Nations in a timely manner; was that really *her* fault?

Apparently so. Certainly, James had believed it to be. Or he decided that the evil of these two things in combination was somehow greater than the mere sum of their parts would suggest. And since she had inspired only bridled passion in his breast, he was now pursuing a wealthy English girl who did not work for her bread.

Probably the new girl had personally signed the peace treaty as well.

His third complaint against Hexy had been her name. Saddled with the ridiculous family name of Hesiod, she had gone by Hexy since childhood. Neither name had suited James. He had demanded that she change her name to Helen and had introduced her to everyone by that moniker.

And the last problem—the *crux criticorum,* he had informed her—were her humble origins. Those were not corrigible. Her rudimentary knowledge of the upper-class English mind should have been sufficient to warn her of the impending doom of this relationship, but somehow she had managed to delude herself about the odds of their survival, and actually had felt something for Mr. Fourth.

Hexy sneezed violently, and two more hot tears tracked down her face.

Relationships, she decided, were senselessly complicated when one side was dealing in emotional currency and the other side was dealing in . . . well, *currency.* Frankly, she was baffled—and more than a little disgusted—by the modern transactions of man and maid. It used to be that a man worked to see a bit of a girl's leg or bosom. Now he spent his time trying to see a girl's bank account and her family's politics.

Hexy smiled and suddenly slightly misquoted her favorite poet, Heine: "Ordinarily she is insane, but she has lucid moments when she is only stupid."

Times were changing now that the war was

done, and so were standards. That was progress. The bad thing about changing standards was that suddenly there were too many of them about, and one never knew by which set another person might be playing. And many people changed them as convenience dictated. And when standards changed, sometimes a true diamond was overlooked in carelessness just because it didn't come in the right velvet-wrapped package.

But the positive side of her era's ever-changing morality, she reminded herself in an effort to be fair, was that she was also presumably free to choose whatever moral system she favored at any given moment, and the devil take the other party and their feelings!

Hexy said a bad word. Another pair of stinging tears escaped her enflamed eyelids, urging her to be aware of her surroundings, which included vast stands of cotton grass and some stunted yews that spewed yellow pollen into the wind.

"Stop maundering," she ordered herself. "So you've a distaste for modern morals and find them indigestible. It isn't as though your heart is broken. You haven't been *defeated* by this defection. You are merely adding to your list of known stratagems that don't work. Someday this knowledge of how *not* to attract men will prove useful. Perhaps you will grow a mustache and become a poetess, and speak to the liberation of women from the bonds of love. You will have both fame and fortune then, and a whole string of lovers."

The tide, slapping against her rocky perch, sighed over her petty worries and improbable ambition.

"Thank you," she answered it politely. "It is kind of you to take an interest in my dreams."

And they *were* merely dreams. She hadn't even a sound notion of what men over here wanted in a face or figure, let alone a personality. Jillian Foxworthy was blond, had a peaches-and-cream face and an exuberant bust that defied any restraint, a nipped-in waist, and *haunches*. She was, according to the mode of the day, most unfashionable. But men seemed to love her. They raced after her like an iron horse held to a narrow track, their usual built-in emotional brakes apparently disabled by her aura.

Hexy looked down. She herself was auburn-haired, at last look that morning, green eyed, and built along slightly less belligerent lines. Except for her slightly pointed ears and the faint childhood scars between her fingers, she was exactly what the fashions called for. Yet men seemed to look right past her. At least they did when Jillian was around. And no one had yet claimed to be driven beyond all control by either her face or body.

"And what are you describing?" she asked herself, blotting her eyes but missing a seventh tear, which joined the others on her rock to complete a perfect damp circle. "Are you talking about love, or a locomotive—Oh damn it! I am talking to myself again. I may as well be a spinster, for I seem to act like one so much of the time."

The sea sighed once more. This time a little more loudly. The strange piping had also ceased. She was truly alone. It was just she and the teasing ocean that she couldn't seem to make peace with but never found a way to move away from.

"Well, whatever the male population's opinion, I am quite indispensable around here, at least for today. That is *quod erat demonstrandum. I mean, QED! It wouldn't do for anyone to suspect that you have a brain or education." Hexy mimicked Miss Flattery from the employment office: "*Advanced education is unbecoming in a woman and completely inexcusable in a concomitant. Even a well-paid one. It is enough that you speak well and present a neat appearance. Do not rise above your station.*"

This was not a sentiment that sat well in an American girl's ears.

The sea's next sigh was a clear warning that,

though sympathetic, her seat was about to be overtaken by an anxious moon-driven tide.

"You are completely correct. It is time and past for me to be getting back to the castle. Jillian will have out a search party to look for me if I'm not back by dark. And then the villagers would start telling stories about me being carried off by mermen." Hexy stood up and sneezed again. She reached into her pocket for a handkerchief and dabbed at her nose. As an afterthought, she reached down and scooped up a small stone to toss at the sea. It was a ritual that her grandfather had taught her and Rory Patrick, and one which survived here among the locals. For some reason, casting stones at the ocean was supposed to keep sea monsters away. She hadn't thought about it in years, but Jillian's vague, half-amused warnings about skulking males hiding on the beach must have brought it back to mind. Really, Jillian's late husband had done a wonderful job of filling her head with ridiculous stories of sea folk who seduced women, even Hexy herself was half-beginning to believe them!

"Though perhaps I am being hasty in driving any male away. Heaven knows that I have had no luck in finding an earth-bound sort that I can love," she muttered. Then she cast the stone.

Ritual seen to, Hexy murmured: "Now, where

might Jillian have left that wretched coat? She said that she was sitting up on a tall, brown rock and watching a seal. Watching a seal—Ha! More like watching some handsome fisherman."

Hexy turned about slowly and said another bad word. There were any number of tall, brown rocks to choose from, and as they were taller than she was, she would be obliged to clamber up all of them until she found the blasted coat.

"Damnation."

She might be invaluable, but she was still an employee. Hexy selected a boulder and began looking for handholds.

Hexy stood in her damp shoes a short time later, the missing coat draped over her arm. As eager as she was to change, she still stood in Fintry's hall looking at the soot-laden ceiling above its smoldering fireplace and shaking her head.

It was hard to imagine, but this relic of the Dark Ages was to be her home for the next several months. The thought was lowering. A prison couldn't be more bleak.

She turned to examine the entire chamber. The one wall had been most insensibly paneled floor to ceiling in rich carved wood imported from Africa, which gleamed beautifully for the lower six feet. The rest was an ashen gray that quite matched the rest of the stone of the other three walls.

Fintry was old, a relic from the days when Scotland still needed defensive fortifications. Jillian hardly ever visited it, except in summer months, when the drafts were not too terribly chilly and the weather not too hostile, and even then she stayed only for limited periods of time. Life here was not comfortable. The gas had never been laid on, and no one beyond the village had electricity. She probably would have rid herself of the place if she could have found a buyer, but none had yet offered themselves to the lovely but impoverished widow.

And, it had to be admitted, there was a certain cachet—especially among wealthy Americans, without whose backing her career would end—to mentioning that one was popping up to one's castle for a fortnight. It made an impression on naive foreigners who had never had to care for a moldering ruin, and lent Jillian an air of breeding that other actresses did not have.

Ah well, the place would be getting a spot of titivation now. Miss Foxworthy had found one of P. T. Barnum's favorite people and convinced him to cough up the money needed for some of Fintry's more pressing renovations.

And lucky Hexy; she was getting the fun of

18

staying in Scotland to oversee the renovations instead of going to sunny Italy, where she might collect more material on how *not* to attract decent men.

"I should have enjoyed being seduced and rejected by a dark, foreign man. I believe that I am finally ready for a truly exotic lover," she told the sullen fireplace, and gave a last small sneeze. Her violent allergic reaction was thankfully fading now that she was again indoors.

As was to be expected, when Hexy looked most ragged, the lovely Jillian came tripping downstairs, her stacked heels clattering loudly on the naked stone treads. Jillian changed shoes several times a day. She had a voracious appetite for all clothing, but especially footwear. She was, in fact, a shoe glutton.

Hexy went to meet her employer, her moss-stained palms tucked into Jillian's fur's delightful folds.

"Darling! You found it! How clever of you. I don't know how I manage to lose things! Was it on the rock, like I said?"

"It was on a rock," Hexy admitted, eyeing Jillian's ensemble. "You are going out."

"But of course, darling! You know this pile is just too dreary at night. Donny and I are going to dash over to the hotel and have a few gin and tonics and soak up some light and what passes for music around here."

Jillian was wearing a stunning black-and-gold-sequined cloche and a black satin flapper coat covered in two-tone gold fringe and embroidered in gaudy Deco designs. Beneath it was an eye-popping gown of gold lamé and black velvet equally encrusted with bead and fringe. The whole combination looked lovely by candlelight but was rather loud in anything brighter.

It was one of Hexy's least favorite outfits in Jillian's collection; but then, she did not care for many of Beer's dresses, which Jillian adored.

Little as she cared for the dress, Hexy liked its purchaser even less. Donny, known to the rest of the world as Donald Mitchell Healey, wasn't a bad sort, but he was egotistical and obsessed with things mechanical, and he tended to bore on about his specially designed motorcar, which had just won him some RAC race. He also tended to go about in the evening in tuxedos with silk shirts and shoes with high gloss.

Scotland, especially so soon after the war, did not run too much toward fashion exotica. This was not a wealthy place, and Jillian and Donny were examples of the tasteless but fascinating rara avis that sometimes visited there.

Donny had another flaw. He seemed incapable of remembering Hexy's name, preferring to call her Hussy, a quip he found uproariously, and apparently endlessly, funny.

Before Donny's time, the one in the driver's seat had been William Morris, of MG Special four-seater Sports fame, the car that had taken first the racing world—and then Jillian—by storm. Jillian liked men who built automobiles, probably because they lent them to her. Until they actually saw her driving. After that, they always offered a chauffeur along with the automobile.

Hexy had rather liked William, though she'd found his new lower-chassis cars to be alarming to ride in. It was a pity he hadn't been able to see his way clear to putting up enough funds to keep Jillian, her new show, and Fintry all in the style to which they were accustomed; but, selfishly, he had wanted to spend most of his money on developing his automobiles.

"Well, I'll just go and pack your coat, shall I?" Unable to stop herself, Hexy gave the fur a small caress.

"You might slip on that yummy black chiffon gown and come with us," Jillian suggested. And then, with a closer look, she added with masterful understatement: "After you powder your nose a bit. I think you've had a bit too much sun and wind. You—you didn't run into anyone *unpleasant*, did you?"

Hexy shook her head, almost smiling at Jillian's nervous question. "Didn't see a soul, with fins or without. And no, thank you. You and Donny have a grand time."

Hexy didn't tell the relieved-looking Jillian, but she didn't plan on wearing that black dress ever again. It had been the black chiffon gown that had gotten her into trouble with James. It didn't look like something that would belong to a working girl, and she didn't want any more mistakes being made about who and what she was.

"You're certain? Things are so dull here at night."

"Absolutely certain. There isn't much room in Donny's auto, and I want to make sure that you are all packed up and ready to go when you leave tomorrow morning. You know that Donny gets impatient when he's kept waiting."

"Dear Donny." Jillian's tone wasn't as caressing at it might have been. "Well . . . as you like, darling. It is grand of you to give up your evening to see to my things. Marthe is good about packing, you know, but she doesn't have your touch."

Or patience. She needn't have, as her job was secure. Getting anyone to work at Fintry now that the MacKenzie owner was dead, even with the depressed economy, was a Herculean task. There were too many wild stories about the castle being haunted. What few servants there were at Fintry got away with everything up to bloody murder.

"Have a good time. I'll see you later this evening," Hexy said, picking up one of the oil lamps on the downstairs whatnot and turning up its flame.

"Do you think it will rain? Should I take my fur?" Jillian asked, peering over her shoulder at her dainty slippers in a vain attempt to see if the seams in her stockings were straight.

They were. Her stockings were always perfect.

"It is April in Scotland," Hexy reminded her. "The odds of rain are about fifty percent. But your fur doesn't go with that outfit."

And she didn't want to let it go. It would be wrong for Jillian to wear the coat right now. Hexy needed to keep it with her.

Jillian sighed.

"You are probably right. It will make Donny cross, but he'll simply have to put the hat on the car."

"The *top*," Hexy corrected. "And I am sure that he will have done so. He was quite upset at having his upholstery soaked last week."

"He was, wasn't he? Men are so temperamental. Well, good night, darling. Don't stay up too late fussing with the luggage," Jillian instructed, magnanimous since she was going out.

Hexy sank her fingers into the fur coat.

"I won't. Good night."

23

She picked up the lamp and hurried upstairs. It was suddenly imperative that she take the coat away from Jillian before she changed her mind and decided to wear it. It was wrong that such a coat should belong to someone like Jillian Foxworthy. It needed to be with someone who would guard it and care for it—and love it as it was meant to be loved.

Someone like you?

"Yes. Why not me?" she muttered.

Chapter Two

Jillian waited in the hall while her bags were carried out and stowed in the motorcar. She had no choice but to stand by and look ornamental because she was wearing a silly blue hobble gown, which forced her to mince when she walked. Of course, it did show off her figure to perfection, and she didn't really want to be useful anyway, so being idle while others worked didn't matter.

Hexy embraced her employer carefully, keeping a safe distance from her finely executed maquillage and the silver net collar that stood out like an Elizabethan ruff and framed her immaculately groomed face.

"You know, darling," Jillian breathed in an undertone, "I could marry again, for he has asked me and it would be most convenient, but I just can't stick that awful word *obey*. If only I thought he had a sense of humor about it! But he always does what the earl says, and his father hasn't any sense of humor at *all*. I fear this may be a tedious vacation if he is forever importuning me for an answer."

"If you can't bear to repeat the vows with Donny, then you had certainly best wait for another rich orphan like Mr. MacKenzie to come along," Hexy murmured absently, distracted from the conversation by losing sight of the trunk in which Jillian's fur coat was packed.

It had taken an act of will to close the lid on the fur and then to latch it. She'd slept with it last night, rolled in it tightly as if in the arms of a lover, and hadn't been able to bring herself to actually pack the thing until a few minutes earlier. The pangs of separation were strong.

She certainly missed the fur more than she did James.

"I quite agree, darling. I'll be working on it in Italy. There must be some agreeable rich orphans there."

"I'm sure there are."

"Now remember what I said. I know you think it's all just superstition, but—well, stay

26

away from the beach at night. Mr. MacKenzie was always very firm about that."

"I know. I won't let the sea monsters get me."

"It's the lovers, not the monsters, that I worry about. They sound lovely, but apparently they never stay for long, and that won't do, you know. One doesn't even get any property out of the arrangement," Jillian muttered, leaving Hexy slightly nonplussed.

"Uh—"

"Anyhow ta-ta, darling." Then Jillian added mendaciously, but with genuine goodwill: "I'll write soon, for I know I shall miss you."

Jillian stepped back and pulled on her gloves. In another moment she was out the door, her heels making a staccato burst of sound on the flagstone floor.

Hexy walked out onto the terrace and waved her employer off, uncertain whether she was sad or relieved to have her gone. In this mixture of sentiments, she suspected that she was a great deal like her new northern neighbors.

Hexy smiled suddenly. Probably she should order up a vast number of willow wreaths to distribute among the abandoned locals, as they had just been deprived of their favorite entertainment and were likely to feel the loss. Gossip about the cost of repairs at Fintry could only come in a distant second to the fun of repeating—and probably embellishing—the salacious details of Jillian's love life and the goings-on of the London riffraff she invited to visit at her late husband's castle.

They would be quite disappointed by Hexy. She was such a boring proxy that they might, in fact, not be interested in her at all—unless she actually was kidnapped by a sea monster. Living here for the summer was going to be a strange sociological experiment. And possibly a lonely one, unless some of the workmen hired to do the repairs on the castle proved to be either very handsome or brilliant conversationalists—something most unlikely, as there were very few able-bodied men left in the village.

Ruairidh looked about in bewilderment and some alarm. His skin was nowhere to be found. It should be atop the very rock he was standing on. Quite obviously it had gone astray—but *how?* The tide had not yet turned its course. There had been no wind to blow it away. No one ever visited this beach at this time of year.

And yet something or someone had taken his skin.

For a moment, he wondered if it was the finmen he had smelled up at the furrier's cottage.

He knelt down on his hands and knees and lowered his nose to the rough stone, searching for their foul scent. He knew it now, for it had been all about the grounds of the abandoned Crot Callow.

Instantly he reared back, shocked at the scent that was at once foreign and yet completely recognizable. No one among his people had had firsthand experience with it for several generations, but he knew it all the same. The smell tightened the hair of his scalp and sent shivers over his bare flesh.

A woman had been here and performed the ritual of summoning! She had come to the sea at sunset and shed her requisite seven tears onto the sea's stones where they were collected at the high tide—and then she had taken his skin away with her!

It seemed unthinkable, but there was, at this very moment, when he needed urgently to return to Avocamor with his news, some brash female demanding that he join her in an affair.

Ruairidh muttered a phrase he had learned from some drunken Orkney merrows and then started angrily up the trail that led to Fintry Castle. This was an outrage! It wasn't even Johnsmas eve—midsummer eve, the humans called it. The People should be free to bask on the skerries and rocks for weeks yet without being molested by aggressive females! But this one had obviously decided to get a head start on her peers and resorted to the old trick of stealing a selkie skin to get herself a lover.

What was the world coming to that first a fisherman's father should violate a century-old pact against hunting, and then some over-bold female should steal his skin before midsummer eve?

Probably she is very ugly and shrewish and had need of such vile trickery to get a mate! Or maybe she was an earth witch!

The thought made him wince. It was unjust, but the rules said that he was bound to her until his skin was returned or she was with child. The consideration of her ugly nature added to his infuriation with the situation. It would be even more difficult if she knew some magic. Witches were the worst—hard to control, tricky about trying to trap selkies by feeding them land salt and hiding their skins in clever places—and they were nearly always barren. He couldn't afford to spend his life with a barren woman.

Well, he simply had to get the fur back. He was needed in Avocamor! The People were on the verge of being attacked by the finmen. He did not like being sneaky with women—especially not elderly ones—but he would compel her to give back his skin even if it meant cheating at the traditional bargain. There were things that could be done to bring a female under control without actually making love to her.

Ruairidh leapt from the rock and landed a dozen feet below on the grainy sand, his ankles untwisted and his joints unjarred. Taking a deep breath of air, he turned into the scent and followed the trail of the fur thief.

Hexy jumped at the sound of angry pounding at the castle door. The old knocker had finally been eaten away by corrosion, and they had temporarily installed a hammer by the strike plate. The noise was always loud, but whoever had come to visit was clearly very agitated and determined to call immediate attention to his presence.

Knowing that Marthe and Robertson were both busy and would be slow to answer the summons, she went herself to answer the door, hoping that it wasn't anyone she knew socially; her eyes were itching fiendishly and were probably quite red.

The ancient door's bolts were rusted; it took a bit of effort to unlatch and open them. Thus she had a moment to take in her visitor through the growing crack before he strode over the sill on long, lithe legs, a fair stretch of which showed beneath his rumpled kilt.

"De tha thu 'deanamh?" the man demanded of her, his bottomless brown eyes framed in the longest, silkiest lashes she had ever seen.

"What?"

31

The eyes narrowed, but he repeated the question.

They were beautiful eyes, Hexy thought, but they were also alive with a hypnotic ire that did not seem entirely normal.

Hexy blinked once and laid her hands on the reassuringly solid wall behind her. Her heart began to beat heavily and she felt a little dizzy. Something about this man was very familiar, but also a bit frightening in a delicious sort of way.

"Are you the carpenter from Aberdeen?" she asked, rather hoping that it was the case even if he was somewhat alarming, because she had not seen such a splendid specimen of Scottish manhood since crossing into the north.

His coffee brown eyes finally blinked back at her, his dark brows drawn together beneath his glossy, unbound hair—which in spite of being unrestrained still managed to look kempt as it grew straight back from his face and spilled down his back in a neat line showing small ears laid nearly flat against his head.

"*A bheil ghaidlig agad?*" he asked her.

"I'm sorry," she answered, trying out a smile of welcome and offering her hand. Unaccountably, both lips and fist trembled noticeably. "I don't speak Gaelic. Um . . . *chaneil ghadilig agam.*"

The long lashes veiled the intruder's eyes for

a moment as he looked down at her out-stretched fingers.

"Ye'd be one of the Sassenach women, then," he said, his deep voice shifting into heavily accented English that resembled the local Scots dialect. He stared at her palm for a several seconds, clearly debating whether to take it.

"Actually, I'm American. My ancestors may have had the Gaelic at one time, but we've been in the States since the Revolution. I'm afraid that I don't know much about the language or customs of the north." The need to babble to this handsome stranger was involuntary and undeniable. Hexy had just noticed that he wasn't wearing a shirt, and she was having a difficult time keeping her gaze on his face. Without a doubt this was the most beautiful, most compelling man she had ever seen.

The tall visitor digested this and then asked with a shade more patience, "So if ye do not know the customs, and 'tis all a simple error, will ye not return my fur tae me?"

"What fur?" Hexy noticed that her fingers were covered in gray dust and quickly let her hand fall. Between her red nose and dirty hands, it was no wonder this stranger wasn't anxious to touch her.

"My fur. Ye took it from the beach. I want it back. Now."

"I didn't take—" she began, only to stop

when he leaned over and sniffed at her. "What are you—"

His tongue darted out, and he tasted one of her allergy-induced tears as it welled out of her eyes.

She stood still, shocked into immobility and incredulity as she watched his pupils first expand and then contract down to pinpoints.

"Aye, yer the one. There's nae point in denyin' it. I'll dae my duty by ye, lass, and lay wi' ye if that's what ye wish. But I want my skin back first." He looked stern as he straightened to his full height. "Though why a bonnie lass like yerself would be out fishing for a lover . . ."

Hexy gasped and prayed she wasn't blushing. Allergies had made her quite red enough. Embarrassment was simply adding insult to injury.

"Look here—*what is your name?*" she belatedly asked. "And who are you? And why are you being so—so rude to someone you don't know?"

The man struggled with himself, clearly not wanting to respond to her question, but finally answering, "Some in these parts call me Ruairidh O'Uruisg. And I'm no ruder than ye've been yerself. Ye know that yer not supposed tae be askin' my name yet. Why did ye call me by ritual if it means sae little tae ye?"

Hexy blinked, taken aback. *Had she been rude?* Marthe was always saying failte when strangers came into the house. Had she insulted this man by not obeying the local custom? Had she truly outraged Gaelic social convention by asking for his name too early in some greeting ritual?

"Roaring Oorushk? I can't call you that," she objected, speaking her thoughts aloud as she pinched her nose, fighting off a fit of sneezes. "Haven't you some normal name?"

She regretted her thoughtless words as soon as she saw his offended expression. Her habit of talking to herself had once again landed her in trouble.

"Look, I am sorry. That *was* rude. But I told you that I haven't the Gaelic and don't know all your customs. I'm foreign. Take pity on me. Haven't you an English name I could use?"

"Aye." The man seemed to be chewing his tongue, but eventually he spat out: "If ye must know, some here have called me Rory."

"Rory?" Hexy repeated, feeling suddenly feverish. She hadn't thought of her brother for months and suddenly his name and image were everywhere around her. Another tear slipped from her eye and she raised a hand to wipe it away. "That's . . . that's a nice name. It was my brother's. He—he's gone now."

The stranger watched her hand as she rubbed at her cheek. His tense expression finally relaxed a trifle and his nose twitched. His lips eased into an almost smile. Belatedly, Hexy recalled how dirty her hands were and realized that she had probably just smeared gray dust all over her cheeks.

"I am starting tae believe in yer innocence," he told her, his voice gone soft as a lullabye. It was mesmerizing, somehow spinning cobwebs over her mind. "Ye may be daft, but I dae believe yer guileless."

"Why are you smiling?" she asked, fascinated by the sight of the corners of his mouth curving upward. She had never seen anyone smile that way. Unable to control her thoughts or speech, she added, "It isn't because I'm a mess, is it? That would be mean."

More confident now, he ignored her question.

"It's a strange accent ye have, mistress. And what might yer own name be, O thief of furs, whose brother was also called Rory?"

"Oh, I'm Hexy Garrow. Hesiod Garrow, actually, but everyone calls me Hexy." The words spilled out as if compelled by some unseen force.

"That's a bit of an odd name, Mistress Hesiod. *Hexy*." For the first time, her name on a man's lips sounded like a caress. "There's something almost *pixiating* about the sound of it."

"*Pixiating?*"

"Enchanting."

"Oh."

Hexy stared at him. The man's deep, un-blinking eyes seemed to call her into a mes-meric trance. *Come drown in me,* they seemed to say. *I'll keep you safe.*

But I don't want to drown, do I?

It was difficult, but Hexy gathered her scat-tering wits. She really wanted to close the door on whatever was making her sneeze but didn't feel quite comfortable shutting herself in with this half-naked man who clearly affected her senses in some powerful way.

"Never mind about my name," she said briskly. "What is this nonsense about a fur? Yours has gone missing, I take it? Along with your shirt."

Hexy knew she sounded incredulous, but the ill-folded plaid barely held in place about Rory's naked waist did not suggest the sort of wealth that produced fur coats.

Unless they were supplied by rich women.

The thought made her scowl.

"Aye, it has, and my sark tae. Ye gathered mine up from the beach last evening and brought it here." The stranger raised his head and sniffed at the air. There was no other word for the flaring of nostrils and the deep inhala-tion that followed.

A second frown began to descend on his brow. His voice lost some of its charm. "It isnae here now, though. Where have ye taken it?"

"I haven't taken your fur anywhere. The only fur I touched last night was Jillian's new sable coat and that—*oh, dear!*" Hexy closed her eyes. "That wasn't Jillian's coat, was it?"

Rory shook his dark head, smiling that strange smile again when she cracked open an eye.

"Nay, it wasnae. 'Twas mine. And I should be right angered about this, for I am here on urgent business and need my skin."

"But how was I to know? Yes, it felt strange—wonderful even," she added plaintively as a huge sneeze began building in her. "But why would there be more than one fur coat abandoned on a private beach? *No one* would question that it was Jillian's coat."

"This Jillian left her skin on the beach as well?" Rory asked, his posture finally relaxing. Then: "Lass, why are ye crying? I'm nae sae angry as to call forth yer tears. Just fetch my skin and I'll be off until Beltane. I'll come back and see ye then, if ye wish it."

"I am not crying." Hexy reached into her shallow pocket and pulled out a handkerchief, which she used to blot at her eyes and scrub some of the smudges away. "I am allergic to something outside, the cotton grass maybe. Or the yews. They are starting to leaf out now and dropping pollen everywhere. My eyes are like watering pots."

38

"Then shut up the door." Rory's long arm reached out, and with very little effort, he closed the heavy panel, cutting out the daylight and the irritating air. "Ye cry everytime ye step outside?"

"Yes. I can't help it."

Feeling silly about standing in the dark of the foyer, Hexy retreated into the main hall, gesturing for Rory to follow.

"Look—"

"At what?" Rory asked.

"At nothing. That is simply an expression. It means pay attention."

"Ah! Well, ye've got my attention. Gae on with it. Where's my fur now?"

Hexy fought down her annoyance at the repeated question. It was somewhat easier to do now that her need to sneeze had subsided. "Rory, I am sorry that your coat got packed by mistake, but—"

"My skin has been *packed*?" he interrupted. "Packed where?"

"Yes. I'm afraid it is packed into Miss Foxworthy's trunk and is on its way to Italy via Wales," she said unhappily.

"What?" The deep voice was almost a shout, the beautiful eyes as baleful as handsome eyes could be. The stranger leaned down until they were face to face. "My skin is where? How could ye let it gae? Did ye no sleep wi' it?"

"Don't glare at me! It's perfectly safe." Hexy leaned forward until their noses all but touched. She did not for a moment consider admitting that she *had* slept with it wrapped about her, pretending it was a lover. It was too embarrassing. "You are the one who was trespassing on the beach. What were you thinking, leaving a fur coat out like that? How could you be so careless with anything that precious?"

"Trespassing!" His breath washed over her. It wasn't unpleasant, smelling as it did of the sea, but the intimacy was unnerving. "There's a Sassenach word fer ye! As if any man can own the sea. That beach has been used by the People fer centuries—"

"That may be so," Hexy interrupted, stung at the accusation and also using a voice that was one step below a shout. "But this is Miss Foxworthy's beach now, and you were trespassing."

"Foxworthy!" The name was repeated with scorn. "And where are the MacKenzies of Fintry?"

The question brought Hexy up short and caused her to immediately abandon the impulse to either kiss or bite the nose in front of her.

"Mr. MacKenzie," she began, then said gently: "I am sorry if he was a friend of yours, but Mr. MacKenzie died late last year. He left Fintry to his new wife."

"Miss Foxworthy?"

"Yes."

Rory clapped a hand to his head, hiding his beautiful eyes. He said something in a strange dialect that didn't sound entirely like Gaelic. It didn't, actually, sound like human speech at all. It was more of a strange barking chuff, followed by a string of vowels.

He finally straightened and took a step away from her, taking his nose and lips to a safe distance.

"And when dae ye expect Miss Foxworthy tae return?" he asked, his voice level.

"I—I am not entirely sure. Whenever Donald Healey stops winning races, or she gets bored, I suppose." It didn't seem a good moment to mention the potential of an Italian lover, or that Jillian would likely return to London rather than Fintry if either of these things occurred.

"Can ye get word tae her of the mishap somehow? Perhaps a letter, or might a messenger be sent by pony?"

Now that her annoyance had cooled, she could sense the urgency that underlay his request.

"If it is so important to you, why did you leave that coat on the beach?" Once again, she spoke her thoughts aloud.

"Because I couldnae very well bring it tae the

41

thieving furrier's house, now could I? The temptation would hae overcome him and made him brash. Could ye nae tell that that fur was special? 'Tis unnatural that ye let it go." He sounded insulted.

"No, of course not. Why would I think it special?" she answered. But they both knew she was lying.

"We'll talk about this later. Now, about that summons tae Miss Foxworthy . . . Fetch a pony up tae the house and let us hae a rider on his way."

Hexy looked away from Rory's long-lashed eyes and tried to think. It was difficult, as the allergies, or something, had befuddled her brain.

"I have a better idea!" Hexy exclaimed at last. "I've just recalled that they have a phone down in the village post office. Fortunately, Donny and Jillian are traveling cognito. We can telephone the hotel in Edinburgh where they plan to stay the night and leave a message for her. If we reach her there she can send your fur back at once."

"A *tell-a-fone?*" he repeated.

"Yes, a telephone. Come along." Hexy touched Rory's arm briefly, no longer able to resist the impulse to make physical contact with him. "We need to hurry. The post office closes at four for tea."

"Post office," he repeated.

42

* * *

Ruairidh looked about with a cautious eye. The village had not changed. It was made up of the same antique cottages, too weathered to be an ideal example of human pastoral charm. They huddled together around what had been a small green planted in the time of the Norsemen, but was now barren except for a few determined buttercups that bloomed every spring.

There had been a lowland church there once, which was surrounded by the remains of an unprosperous orchard that had been left long unattended; the wind-bent trees produced nothing but bitter, stunted fruit. Only a few identifiable ruins were left, a crumbling terrace of some sort and balustrades, and even parterres where black-faced English sheep grazed on wild vines and grasses. Still, for all it survived, it was not the sort of agreeable garden that thrived on neglect.

As the wooden shutters rattled under the wind's late afternoon assault, Ruairidh stared suspiciously at the metal and wood instrument they called the telephone. A gramophone he had seen once and understood. This device did not look so straightforward and pleasant. He could hear the wind singing eerily in the wires that attached to it.

"What is that thing?" he asked of Hexy, firmly

resisting the urge to touch her auburn hair. It was probably simply a matter of her having done the summoning ritual that made her so very appealing—though he now had some doubts about whether she had actually intended to summon him—but something about her called to him at an instinctual level.

"It's the telephone. We shall use it as soon as Mr. Campbell returns from his walk."

"Aye, you said that before, that it was a telephone," he answered, looking up. A short, stout man bustled in through a small door, tiny spectacles glinting on his reddened cheeks. *A Campbell!* Ruairidh could tell his clan by his lowlander face and his broad feet. The People had been wary of Campbells since one of their females had committed suicide when her lover left her and there had been bad blood.

"But what does this telephone dae, lass? How does it work?"

Hexy stared at him.

"I forget how remote we are sometimes," she said, apparently addressing herself.

"Ach, laddie!" Mr. Campbell answered, setting down his walking stick. He rubbed a hand over his bald pate and limped forward. "As well to ask how the sea works. In principal 'tis simple enough. Think of this wire as being a very long horse wi' his head in me shop and his arse in Edinburgh. The lassie shouts her message into this end and it's delivered out the other a short time later."

Hexy picked up the handset, ignoring Mr. Campbell's vulgar explanation.

"Well, it's right glad I am that we hae the head end of the horse here," Ruairidh finally said, watching intently as Hexy began cranking the handle on the side of the wooden box. "I'd nae like to see the other when the message arrives."

Mr. Campbell laughed, but he eyed Ruairidh curiously.

The shouted conversation with the Edinburgh hotel manager that followed was confused, and Ruairidh suspected not likely to lead to the prompt return of his skin. The most he could hope for was that Miss Foxworthy would discover that there was an urgent message from her secretary—whatever *that* was—and somehow contact Hexy at Fintry.

"Well, that is all I can do for now," she said, hanging up the thing she had held to her ear. "As a precaution I'll post a letter to Wales straightaway if Mr. Campbell . . . ?"

"Certainly, lass. I have some paper to spare." The postmaster began rummaging through his desk. His gaze was curious as it rested on Ruairidh, but he asked no impolite questions.

"Thank you. As you have gathered, the matter is an urgent one."

"Aye, I gathered so." He handed her a paper, a quill and a pot of ink. He added rather pointedly, "Missing furs are always a problem in these parts."

Hexy nodded absently as she seated herself and began writing. Ruairidh knew that she found his presence to be a distraction, but she didn't ask him to step away. His kind were comforting in their warmth. And he knew that his attention made her feel beautiful and important, in spite of her red nose and apparently domestic position. It was a gift that the People had, and he was happy to share it with her.

"So this is about *poaching*, or whatever you call it? I am relieved to find that you are actually a savory character and not here for some nefarious purpose. I had my doubts about you in the beginning," Hexy told Rory happily, as they left the small cottage where the postmaster lived. She had left some money on the desk to pay for the call and the postage for the letter. "I even wondered for a moment if you were maybe a little mad."

Rory blinked, a slow closing of the lids, that showed off his lashes and that Hexy suspected was habitual. It was also quite alluring.

"Savory, am I? Surely that is what ye call yer meat pasties made frae these balls o' fur?" He gestured at the black-faced sheep nearby.

Hexy laughed. "It is also the name of an herb."

"So now I'm a plant. Are ye by chance having a game with me? Playing with Sassenach words and such?" he asked, looking down at her from his superior height. His lips made their odd curl.

"Perhaps a small game," she admitted. "The language is still rather new to me. It all sounds very strange and even funny. I've only just gotten accustomed to *English* English, and now you speak Gaelic and Scots at me. You must remember that I am but a simpleminded female."

"Aye? Then allow me tae tell ye in yer *English* English that yer one of the least simple women I've ever met—and it has been my luck tae not avoid an acquaintance with ye." He added on a mutter, "And tae think that it was all brought about by the drowning."

Hexy blinked and sorted out his periods. She smiled slowly.

"I am not especially good at puzzles or mathematics, but I do believe that that was a compliment. Except maybe the drowning part. What does that mean?"

"You must be very bad with sums and plussages. But mayhap you should be forgiven this once, since it was all said in the confused Sassenach tongue," Rory answered. He shook his head, but he said it with a small smile. He did not answer her question about drowning.

"Rory, would you perhaps like to come back to Fintry and have some tea with me?" Hexy heard herself asking.

The question shocked her a bit. She knew that they were being observed out of every door and window. The village was the repository of all the castle gossip. The inhabitants were a high-minded, moral people in all respects save one: They were inquisitive. Of course, that was universal. In a small village, rumor-mongering was almost compulsory.

Hexy realized that she was holding her breath, waiting for an answer—though whether she hoped for a reply in the affirmative, she truly could not say.

"Aye, that I would. As long as ye put nae salt in the brew," he added, his tone suddenly warning. "I cannae abide land salt."

Hexy stared at him, trying to decide if he was making a joke. She thought he must be. Who had ever heard of putting salt in tea?

"Well, that's what we'll do, then." She confided, "I was a little afraid that you would hurry straight off again."

"Oh, I shan't be doing that," he assured her. "We shall be quite close until my fur is returned tae me."

Hexy again turned to stare at him.

"Of course, I am certain that Jillian would

like to offer the hospitality of Fintry to any of the late Mr. MacKenzie's friends, but—" A sudden sneeze interrupted her. Two fat tears rolled out of her eyes.

"Guid. I shall be happy to accept your offer. Best we get on tae the castle now, before ye get bad again. Something here has ye weeping like a banshee."

Rory leaned over, and for one minute she thought he meant to again lick the tears from her cheeks. But instead he brushed them away with his thumbs. The touch seemed to make him tremble.

"I think I'm allergic to Scotland," she complained, unable to find the words to contradict Rory's self-invitation, and not truly wanting to, in spite of the potential for the sort of gossip that would make her notorious. She added with an air of thoughtfulness, "Or maybe it's just you."

"Nay, it isn't me that has set you tae weepin'." He added under his breath, "At least, not yet."

"What?"

"I said that I like ye."

"We'll see how you feel after I put pepper in your tea," Hexy muttered. She bent down and picked up a stone to hurl into the sea.

"What are ye about, lass?" Rory asked her as she threw her rock with special vehemence.

"Oh." Hexy blushed as she realized what she

had done. "It's just a local custom. It's supposed to keep the sea monsters away. I thought I'd make sure that none were creeping up on us. I'd hate to lose you so soon."

Rory shook his head, his tone serious as he answered. "Those gray rocks willnae keep any monsters away—unless they are wee, timid beasties. What ye need is one of those red stones filled wi' iron. Even then, ye'd best hit what yer aiming at, fer casting rocks will only make the monsters wroth wi' ye."

Hexy smiled and shook her head. "It isn't nice of you to tease the Sassenach, you know."

"It isnae nice of the Sassenach tae be teasing me," he pointed out. "But ye dae it anyway."

"You have a point," Hexy admitted.

Chapter Three

It was after four when they returned to Fintry. The sky was nowhere near dark yet, but the sunlight was definitely on the ebb, and Helios's fiery chariot was descending toward the ocean. The tide had turned and with it the breeze, bringing inland both the salt tang of the cold gray water and the murmur of the tidal lullaby.

Hexy's footsteps slowed as they mounted the uphill drive to the castle. Here the wild ocean could be heard plainly as it threw itself on the granite shore.

Yesterday, the sound of the waves had seemed an unhappy one, haunting even her dreams. But for some reason, the shushing wa-

51

ter and seabirds' cries no longer made her feel cold and lonely. The sound was, in fact, alluring. She had an urge to slip off her shoes and go back down to the rocky beach and wade in the cold surf. The froth would tickle her skin as it inched higher. If she went out far enough, the waves would pick her up in salty arms and rock her—

"Are ye coming, lass, or hae I lost ye tae the sea?" Rory asked, his voice as gentle as the ocean but deeper than the shallow waters that whispered on the sand. He watched her with his bottomless eyes, looking oddly sympathetic to her abstraction.

"Yes, of course I'm coming." Hexy shook her head, scolding herself for letting her mind wander. "The sound of the ocean is hypnotic though, isn't it?"

"Aye, that it is." Still smiling at her air of pensiveness, Rory held out his hand to her, pretending once she took it that it required great effort to tow her up the steep hill.

"I wonder why others here don't seem to feel it," she puzzled, happy to have her fist tucked into Rory's palm. "And the people inland don't seem to like it at all. Many are even afraid."

Rory smiled, obviously pleased with something, but Hexy couldn't guess what.

"Ye maun be here in the awakening season to appreciate it."

"Awakening season? Oh—spring!"

Rory nodded.

"Most people willnae come here because this isnae a great city, and it is these sheltered inlanders who are used as a country's eyes and mouth. And they use their inlanders' beliefs and impressions tae judge the rest of the world, and tae tell the world of us. But what they hae forgotten is that it wasnae always sae. Once, before man had the way of growing the crops, all lived near the sea, because it was here that there was the bounty needed tae live."

Hexy had a sudden vision of an ancient people huddled around a giant fire as they pried open black mussels.

"They forget—or choose tae ignore—that we of the sea are the first tae see all wha come tae this island. We are the first tae know when change comes frae the sea." Rory laughed, a strange but joyous noise that rose from the back of his throat. "And mayhap a passage on a rough sea gives some arrogant outsiders an incurable dislike of the coast, and they never again try tae embrace the deep and her mysteries . . . and mayhap we prefer it that way."

Much of what Rory said seemed to be non sequiturs or even nonsensical, and yet it appealed to Hexy on some subconscious level. He conjured up more visions of bearded men, sitting by a watch fire as they looked toward the water for invaders, some human, some not. The image stayed with Hexy until the sound of the ocean faded completely.

Fintry Castle was waiting for them at the edge of the plateau, and though Rory was with her still holding her hand, and she felt a sort of unfamiliar inner happiness, the building appeared no more welcoming than it ever was.

The castle was not some pretty pleasure palace that left one feeling enchanted or bemused. The emotions it engendered were closer to grim foreboding, for it had about it an air of ancient misfortune that colored the nearby land like a northern winter even on a fine spring day. Those ancient men hadn't huddled on this beach indefinitely. Soon they'd learned the art of building walls of stone to keep themselves safe.

Hexy recovered from her odd reverie once the spell of the ocean was pulled from her ears and the sun's rays taken from her dazzled eyes. She quickly showed Rory into one of the less disgraceful parlors the derelict castle had to offer and bade him make himself at home.

After fetching her guest one of Mr. MacKenzie's shirts to replace the one that had been purloined, she hurried for the kitchen to put together a tea tray.

She shivered as she worked. It wasn't that the castle's interior was especially cold, but away from Rory, it felt dead, as if she was standing inside the rotting stone heart of an earthly corpse. The whole castle smelled of age and perpetual damp, and the atmosphere sometimes affected her with its air of dank oppression. It was as far from paradisiacal as she could imagine any place to be.

However, she did not complain aloud. Mistress Maggie, the cook, in a rare showing of leniency, had kept the kettle on for her, and it took Hexy only a moment to arrange the tea things on a tray. She wished that it was acceptable to serve tea in the kitchen, where the room was warm and full of the scent of scones, but Rory was company, a friend of the late Mr. Mackenzie's, and as such was entitled to crisp linens, silver spoons and tea in the best parlor.

Inexplicably uneasy about leaving her unusual guest for too long, Hexy quickly added a small bowl of sugar and a pitcher of milk to the waiting cups and teapot and then hefted the silver tray. Charles II was said to have thought tea capable of vanquishing heavy dreams, easing the brain and strengthening the memory.

"All consummations devoutly to be wished for," she thought with a smile for the Bard of Avon who, like tea, was useful in almost any situation.

Humming under her breath, and quite forgetting to check that she was in her most kempt state, Hexy carried the tray in front of her and started cautiously for the shallow stairs.

"Here we are, then," she said, pushing open the door of the parlor with her hip and easing the tray onto the tiny table near the room's empty hearth. Rory stood there, one foot propped against the tender where he examined his crude shoe with a sort of horrified fascination. "It isn't the most sumptuous tea ever, but the cream scones and marmalade bitters are very good."

"Ye've come tae gruntle me up?" Rory turned from his pedal examination and inhaled. His dark eyes gazed into hers and he asked solemnly, "There isnae salt in it? In this brew or in the bread?"

Hexy blinked and thought back to earlier in the day, when she had watched Maggie mixing the dough. She had used flour and sugar and heavy cream. And there must have been baking soda, though she didn't recall seeing her add it or salt into the dry mixture.

It seemed a silly, pointless thing to worry about, yet under the force of that dark gaze she found that she could not lie. Especially not after he reached out and ran a finger along her neck.

"Tell me true now, lass." His voice seemed to

come at her from a long distance and she felt momentarily dizzy.

"I am not certain if there is salt in the scones," she answered finally as the room righted itself and stopped quivering. "But I am quite certain that there is none in the tea, for I have just made it."

Rory nodded. "I will join ye, then, in a cup of yer brew."

Still feeling somewhat off balance, Hexy reached carefully for the squat pot.

"Are you chilled? If you like I could light the fire," she said, glancing at the narrow window, which let in only a small amount of light.

"Nay. We've nae need of fire." His tone suggested distaste. Perhaps he was one of those Scots who saw concern for the comforts of the flesh as a form of moral weakness.

"Cream?" she asked.

"Frae a cow?" He sounded horrified. "Nay! I'll not drink the milk of some stupid, lumbering animal."

"Hm—I hadn't thought of it that way."

Hexy handed him the cup and saucer, watching the way he examined the cup, turning it about carefully, as though it were a completely alien thing.

Seeing her eye upon him, he said easily, " 'Tis much like a shell. I've nae seen a thing so delicate upon the land—unless it be yerself. Yer skin has the same glow."

Hexy blushed, not so much at the compliment but because, without giving any sign of interest in a standard flirtation, he still seemed to mean it.

"The porcelain is very fine. It is Limoges, in fact," she said to hide her discomfort. The subtle inlay covered in gold twinkled in the late afternoon light. Ridiculously, she heard herself add, "It was one of the first hard porcelains manufactured in Europe."

"Aye?"

"The first porcelains came from China. In the East."

He nodded, but she had the oddest feeling that her words didn't mean anything more to him than her description of the telephone before he had seen it used.

Vaguely baffled but unable to follow the meaning of these thoughts, she poured out her own tea.

"Sae, ye were born across the ocean?"

"In America, yes. My family comes from Philadelphia, the City of Brotherly Love."

"Ah, a city of love? That maun be a nice change frae the usual city. Ye liked it there?"

His eyes were calm, beautiful. And they made for disjunctive thought.

"I think it must be less affectionate than in

58

the days of yore. I did not find the people there particularly loving. Or lovable," she answered, more or less at random. "I moved closer to the coast when I could. Then my brother died."

"Ah. And then ye came here." Rory inhaled the steam from his cup. "Tell me now, lass, dae ye ken the words tae the tune ye were humming?"

Rory's eyes snagged her as he asked this, his gaze soft but oddly compelling as it rested on her face.

"Humming?" Hexy thought about the question. "Oh! You mean just now? No, I don't. I am not even certain I know the name of the song, though it seems as if I should. It has been in my head for a day or two now. It's strange, isn't it, how something can be so familiar and yet so elusive? Do *you* know it?"

Rory lowered his eyes to his teacup and said casually, " 'Tis called 'The Great Silkie.' It is about the selkie of Sule Skerry. It is a special song sung on the coast, made up of what we call a humpbacked rhythm."

"The great *silkie?*"

"Aye. 'Tis about the seal man and his human love." He lifted his eyes, studying her face for a reaction.

"I think I heard something about the seal people of Scotland many years ago. My granddad was always telling us wild stories. He said

59

we had to leave Scotland because the women of our family were followed by a bane that stole them away, and that any fate that was corrigible should be avoided. Imagine being that superstitious! And he was a doctor too."

Hexy shook her head, but even as she did it, a voice reminded her that her brother, also a doctor—and not raised in a small village—had not thought the family legends so outrageous. Nor had the late Mr. MacKenzie, if she now understood Jillian's cryptic warning about lovers rather than monsters coming from the sea.

"He studied the leech craft, did he?"

Hexy nodded. Then, tired of moving her head, she said, "It's a tradition in our family. We used to tease him and call him Sawbones, though he was a very good and learned doctor. But the rest of his hobbies—well, they are just silliness. I've spent a deal of time in Scotland now and the only thing that bothers me here are my allergies, and I've about decided that they are the fault of the yew trees. I've noticed that I am much worse whenever I get near those."

"Aye, the yews are a bane tae certain of the people," Rory agreed. "The wood can even blister the skin if the allergy is strong enough. Mayhap yer family suffered frae this."

"Truly? The wood can actually blister? But that is hardly an adequate reason to leave Scotland. Anyway, Granddad was talking about sea monsters or some other nonsense." Hexy shook her head at such silliness, but then asked with a trace of nervousness, "Will you sing 'The Great Silkie' for me? I should like to know how the song goes now that I have it in mind."

"I cannae sing here," he said gruffly. "And the song is muckle nonsense tae boot. 'Twas made up tae scare the lassies from taking lovers. I was just curious about where ye'd heard it. Nae many people sing that auld song anymore."

Hexy shrugged and sipped from her cup.

"I'm not certain where I first heard it. I think perhaps I heard the tune one evening when I was walking down on the beach. I often think I hear music when I'm out there in the evening. Or maybe my grandfather sang it for me when I was little. Or played it. He used to play the pennywhistle." Hexy put her cup aside and reached for a scone.

Rory watched intently as she set the pastry on a small plate. Self-consciously, Hexy broke off a diminutive piece and tasted it.

"Ugh!" Hexy grimaced involuntarily. Swallowing hastily, she put the scone aside in favor of having a swallow of tea. "The cook must have been having an off morning. It tastes like she emptied the entire saltcellar into these scones."

"Ah!" Rory sat back. Hexy couldn't swear to it, but it seemed as if he were both satisfied and yet also filled with nervous anticipation.

"Maybe she confused the salt with the sugar." She explained, "Maggie's eyesight is not what it used to be."

"I dinnae think so. 'Tis often the case that those who are sensitive to yew can also taste the salt most strongly. Ye'll hae a care now, won't ye? The salt they use here isnae healthy for everyone. It does nae come from the sea, you ken. This land salt can make the body behave oddly. Some think it is even bespelling, chaining souls tae the earthy places. Ye'd nae want tae be imprisoned here, would ye?"

"No, not at Fintry." Hexy shuddered. "But I don't know about that legend. It sounds like more of my grandfather's superstitions, though I do recall that salt is a traditional way of warding off evil and bad luck, isn't it?"

"Aye."

"But that can't be what Maggie had in mind. Why would she want to ward off you or I?" she asked.

"Whyever?"

"Well, I shall certainly make my own scones for a while. Obviously, Cook isn't to be trusted. Truly, none of the servants are. They don't like it here and take out their resentments by being lax and careless."

Hexy took another swallow of tea, trying to banish the last of the briny taste from her mouth. She added fairly, "Not that I entirely blame them for that attitude. Fintry is a cursed uncomfortable place much of the year. In the winter, it must sometimes seem like the wind and rain are going to drive it straight back into the sea. There was a bad winter some decades ago when the sea is supposed to have actually pounded on the castle door!"

Rory nodded. "Aye. It shall likely happen one day that the sea will take back her stones. That is the way of things."

Hexy had a sudden thought. "You suspected that the cook would do this, didn't you? But how could—oh! You've been here before." Hexy laughed once, a little relieved at the commonplace explanation for his seeming prescience. "Of course that's why you knew. I am surprised that Mr. MacKenzie tolerated such carelessness in his cook, though. He was supposed to have been a bit of a tyrant with the staff. Or so Jillian said. I did not know him well."

"Mr. MacKenzie was a man filled wi' a deal of decision and was stern wi' his people," Rory agreed, finishing his tea and setting the cup aside. "But he had his virtues. He lived on good terms wi' his neighbors. My people always appreciated that."

"Your family lives near here?" she asked, pleased and vaguely surprised.

Rory smiled his odd, secretive smile. "Aye, we're a bittock distance away, but we hae shared a boundary wi' the MacKenzies fer nigh on eight hundred years."

Hexy blinked. "That's a long time."

"Aye, long enough tae miss the MacKenzies' presence." Rory sat forward, his voice and face earnest. "Lass, I maun gae down to the sea for a spell. 'Tis time fer my brother, Keir, tae return frae his fishing. And I waud hae a word wi' him. Someone's been attacking seal pups near our home and I maun find out the latest news. Also, my kin need tae know that Mac-Kenzie is gone and his widow is sometimes here in his place."

"But it is nearly dark," Hexy protested, feeling sudden dismay. That wasn't strictly true, as there was still perhaps an hour of light to be had, but she didn't want Rory to go down to the sea without her. She had a ridiculous premonition that he would climb into his brother's vessel and never come back. "And the beach is hardly a safe place to try and put in a boat. He'd do better to come by land. He could come for dinner. I'll make it myself, so you needn't worry about the salt."

Rory shook his head. "Keir will be in his fishing garb and in no state tae dine at a table."

"But—"

"And believe me, there are safe harbors tae

be had fer those wha' ken the coast as we do,"
Rory added gently. He rose to his feet. "Dinna
be distressing yerself wi' worry o'er me and my
kin. The People will never be hurt by the sea.
And I shall be back, lass. I'll gae nae distance
frae here without my fur, be sure of that."

Unhappily, Hexy nodded, accepting the teacup from Rory's smooth hand and watching uneasily as he left the room.

She was not left long to anxious musings.
The moment Rory left the house a long-faced
Robertson presented himself. He was accom-
panied by a somewhat dusty man who looked
to be a silver-whiskered biblical sage but was
soon revealed as a more important personage,
the local joiner. She had noticed that all the
workmen about the castle were elderly and supposed it was because the younger men were all
either out fishing or had perished in the war.
A more involved landlady would have sent her
secretary to check on these things, but Jillian
did not care to involve herself with the village.

The aging carpenter was apparently mute, or
perhaps simply loath to try to explain himself
to a female Sassenach, for it fell to a reluctant
Robertson to make an exhaustive explanation
of why the men would need to put in more
costly beams instead of joists in the lower floor's
bathrooms, where plumbing was finally being
installed.

The explanation was a long one and made Hexy stare in disbelief. The butler was not an eloquent man, and contrary to the vogue of some career domestics, Robertson had always practiced the exemplary caution of not being too efficient in his job, and therefore having his employers expect too much of him on a regular basis. The rest of the staff, taking their cues from the butler, had followed suit, the house-keeper and cook adding the refinement of the use of a local dialect that was so far removed from English that their speech was nearly always incomprehensible to their employer. Thus, communication, when it could not be avoided, nearly always fell upon dour Robertson.

Today, the butler's long face was looking unusually morbid and his tone was one of a man sorely tried by unfair vicissitudes. Hexy withstood the long-winded explanations of privy enhancement bravely until Robertson launched into a second and more detailed clarification of why certain seats were to be preferred in the newfangled commodes that were to replace the old style cesses.

"Fer ye'll want tae keep visits prompt. But there's nae reason fer people tae actually suffer. The old privies were a horror, mistress! I tell ye, a Scotsman's heroism is nae always limited tae the battlefield. The bravest man would sob at the feel of those icy seats frozen ontae his bare backside on a wintry day. I recall occasions when flesh was actually left behind!"

"I see. How unpleasant for you," was Hexy's only response.

The joiner nodded in solemn agreement and then let loose with a powerful yawn, which revealed a mouthful of teeth and a breath that were both malodorous and ominous in size. Whatever his care with his professional obligations, the joiner's self-maintenance had not extended to dental hygiene. That was one thing she had noticed about Rory: He had perfect white teeth behind his odd smile.

Before she was called upon to answer this unwholesome and impolite observation about chilblained bottoms, their ears were assaulted by the horrific clatter of pipes falling down stone stairs, and then the hollow sound of anger-begotten swearing.

"Robertson," Hexy said, looking uneasily toward the door, where the thankfully incomprehensible voice was berating someone or something with notable vigor. "I trust your judgment in this matter. You are the senior member of the staff. We'll let this be your particular project. Please choose whatever—uh—fixtures you feel would be best and we'll tell Miss Foxworthy about it later."

Robertson opened his mouth either to thank

her for her trust or more likely to argue about whom was to be responsible for the costly decision, but the sound of the hammer being applied to the strike plate at the front door forestalled further argument. It was, after all, the butler's primary duty to answer the summons, at least when eyes were upon him.

Their last visitor of the day proved to be one of Mr. Campbell's sons, sent up from the post office to say that Miss Foxworthy had telephoned and promised to send the missing coat back promptly. She also wanted Hexy to go back to the beach and see if her own coat were still somewhere about, though she was thinking now that perhaps she had left it down on the one sandy beachhead, or maybe at the hotel when she had gone there for tea. The boy added that his da said would Mistress Garrow be pleased to come visit the post office some afternoon for tea, as Mr. Campbell had some old books he wanted to share with her.

Relieved at hearing that Rory's fur would be returned, but also annoyed at the prospect of a further search for her careless employer's missing sable, Hexy escaped from Fintry and the hovering Robertson as quickly as she was able. Pulling an old woolen shawl about her shoulders to ward off the evening mist that would soon fall, she allowed her footsteps to lead her down the narrow path that twisted toward the second, smaller beach, whose tiny, sharp shoals lay between two deep sea caves.

She couldn't know for certain that this was the place, of course, because it was a peculiar place to visit when Rory said that he was going to meet someone with a boat; but her instincts insisted that this was where Rory had actually gone when he left the house rather than the more public beach. She couldn't explain the origin of this odd certainty. It didn't feel like something her imagination would invent, but its fanciful shape certainly did not fit properly in her orderly brain's usual inventions.

But where else could it come from, except her imagination?

Hexy shrugged.

Whatever its origin, it was as though something had forced a hole in the shield of good sense she kept around her mind and this idea had wormed its way inside to incubate and probably eventually hatch into some lunacy that would haunt her dreams.

Yet in the meantime, it compelled. It wasn't a reasonable impulse, but to the smaller beach she would go.

Not that there was an urgent reason why she needed to see Rory again before dinner, she assured herself, but he would certainly be relieved to know that his fur was being returned to him. And it was only polite of her to tell him at once and set his mind at ease.

It was also a fact, she admitted to herself, that Rory elicited some sort of euphoria in her brain. She understood that she was getting involved in something—and with someone—beyond her previous experience, but the loss of life and love that had dimmed her world with grief was suddenly gone. In the space of a few hours, her soul's winter had turned into spring. She felt emotionally resurrected. The cause of this revitalization deserved further detailed study, and it would get it.

The first confirmation of Rory's presence on the smaller beach was a cast-off plaid abandoned in the gritty sand in a careless pile.

Hexy smiled in satisfaction.

The plaid was soon followed by a pair of crudely stitched leather shoes, also flung away by a hasty hand so that they'd fallen upside down and unmated; and finally by the finely made borrowed shirt, which had been dropped too near the tide line. The latter was now being taken out to sea by the cold, thieving waters that had crept up on the land.

Slowing to a stop, Hexy stood over the dead-white shirt, mesmerized, watching its gaping neckline slowly drawn down into the water, where it gasped like a drowning man for a last mouthful of air. It brought to mind the many fishermen who had died in this very sea. And also men who were not after the sea's bounty, but were simply unlucky in encountering rough waves and had been battered on this cruel, cold shore. She knew firsthand that not everyone escaped such storms with a mere mal de mer. Her own brother had not.

Something moved at the base of her brain, and a terrible thought about her brother began to stretch its curled limbs and claw at her mind. The intrusion of the expanding notion threatened great pain, and Hexy found her heart racing and her breath coming in gasps. Her brother's bloodless face rose suddenly in her mind.

Hexy, help me.

"Rory Patrick?"

Help me. It's dark here and I am alone.

"Where are you?"

Unexpected, and perhaps even imaginary laughter floated over her, breaking the conjuration and sending the dark hallucination back into hiding before it overwhelmed her. The laughter was odd, a sound she had never heard before.

Hexy exhaled sharply. She had to stop this. She had grieved long enough. These nightmares had to end or she'd become one of those hysterics who couldn't stir from the house without smelling salts.

Shaking off her sudden morbid thoughts, she waded into the surf and retrieved Mr. MacKenzie's borrowed shirt. Once lifted from the water, it was no longer sinister. It just looked like an empty, wet shirt.

"Rory?" she called softly, looking about uneasily for the garment's missing wearer. The water lapped at her own clothing and invaded her slippers with cold and grit. There were a few places that he might be, and she didn't want to look into any of them.

Disgusted with her alarm, and with what was shaping up as an inconvenient infatuation with a slovenly stranger, she began wringing out the sopping garment and retreated up the shore, hoping to escape the water before the sea had climbed all the way up her skirt.

"You are making a bad habit of leaving your clothes on the beach," she told him, as if the air would carry her message to his ears. "One of these days you'll be caught stark naked somewhere—and then what shall you do?"

In timely answer, a movement out at the surf line caught her eye. Two figures, one pale and human, one darker and larger, seemed to be grappling in some playful embrace.

"What?"

The rollicking bodies cut and then recut the sea's delicate silver line as a peculiar sort of barking reached Hexy's ears over the waves' shushing. The sound of the inhuman voice seemed to grasp her ears, to catch her attention in some invisible but inescapable net. This had been the laughter that disturbed her morbid reverie.

Unaware that the tide was again slowly creeping up her calves and wrapping her skirt about her legs, Hexy stood for several minutes, watching in charmed fascination as the two figures played, then finally parted. The paler one, whom she was certain was Rory, began to wade back toward the beach. With a last high bark that raised the tiny hairs on her nape, the darker figure waved a flipper and then dove beneath the surf.

Hexy turned bemused eyes on Rory.

Several things about the emerging Scotsman struck her as odd, the first of which being that he was actually wading nude in a very cold sea. She had known that he was without kilt and shirt, of course, but for some reason it hadn't occurred to her that he would be completely without clothing. That he would look as naked as—as a newborn coming from a mother's womb.

How could he not feel the cold and wet? He didn't seem aware of the sea's freezing caress. It was as though he were impervious to the usual afflictions of men.

The second thing she noticed, as the setting

sun painted him in a backlight of glorious bronze, was that his skin looked smooth, flawless even, like the finest kidskin gloves, and that there was no hair on it, except for the locks on his head. None. He looked like an infant, except that no baby had ever moved as he did, with an undulating walk that was as graceful as an otter at play.

Not an otter—a seal, her inner voice corrected.

The final thing, and oddly the most incongruous, was the bit of silver Rory had in his hand. She watched in disbelief as he raised it to his lips and took a large bite from the flopping carcass, chewing on the fish with obvious relish.

Some cautious part of her brain, still mostly untouched by Rory's odd charm, and perhaps accustomed to the dark thoughts that went with a history of disappointment, uttered another warning about getting involved with such a strange man. But Hexy, in no mood for unhappy caution, told it to take its dire mutterings and go to Hell with them.

Startled by a stray wave, which shoved at her rudely, she took a tumbling step back, nearly sitting down in the freezing surf as she turned an ankle on the edge of a submerged stone.

Just as Rory's movements had betrayed him to her searching eyes, so her own careless movement gave her away to him.

"Dae ye plan tae run from me, lass?" he asked, tossing his fish aside. "But why? Yer drawn tae the sea as well, are ye not? And ye seem tae find me pleasing."

Hexy shouldn't have been able to hear his voice, but somehow it carried to her over the sea and stroked her ears.

She swallowed twice and cleared her throat, but found that she could not answer.

"Listen now. The sea has a music tae it," he said softly. "And the music is like the People. It was born wi' us; we grew as it did, married with others, mingling our waters and blood, and we both gave birth tae new songs and new lives."

Rory drew closer, his great, dark eyes unblinking and filled with heat.

"But then the waters and the People ceased tae thrive. Little new music was written, and what there was of it became sad. Still, the sea can renew herself and sae shall the People. And ye can be of help tae us both."

Part of Hexy understood what Rory was saying and wanted to run, or at least avert her eyes from his, which were fathomless in their depths. Another part wanted to rush forward and throw herself into his arms and maybe into the sea. But she did neither. Instead she stood calmly, ignoring her twinging ankle, and even offering him his damp shirt as he reached her side.

"I think we know what happened to your last shirt," she managed to say at last, amazed at the tranquillity of her voice and proud that she could still speak sensibly after the spell of his words had enfolded her. "Your kilt is safe enough, but I don't know about your shoes."

Rory studied her for a long moment and then turned to look out at the sea. He nodded once at something there and then reached out for her with his hands and eyes.

"Ye didnae run from me, but ye'll not come willingly tae the song, will ye, lass?" His voice was whimsical, yet also deadly serious. "Yer resistance is strong. Someone gave ye a reasoned mind. This is new tae me."

She gave up trying to change the subject.

"Yes, I have a mind. And I'm not going anywhere until I am certain it is where I want to go," she warned him.

"Then sae mote it be. I'll just hae a talk with yer blood and the memories therein, instead of yer shut-up mind."

Run, a voice whispered.

I will not!

But even as she thought this, fingers, incredibly strong and yet gentle, curled about her nape. He touched a place behind her ear and pulled her forward so that he could bend down and kiss her there. He touched her with the tip of his tongue. The kiss startled her into immobility, and after a moment, Hexy's legs began to buckle.

Rory quickly caught her, pressing her against his body—impossibly warm, even after his prolonged immersion in the sea—and held her until she had regained her balance. As soon as she was steady, he turned her so her back was to the ocean and the disappearing sun. For one moment, she feared that he was going to carry her out into deeper water and perform some sort of strange baptism that would completely subjugate her will.

"Ye've questions about what ye've seen?" he suggested, his face buried in her tangled hair. The intimacy seemed normal. "Ask me, lass, fer I'll tell ye anything ye wish tae know, teach ye anything ye need tae remember."

"No, I have no questions," Hexy denied, leaning against Rory because her own limbs seemed unable to support her. But she lied. She did have questions, if only her sluggish brain could sort them out!

"It must seem passing strange, what ye've seen and felt this day. But 'tis not sae odd, Hexy lass. Sometimes I ween the old smell and come down tae visit here. Through the years I've made friends with the ocean and almost all who live in her." His voice was persuasive. "Ye can understand that, can ye not? Yer brother loved the sea tae, did he not? Sae talk tae me. Tell

77

me yer thoughts, yer memories, what ye see when ye dream. Ask me what ye wish tae know."

Hexy swallowed. Though it was silliness, perhaps it *was* better to ask Rory about what she had seen—what she was feeling. Maybe he could explain the incredible thoughts running through her head.

"You were playing with a seal." It wasn't exactly a question, but not strong enough to be a declarative sentence either.

"Aye, I was. He's a young one yet and still a wee bit frolicsome." Rory fisted a hand in her hair and tilted her head upward so their eyes met. "Were ye frightened? Ye shouldnae be. Seals are gentle creatures, nae threat tae any man. They shouldnae disturb ye."

"I'm not disturbed. I—it was fun to watch. I would have liked to have come, too, but I was afraid of the tide." And she was not ready to put off her clothes and wade into the cold.

"Would ye have liked tae come wi' us? Well, mayhap one day ye will." His hand loosened in her hair, and he caressed her gently. His smile was pleased. "And when ye come ye'll hae nae fear. I promise this."

"You saw your brother, Keir, too?" she asked, aware that she was standing in the arms of a naked man—a very strange naked man—but finding it beyond her power to move away.

"I did. He was settin' out on yon rock,

croonin' like a daft mavis. He never could sing."

"And he had news?" In spite of Rory's heated flesh, Hexy was beginning to tremble with cold. The ocean was draining the very life out of her through the soles of her feet.

"Aye." Rory frowned, noticing the tremors that were moving through her body. His voice was brisk, yet suddenly more normal: "Come out of the water, Hexy lass. Ye'll catch yer death. Poor love! Ye look as miserable as a sheep in a snowstorm. Mayhap a bit sadder even."

Not waiting for her to move, Rory lifted her in his arms and walked swiftly up the beach, apparently unbothered by her wet weight or the sharp-edged grains of sand beneath his naked feet. They were jagged enough to cause lacerations, but perhaps he always went barefoot and his soles were more calloused than usual.

"Wring out yer skirts and empty yer shoes whilst I dress in this sheep's clothing," he instructed her, setting her on her shod feet. His voice was very practical. "Keir tells me that the circus has come tae town, and I need tae see something that they have wi' them."

Hexy found his words bizarre, but no more so than anything else she had experienced that day.

Finally finding some inner strength and a

soupçon of modesty, Hexy turned her back while Rory dressed. As she wrung out her waterlogged skirts, it unhappily occurred to her that her outlandish actions—like watching a strange man bathing in the nude—required some explanation.

"The reason I came to find you," she began, standing carefully on her twisted ankle, "is because there was a message from Mr. Campbell at the post office. Jillian has discovered the mix-up with the coats and is returning yours right away. It should be here in a day or two."

"Aye?" Rory didn't sound as happy as she had expected him to be, and she risked a quick peek at his shadowed profile.

"I thought you'd be pleased," she said. "You seemed so worried earlier."

"That I am, lass—more pleased than ye'll ever ken." Rory belted his plaid in place and pulled on his shoes without bothering to brush the sand from his soles. "But things hae happened in the last day, and there's something else we maun dae right now. Something just as important tae me as finding my skin, and more urgent tae the People."

"Yes?" she asked, meeting his eyes squarely as he came to her, holding out his long-fingered hand. It seemed only natural that she should take it.

"I'll tell ye about it after we've climbed the

trail." Rory jerked his head to the left. "Up wi' ye, now."

"The trail?" Hexy asked, confused. "But the path is that way."

She gestured in the opposite direction.

"I ken a shorter way through these caves. We maun hurry. Haste ye now, lass. Just stay behind me and dae not let go of my belt for even an instant."

"But, Rory, it's dark in there—and the tide is turning—" she protested, for some reason greatly fearing the sea cave he indicated. Perhaps she had dreamed of one after her brother died. After his death she had had many bad dreams and many new fears about the ocean.

"I'm sorry, lass." Rory touched a finger to his lips and then touched her again behind her left ear, pressing on the spot he had kissed earlier. This time her legs did not buckle, but she had another moment of weakening vertigo that sapped her will to argue. Fighting dizziness, she shifted more weight onto her left foot and winced.

"What ails ye, lass?" he asked, frowning. "Are ye injured?"

"I twisted my ankle on a rock," she answered, waving at the stony ridge as it disappeared into the sea.

"Let me hae a look at ye." Rory knelt down

and shoved her clinging skirts aside, then rolled down her stocking.

Hexy watched, slightly shocked, as he reached inside his already drying shirt and ran his palm down his chest; then, withdrawing it, he laid his warm hand over her right ankle and rubbed gently, as though spreading an unguent.

Immediately, inexplicably, the small pain there faded. Warmth traveled up her body, flushing her skin.

"How did you do that?" she asked. "What . . . ?"

Rory quickly pulled off her slipper and brushed the sand away from her chilled toes. He did the same for her other foot. His touch was matter-of-fact through the stockings, but it still made her feel weak and trembly, and far too warm. And it got worse as he smoothed the stocking back up her leg.

"That shall dae for now." Rory stood up. Looking into her eyes, he said with the air of a man taking a solemn oath, "Stay close, Hexy lass, and hae no fear of the cave. I swear by all I hold dear that darkness or not, tide or not, I'll never let anything happen tae ye."

Quite without reason, the unusually docile and feverish Hexy believed him. "Wither thou goest," she answered, reaching out for Rory's hand.

Chapter Four

The last thing Hexy expected to see at the head of the beach trail when they finally emerged from the black of the cave was a torchlight procession of colorful strangers. The huge, garish wagons were easy to recognize even in the twilight, as were the parading plumed horses. But even if they had not been visible from the cliff trail, Hexy and Rory would have known that the circus was in town. There was no escaping the calliope's shrill, steam-driven notes once they were outside the hidden tunnel, where they'd heard nothing except the sea's tidal roar.

They stood quietly and watched with interest—Rory's more critical and focused—as first the bright clowns and then the jugglers came marching by. There were tumblers, too, but they had abandoned their acrobatics once the procession started up the hill and their followers from the village forsook their escort.

Aware that Rory was sniffing the air and suddenly frowning, Hexy turned to examine his face. He glanced down at her, his expression abstracted in the torchlight, and then urged her toward the parade.

"I need tae see something here, lass," he told her again. "Ye'll speak wi' the men there beside the wagon and keep them occupied for a bittock whilst I look about."

The tone was something more than a request and Hexy felt obliged to protest. "I—"

"Please, lass. 'Tis important." He touched her behind the ear again, causing her a moment of vertigo. She tried to look into his eyes, to see the thoughts and plots that lingered there, but he dropped his long lashes over them like a widow's veil. "Lass? Will ye nae help with this small thing?"

"Very well," she agreed, feeling disoriented and more baffled than ever, but willing to help Rory if it was important.

"*Tapadh leat*," he murmured.

"Speak English," she said absently, the only tone her voice seemed to have that evening.

84

"This is the one," Rory whispered, placing a hand to the small of her back.

At his urging, they fell into step beside two slightly muddied tumblers who were bringing up the rear of the procession, save for two wagons, one of which was a droll booth, presently without puppets in its curtained window. At Rory's nod, Hexy engaged the two men in polite conversation. She hoped that in the dim light her damp skirt, wet to the waist in the back, and her sagging hose, peppered with sand and sea wrack, were not apparent, because there was no respectable explanation for their condition.

"What is the name of your circus?" she asked, her eyes wide and her voice loud enough to compete with the music. It took some effort to pretend that she didn't see the very large sign on the side of the yellow wagon that proclaimed HECTOR'S GRAND CARAVAN CIRCUS SINCE 1894.

"We be the Grand Caravan Circus, missus, up from Lunnon way, and making our long-awaited reappearance here in the wilds of Cal-e-don-ia," the elder of the two tumblers announced proudly.

"From London!" Hexy shouted admiringly, glancing back once at Rory as he stepped closer to the yellow wagon. She added the next thing that came into her head: "That's a long way. It must cost a great deal to travel here to Scotland with all these people and wagons."

"Aye, it do. It do. But we aren't worrit about making the nut here, mistress. Folks in the north is real friendly—"

"And bored. People get a little weird up here after a long winter with just theirselves for company," added another man, an impertinent youth, also dressed as a tumbler but rather taller and more mud-spattered than his companion. His comment seemed a bit disrespectful as he was staring at her squeaking shoes as he made it, but she supposed she couldn't blame him for being interested in her odd appearance.

"—so we always makes good money on the Scotch run in the spring. Manny!" The older man reached out and cuffed the teenager, who'd started to turn and look at Rory, who had fallen back to the rear of the yellow wagon.

"Ow!" The youth grabbed his ear and glared. "I was just lookin' at that odd man what—"

"Ain't I told ya that lookin' backward durint the parade is bad luck? Leave that odd man to hisself and mind yer marchin'."

Hexy, not wanting to be cuffed or draw attention to Rory's strange behavior, also refrained from looking back at her now missing companion, though she was horribly curious about what he was doing. She had just noticed that above the Grand Caravan Circus sign there was another banner. This one said FREAKS AND ODDITIES.

"My goodness!" Hexy gestured at the sign. "What sorts of things do you have here? I once saw a chicken egg that had three yolks and a lamb with two tails."

Since it had been her brother's field of interest, and Rory Patrick had never given up his search for a reasonable explanation regarding the creatures of legend their grandfather had talked about, she had also seen some revolting sirenoform fetuses both pickled and waxed while accompanying him on his investigation. *Phocomelus* was the term her brother had used for the poor souls born with foreshortened and sometimes fused limbs. He'd seen some of the crippled wretches in medical school and admitted that short of making a living in a circus, there was very little that many of them could do to earn their keep.

And there had also once been a Frankenstein horror of fish and monkey parts sewn together and passed off as a mermaid. Hexy had been appalled at the display of withered remains, but Rory Patrick had snorted with derision at that one—*see the pelvic fin. It's the same as you would see in a quadruped, but the actual pelvic ratio of transverse dorsoventral diameter is all wrong. It's an obvious fake. Who would be taken in by something so poorly made?*

"Are there a lot of freaks and oddities like those here? I'd love to see a horse with two tails," Hexy lied.

Both tumblers snickered at what they thought was her bucolic naïveté, the younger one going so far as to sniff with disdain that they would have anything so mundane in their sideshow.

"Missus, that's all very well for a small, countrylike fair. But we are pro-fe-shun-els and we have us some world-class wonders in there." He leaned toward her and said significantly, "For tuppance ye can see the taxidermied remains of a two-headed, four-tongued snake from Arabia and the skeleton of the great mythical beast, the merman of Sule Skerry!"

"A merman!" But it wasn't that fantastical word that sent shivers down her spine. Mermen she had seen, and thanks to her brother, she understood the trickery that made them. It was the mention of Sule Skerry that disquieted her. She had an unpleasant premonition that it was this that was attracting Rory's attention and would probably get them both in trouble.

It was a moment's work to force the flimsy lock on the old door and boost himself into the wagon. In the shadowy recesses of the rocking caravan, Ruairidh lifted the cover off the glass-topped display case nearest the door and looked down without surprise.

He'd known what to expect after his brother's warning, but still the sight filled him with rage. He did not know for certain which of the People had been the unwilling doner of these stolen bones, but that they were one of his kin he did not doubt. And some foul magic had been worked upon them.

But how? How had the humans come to possess such a skeleton? Only a selkie or some other sea creature could have journeyed into the deep caves where his ancestors' remains were kept and taken one of them away.

Sickened at the desecration, Ruairidh closed the box and then drew the tarp back over the case. Taking a quick look through the open door, he dropped lightly back onto the road and wedged the door more or less into place. There was nothing he could do about this now, not with Hexy there and so many people about. But he would be back later to retrieve his ancestor's bones and return them to the sea, where they would be cleansed of their taint.

In three strides he had regained Hexy's side. A quick look at her pale face told him that something had disturbed her. He reached out a hand to touch her neck, trying to soothe her in the only way he knew how. The sweat from his palms should have immediately calmed her to a soporific state, but it did not. Instead of immediately soothing her, he found it was growing more difficult to control her the farther they got from the sea. Perhaps it was because his own agitation had increased.

Hexy had had the oddest effect on him from the first moment they met. Perhaps it was the tears that had welled from her eyes—those beautiful eyes, the color of spring when it came to the land in a rush in May. But it was something else as well. The curves of her body, the very feel of her. Everything about her was different from any female he had ever known. His own body was emphatic about its attraction to the variation of woman that was Hexy Garrow. The pleasure of exchanging passion with her would extend far beyond the satisfaction of having done his duty by contributing to the survival of his clan.

The thought of it made him impatient, but fulfillment would have to wait while he dealt with this new outrage. The two facts in conjunction incensed him and made serenity impossible. He would have to be careful. Being separated from his skin was making him irritable.

"Rory, did you know that they have a merman from Sule Skerry in this wagon? Imagine that! We'll have to come see it tomorrow, won't we?"

"Aye," he agreed, his voice a shade grim as he stroked his hand down her nape and then behind her ear. He could almost feel her rebelling thoughts buffeting her captivated brain with their great disembodied wings as they attempted to escape his control. He could not allow that to happen. Whatever else occurred, he could not allow her to panic and run away. "We'll come and see it, there's nae doubt of that."

It was impossible for any of the People's beautiful brown eyes to ever appear cold, but Ruairidh knew from Hexy's reaction that his expression was far from the reassuring one he wanted to wear.

He renewed his petting, stroking salt into the skin over her veins, and forced his features to relax so that she would not be frightened and fight its effects.

It bothered him to do this, to use his gift in this way. Hexy's contentment was something needed for the collective good of the People, and perhaps for himself as well, but this constant interference with her thoughts was too close to the subjugation the amoral finmen imposed on their women.

The People had always prided themselves on their society, which allowed for individual thought and choice.

Of course, some would say that Hexy was not

one of the People and therefore not entitled to the privileges of the clan. And so much was at stake—the selkies very survival, in point of fact—that he could not risk losing her before she understood her importance to the People and to him. And his importance to her.

In the meanwhile, he could not waste time in questioning the philosophies of his clan. There were concerns of more immediacy.

"Where came ye by such a wondrous thing?" Ruairidh asked the young tumbler as the older one stopped long enough to hike up a drooping sock. "It must hae cost ye a shilling or two tae buy something sae rare."

"Nay, it didn't," the youngster said. "Hector never paid a brass farthing for it. It was brung to us last year while we was in Scotland by two bullyboys named Turpin and Brodir—compliments of a Mr. Sevin. Muffled up to the eyes they was—two strange blokes, and that's no lie."

Ruairidh stiffened in shock at the name, and so alarming was his posture that Hexy actually laid a restraining hand upon his arm. At any other time, he would have found the gesture amusing, for the People were not usually violent. But in that moment he was glad of her reminder to use caution. It was improbable that this boy knew anything of importance, but the urge to drag him away and question him roughly was nearly overwhelming.

"Manny!" the older tumbler warned as he rejoined them. "Ain't anyone learned you not to discuss business with the townies?"

"Well, aye, but—"

"But nothing! Shut yer gob and go check on the horses. I think one is throwin' a shoe."

The youngster glared at the other tumbler but went off without protest.

"Boys! They's all chatterers. Ye mustn't mind him."

"That's quite all right. We must be going, too," Hexy said. She offered a smile, which was too friendly, but she didn't want the older man looking too closely at Rory, whose expression was far from calm. "We shall certainly come see your exhibit when you are all set up. It sounds wonderful. Good luck to you."

"Thankee, missus. We'll see you on the morrow. Sir." He nodded to Rory, but true to his lecture about bad luck, he didn't turn his head to look at them as Hexy dragged Rory off the path and into the gradually quieting darkness.

They stood without speaking as the last of the circus disappeared over the hill. Slowly but surely, the shrill music faded.

"Was it really a merman inside that wagon?" she asked at last, looking down at her clammy shoes, which felt as though they were shrinking around her freezing feet. "Not just a seal or a fish, or some cobbled-together horror they've concocted to extort money from the masses?"

Rory hesitated.

"It wasnae a merman, a seal, nor a fish."

Hexy nodded jerkily. What she was thinking was impossible—quite insane. But that didn't seem to matter to her brain. It was beginning to embrace an impossibility, and this fantastical thought made her want to both run and hide and yet also seek out the possible wondrous truth.

For the time being she was caught between the wild conception and the discovery of an improbable reality, stranded between the thought and some moment of inescapable proof. Until she could decide what to do and believe, she would have to manage to live with two simultaneous and contradictory thoughts.

More than ever, she missed her brother and wished that he were there to talk to.

"How is yer ankle, lass?" Rory asked, his tone solicitous. "Shall I carry ye back tae Fintry? We cannae go by the beach as the tide is in now and would be tae strong for ye."

Hexy shivered, her strength draining away with the light. They were half an hour from the castle, and every step of it was steeply inclined, but she had no doubt that Rory could easily bear her up the hill if he needed to.

However, she had had quite enough of being hauled about for the evening. Even if she suffered the agonies of the damned, she would manage the slope on her own.

"No. I can handle it."

For a moment, she thought Rory was going to ignore her words and again force her into doing what he wanted. But he merely nodded and laid a gentle hand on her arm.

"Come away, then, Hexy lass. We'll see ye warm and dry, and with a meal in yer belly."

"We'll have a fire?" she asked, finally looking up at Rory's face.

His nod was reluctant, but he said, "Aye. I believe ye've need of one, and I can bear it if I maun."

"I think these shoes are ruined," Hexy added as they started up the hill toward the castle. The footwear was beginning to chafe and squeak alarmingly when flexed. "And your kilt is about the sorriest thing I've ever seen. It looks like it has seen a hundred years of war."

"True enough. Things frae the land rarely fare well in the sea."

She paused, trying to sort that out. At last she said, attempting to lighten the mood, "It doesn't seem to have done me any harm, though. I am still whole and unscathed except for my ankle—but it was a rock that did that."

Apparently she succeeded in hitting the right note of airiness, for Rory smiled widely, his teeth white in the new moonlight.

"Aye, that is true enough. But, Hexy lass, I suspect that is because ye belong more tae the sea than ye realize yet."

"Perhaps," she heard herself agree. What she really thought was that she might belong to Rory.

The thought was a little frightening and a lot wonderful. She hadn't belonged to anyone since Rory Patrick died.

"Someday soon I maun take ye tae meet my family. Perhaps at the dark of the moon, when the tides are nae sae strong."

Hexy wondered which village they lived in. There were several along the coast that could only be reached by boat or by hiking overland.

"I'd like to meet your family," she answered.

"Da will be delighted with ye—I can swear to that, Hexy lass."

Chapter Five

Westward across the small sound there was a tiny islet, hardly more than an upthrust of pulverized granite slightly taller than most of the sea's waves. It was one of the many bits of land that littered the coastal region, usually pretty places where bog myrtle, crinkle root and odorous cotton grass grew out of the gray stone in delicate-colored puffs. Hexy had visited a few of the islets near *Tresh nish* and knew that there would be small stands of fragrant plumage, as the asphodels were thick on the ground this time of year, when they could find fertile soil for their roots. In summer, Rory said that there would be a profusion of wild orchids, as colorful as exotic butterfly wings, but the season was still too early for them even though there was a tropical flow.

Still, Hexy thought optimistically, even without the wildflowers, it would be a lovely place for a picnic. The sun was shining, the breeze was moderate and she was wearing a pretty frock of lavender silk tulle with a bronze underslip, which brought out a colorful heat in her dark red hair.

Their movable feast, which Hexy had herself prepared, was packed carefully into the hamper at her feet, lifted off the boat's damp floor by a small pile of rushes. The basket was a heavy one as it bore not only the food she had made but also a blanket, crockery and a flask of precious lemonade whose rare, tangy fruit had been purchased at three shillings and sixpence from the village's tiny store.

As they drew closer to the shore, Hexy was reminded that the island would not be a silent one, because there were birds of every kind nesting on these tiny bits of land, and feeding in the nearby waters. The palest blue sky above was full of diving avians that were clearly happy to be out in the gladsome weather. She was pleased that she had planned their excursion with care and had brought a generous amount of food, because doubtless they would be asked repeatedly to share it.

Hexy smiled at Rory, watching the muscles of his arms and chest as he pulled on the oars. One stray lock of hair had fallen over his forehead, so that he reminded her a bit of an affectionate sheepdog when he grinned at her. Though, of course, she had never seen a canine with hair of that glossy brown shade.

Her own hair had worked its way loose and probably looked like a shaggy aster on a windy day, but she did not bother to try and neaten it. That would have been an exercise in futility, and besides, the breeze combing through the loose strands was delicious. She planned to spend the entire afternoon relaxing and getting to know more about the mysterious Rory.

In spite of this resolve, from the moment the boat's keel touched the stony shore of the fisherman's island, Hexy could not shake off a feeling of unease.

Part of her discomfort could be explained by the mission they were on. Someone—this missing furrier, John of Crot Callow, most likely—had been attacking seal pups on Rory's family lands. Rory had said he was not certain whether it was an act of vengeance against his people for the loss of the furrier's son in their waters, or if the man sought to take the pups hostage as a bargaining tool. He and Hexy were looking for some evidence of where he was hiding, and of the missing man's state of mind, since it would determine how the poor soul was dealt with. Poaching was a serious crime here in Scotland.

Rory stepped out into the calf-deep water, and with the casual use of what looked like inhuman strength, pulled the rowboat up onto the gritty shingle with but a single hand. He turned and offered his arm to her.

"Careful now, lass. Yer shoes are lovely but not made for rough sand."

Abandoning the picnic basket, Hexy allowed him to assist her onto shore. His touch, in spite of his previous show of force, was as gentle as sunshine, and as warming. That was pleasant, because she felt a sudden, unexpected chill creeping over her body.

"What dae ye feel here, lass? What dae ye smell?" he inquired of her, his head cocked as he asked that rather strange question. "Ye sense something, dae ye not? Yer kind always could talk wi' the dead."

Aware that she had been holding her breath, Hexy finally released a sigh and sampled the isle's atmosphere. Peat reek was strong in the air, even with the cyclonic breeze that wrapped the tiny island. And though not far from the mainland, the air of isolation was profound. Even the birds had abandoned them once they came on shore.

Hexy turned her head slowly, trying to identify something that was at once foreign and yet familiar. This seemed like a place she might have known long ago in a dream.

There were the odd ruins of eighteenth-century habitation about them, erected when stone was quarried here, and a few shacks along the grass fringes where lobstermen and other fishermen kept their extra nets and pots, but that was all, except for a small stone vault, perhaps six feet by eight, and five feet high.

She recognized the building's purpose and suffered a chill. Such vaults were erected on islands that the tide favored. They were used to temporarily house the bodies of drowned seamen who washed ashore until coffins or shrouds could be brought to the island by the families of the deceased.

Yer kind always could talk wi' the dead.

Nonsense.

Hexy turned away, searching for some sign of modern habitation, but there was none. There was no town, not even a single croft with a friendly chimney. It was, in fact, the loneliest place she had ever seen.

"I don't like it here. It's too quiet. Let's just do what we must and then leave. Where do we start our hunt? He could be hiding anywhere," she added, staring at the roofless buildings and wishing they needn't explore the island.

She didn't bother to protest the search,

though. Obviously Rory took the matter of poaching very seriously. Just as seriously as he had taken whatever had been in the wagon of the circus.

It made her doubly uncomfortable to think about that, because the disappearance of the freak-show oddity was being talked about all over the village and even up at Fintry. The only certain fact seemed to be that the remains of the merman had been taken during the night, before the circus even opened. There was a great deal of speculation about *why*, and the scandal was shaking the village. A nervous Mr. Campbell himself had come to Fintry to tell her of the event and to leave some old books about mermen in her care.

She was certain Rory had taken the merman's body—but why?

Rory took a deep breath of air and then pointed at a sorry-looking structure whose threshold had been swept away, leaving nothing but sand on the stoop.

"Here."

Hexy turned. The building was gray, canted crazily, and had strange wounds in its walls. It was wrapped in an atmosphere of neglect that seemed to repel the sun. No more dismal dwelling could be imagined; just looking at it made the sky seem suddenly overcast with sickly green, and it was easy to imagine that it was lowering upon them, ready to crush them into the earth.

"That is the place. This is where the evil lies. Can ye not feel it, lass? Can ye not smell it?"

Hexy tried to think of something to say to this odd observation, but speech failed her. Evil? No one spoke of evil these days.

She shifted restlessly from foot to foot, uncomfortably aware of the unpleasant chill creeping in through the thin soles of her shoes and ghosting up the back of her legs with icy fingers. She suddenly wished that she were wearing leather instead of thin silk. A tea gown and slippers seemed inadequate protection against whatever was waiting inside that building.

Rory began pacing toward the weathered shack. After a moment, Hexy reluctantly followed.

The warped door opened without any audible protest and Rory disappeared inside, leaving only his footprints in the sand. Taking a final lungful of the clean, outside air, Hexy trailed him into the dark interior.

She paused three steps inside the door, unable to force herself any farther indoors. It was as though she had been entangled in a spider's web.

Danger. Insanity. Evil.

She looked about hurriedly, trying to find

some reason for her growing alarm, but nothing obvious leaped out at her. Nothing touched her limbs or face, nothing spoke into her ears.

Shutters had been fastened over the windows, closing out most of the sun, which made the room uncomfortably shadowy. The paving stones of the cottage floor had been upset, as though heaved about by a fearsome sea. The uneven ground was littered with dark casks, ropes and assorted nets that coiled menacingly like so many snakes. But that was all. No living thing stirred in the room.

It was hard to imagine that any living thing had ever been here.

Hexy looked up into the dark rafters. One particularly large net had been hung on a pulley rather like a stage curtain, partially veiling a small, high table set at the end of the room. She shivered, staring for a long moment at what should have been harmless rope but that seemed transformed into an instrument of torture and death that waited for her to walk beneath it.

And it *was* just that, of course, for the many sea creatures who had died within its grasp. But that was no reason for her to fear it.

Still, fear it she did. Profoundly.

As her eyes grew accustomed to the darkness, Hexy could see that there was actually some order to the placement of the fishermen's goods.

There was also no mistaking the straight aisles with their pews of barrels, or the broken Celtic cross and candles placed on top of the lectern.

"It looks like a church made by insane people," she whispered.

"It is. But I cannae imagine what sort of worship happens here. Look ye! See yon pieces of wood. They come frae a wrecked ship. There maun be the remains of a dozen boats here. I can smell something else as well." He closed his eyes and inhaled deeply. Slowly his head turned toward the darker shadows. For a moment, he didn't look at all human, but rather like some beast of the hunt.

Hexy's sense of sanity and safety began to unravel. They were standing in the presence of lunacy and hatred. She could feel it all around them. The place was haunted.

You don't believe in ghosts, she scolded herself.

I do now, a frightened voice answered. *And I don't want to talk with the dead.*

"Rory," she whispered, her throat dry and constricted as it tried to keep the room's dank, spirit-poisoned air out of her lungs. She couldn't imagine how Rory managed to take in such deep breaths without retching. The atmosphere was vile, venomous.

Rory grunted but continued to walk among the upturned casks that led to the altar.

"Stay away from that net," she warned suddenly. Good sense was shrinking and congealing into a useless mass of quivering nerves, leaving room for fearful speculation to eddy around the edges of her consciousness. Not even Rory's presence could keep it at bay.

"There's a Bible here. 'Tis covered o'er wi' salt," he said, not touching the lectern, which had been fashioned out of a ship's rudder and a rusted anchor, lashed together with rotting rope. He examined the strange, cracked cross with several deep breaths, being careful not to have contact with the icon made out of a ship's wheel.

"Salt?"

A talisman to ward off evil.

"The son was a fisherman. He drowned some weeks past." Rory's voice had to fight to reach her. The oppression was thickening, darkening, closing in around her, and it swallowed light and sound. "Old John thinks that the People took him, but he's wrong. All we did was bring the body home."

"Why?" Hexy cleared her throat and put a hand to her temples, trying to keep the fear at bay and to make sense of what Rory was saying. "Why does he think that your people took him?"

"The son had a red nose and the marks of what looked like needle teeth upon it," Rory answered, gazing up at the fishnet. Clearly disturbed at the instrument of murder, he was careful not to step beneath it.

Hexy stared at him, trying to create order of his gibberish. "What? What has that to do with anything?"

Rory glanced at her assessingly. "Ye ken the answer tae that, down inside, don't ye, lass?" he suggested. "Look inside yerself and tell me what ye feel."

Hexy began to back toward the door. Rory's word were strange and frightening, and the hostile atmosphere was overcoming courage and reason. Her brain was not functioning as it should, but she knew that she couldn't stay in the tiny chapel any longer. Something there hated her, hated all women. Something not dead but still full of death.

"I didnae think on the body's state at the time. Sae many things might have been at it. But now, wi' Wrathdrum awake . . ." Rory's voice faded in and out of hearing.

"Rory?" Her voice was weak. "I have to go outside. Now. You should leave, too. It isn't safe here. Something is very, very wrong with this island."

"Aye, lass, it is far wrong. But ye needn't fret so. I ken this taint. And I fear that John may have the right of it, though he's wrong in blamin' the People for what happened tae his son."

"Rory, please! Come away." Hexy forced herself to stop at the doorway. By turning her head, she could see the sun outside and breathe the clean air. This was enough to keep panic at bay for a few moments more. "What do you mean he blames *the people?* Are you saying that someone actually drowned John's son?"

"Aye, I fear sae. I believe he was wrapped in that very net and left tae the sea. It smells of a shroud. And this whole place has the stench of the finmen aboot it."

"*Finmen?*" A sudden image, dark and horrifying, bloomed in her head. It was another part of some half-recalled nightmare. Knowing it was a completely irrational question she still heard herself ask, "Like mermaids? Rory, is it . . . You are saying that the old legends are real, aren't you? That's what you were hinting at last night."

"Aye, of course I am. These are evil creatures, though, not like the People. They are the sorcerers of the sea come over eons past frae Norway. They've been moving down frae Hildaland, making a new kingdom in Wrathdrum." His voice faded further as he peered behind the altar. "I right pity their womenfolk and cannae blame them for trying to escape their fate by lying with mortal men. But many a time it leads tae trouble."

Hexy turned her head, fighting tense neck muscles all the way. Rory was walking toward her, growing larger and brighter as the gloom surrendered its hold on him. She was both fascinated and afraid. He still did not look as he usually did.

The disparate impulses to touch him but also to flee warred within her.

"What fate? What happens to the mermaids?" Then, with a touch of ridiculous concern: "Are they truly as pretty as the legends say?"

"Aye. They are bonny creatures, even if 'tis all alchemy," Rory answered, stepping up beside her. He took her arm and carefully led her outside into the sun. Pulling her from the darkness seemed to require an effort, so strong and binding was the morass around them. "Frae their eighteenth year, until the nineteenth, they are the loveliest of all the sea creatures. But each year after that, unless they are mated to a human mortal, they grow more ugly, until at the end of five years they are aged and misshapen like ancient crones. It is then that their fathers give them to other finmen as wives. Most finmen chain their daughters up in caves to wait for the transformation. And most finwives defy their husbands and try to hide their daughters away the moment they are born."

His words were nonsense. This was insanity. Or perhaps a dream. She had fallen asleep in the boat and was having a nightmare. She would wake up soon and laugh at herself.

"It doesn't sound like they have a happy civilization. Why don't the women just run away?" Hexy asked as she leaned over, putting her hands on her knees and taking cleansing breaths of sea air deep into her lungs. She coughed weakly. She hoped that she would wake up soon.

Rory's hands caressed her hair, their touch gentle and soothing, though she sensed his underlying impatience with her confusion.

"Where would they run? They are helpless and hunted by finmen and superstitious humans alike—a situation that suits the sorcerers well. Are ye well, lass?"

"No, I am not well. I am dreaming," Hexy snapped. "I don't feel right at all. I want to wake up."

"Aye, lass, I am sure that ye dae wish tae be yerself again. But this is nae dream." Rory's touch continued to be gentle. "And ye will feel better soon. But fer now ye are in a place of inbetweenity. Don't fight it. Ride it as ye would a current. The longer ye go on thinking that it is just a dream, the longer ye shall suffer."

Hexy rubbed her face and tried to wake up. It didn't work. Next, she tried to think. Perhaps she would awaken if she solved the riddle of her dream. And the riddle appeared to be discovering what had happened to John's son.

"So you are saying that it is these creatures, these sorcerers, who killed John's son? But why? Was he trying to run off with a mermaid?"

"I cannae say what the lad did tae earn their enmity. It may be that they simply wanted a soul for some new alchemy and he was nearby."

Hexy straightened, resolved to find the answer to this conundrum.

"Well then, we must—what do you mean *alchemy?*" She stared at Rory, appalled, as his words finally sank into her brain and received recognition. "Are you saying that they can actually, truly steal someone's soul? But they can't, can they? No one can do that. Not even the devil can take a soul without consent."

"It is just legend, you ken, but it is said that they collect souls and keep them in upended pots down in dark grottoes in Wrathdrum. They use them up a bit at a time in their magic spells."

Like eye of newt or tongue of bat.

"But that is—that isn't possible." Hexy added helplessly as the image of her brother again rose in her mind, "I truly am dreaming, aren't I? Please say that I am."

Rory shook his head and took her hand, spreading her fingers so the scars showed.

"This is nae dream, lass. Ye ken what and who ye are. Ye know me as well. Yer kind and mine have met before. When ye are ready tae recall it, then ye'll pass out of inbetweenity."

Hexy shook her head.

"No." But even as she voiced the denial, a vision, something almost like a memory floated up inside her brain. She had lived once in the sea, been part of its tidal rhythms. She took back her hand and went on weakly, "In any event, I have never heard of these soul-stealing finmen."

"Nae many people hae heard of them. They are an ancient race of sorcerers. At the time of yer King Solomon, before the Other People were called the Tylwyth Teg and had abodes on the River Jordan and in the places that would become Rome, these creatures were living in icy caves practicing necromancies. All fear them and leave them be. Who knows what they can truly dae?"

Hexy was shaken, half-believing his words against all common sense.

"And John believes that this is what has happened to his son?" She added in a whisper, "That poor man! No wonder he has gone mad."

"Aye, this is most likely what he believes. Only he blames the People for it, not the finmen."

Hexy wondered why he kept saying *the people,* instead of *my people,* but she left the question unasked. She knew that she was not ready to hear his answer.

"Then we must find him and somehow explain the situation," Hexy said resolutely. "It is the first thing we have to do. This—this whole thing must stop before someone is hurt."

"Aye, lass. But we cannae find him," he said patiently. "The People have been searching. We've sent word all the way south tae our kin in Aberystwyth tae watch for him. But tae no avail."

He waited a moment and then asked, "Dae ye sense where he is?"

"No," Hexy denied, not even bothering to look inside her turmoiled brain for an answer to this question. Instead she asked back, "Aberystwyth? Where is that?"

"Ceredigian at Cardigan Bay—at the confluence of Ystwyth and Rheidol."

Hexy gave up trying to understand Rory's watery geography. Even that was apparently beyond her. "Well, we'll have to look eastward, too, on land," she said resolutely.

"Aye, and we are. But, lass, ye must consider the fact that even if we find him, he willnae necessarily believe us. Even ye dae not believe me."

She could understand John not believing. Rory was right; she didn't entirely accept it as true either. No sane person could believe in such things. Even her grandfather and brother had not talked so matter-of-factly about their belief in legends.

"But what else can we do?" Hexy pulled her windblown hair back off her face. The sun was shining, but she still felt cold, stranded in some stormy, winter nightmare. She wanted to go to Rory, yet was now somewhat afraid—not of what he might do, for he was always gentle with her, but of what he might say.

"Either we stop John before he hurts one of the People—"

"You mean kill him, don't you?" she accused. "But he isn't in his right mind, Rory. He can't be."

Rory looked grim but answered straightly. " 'Tis that, or someone maun gae tae the finfolk and get that soul back for John. If it isnae tae late already."

"Too late?"

Rory spread his hands in one of his odd gestures, which she did not entirely comprehend.

"They may have taken old John as well," he said after a long moment. Then he shook his head and let his arms fall. "We maun start the search for the furrier's body at sea. It'll be in the north, where the finmen live, if it is anywhere about."

"No." Hexy shook her head. It was a contradiction to her stated belief that none of this was real, but she still strove to apply logic. "I know what you are thinking and you can't even consider going. We don't have conclusive proof that this is what has happened. There could be a dozen other explanations."

"Nae, not a dozen. I cannae think of even one. The evidence is highly suggestive, lass, if ye ken what tae look fer. The finfolk never come this far south unless they are after something."

"But—"

"And I've nae choice about this task. 'Tis my duty tae keep the People safe. I am the grandson of King Lachlann. And tae argue against my duty is pointless, a waste of breath," he warned her.

"If you mean that it is pointless to argue with you, then I disagree. You aren't stupid. You must see reason. If what you are suggesting is true, if you really are . . ."

"A selkie," he said, his tone soft but insistent. "That is what I am, Hexy lass, what the People are. It is what your people—"

Hexy swallowed and clapped her hands to her ears. It didn't seem possible that she could hold two contradictory beliefs in mind at the same time, but somehow she did.

"If that is true—" she interrupted, not wanting to hear any more.

"It is."

"Then you can't go. You haven't even got

your skin. Selkies need their skins. Don't they? How could you manage this journey?"

"I shall have it aen the morrow or the day after. That is what the MacKenzie's widow said, is it not?"

Hexy dropped her gaze while she wondered wildly about intercepting Jillian's package and hiding Rory's fur from him. Not that she believed that he would put on the coat and become a seal, but . . .

"Lass." Rory tucked a hand beneath her chin and urged her to look up. He stared into her eyes and then shook his head, smiling slightly. "Ye lie horribly, and plot even more ill. Yer of the MacNicol blood. I feel it. Ye cannae lie tae me."

"I can lie if I want to," she objected, but without force. It was hard to utter the words with Rory staring down at her. "And I'm not a Mac-ni-Col or whatever you said."

"Ye *are* a MacNicol and ye cannae lie. Not tae me. Stop fighting it. Stop fighting me." He shook her once. "Our kind hae always found each other, lass. Think now! Ye've awakened. Ye cannae bear the scent or touch of yew. The land salt is now poison tae ye. Hexy, accept this. 'Twill be easier for ye if ye dae not fight me all the way."

"I can't think about this now." Hexy put a hand to her head where her temples had begun to pound. "Let's stay with the problem of the missing John. It is the most urgent. If you go off to hunt him, then I want to come with you."

"Nay. 'Tis dangerous. Yer nae ready yet," he argued immediately. "The oceans would freeze yer fair skin. Those northern rocks would score yer flesh and break yer bones when the waves battered ye against them." He went on before she could speak: "I am touched that ye wish tae help us, lass, and I tell ye true that I value yer kind heart more than gold or gems, but it is tae dangerous a quest for ye. For any woman."

He didn't add that he could not risk having the finmen steal her soul as well, but it was understood.

But whatever the risks she could not let him go there alone. "But Rory—"

"Yer tae important tae the People," he said with finality. "Yer the first MacNicol female tae be seen in a hundred of yer years. Ye cannae be risked in this endeavor."

"But—" she tried again.

He leaned down, touching his lips to her mouth, nose resting against nose where he could inhale her breath. His kiss felt natural but exotic and foreign. And it was beguiling. Much of her alarm faded away under its influence.

Hexy slowly lifted her hands and touched Rory's arms. The musculature beneath her fingers was different, stronger and more flexible than a normal man's would be.

And he felt that way because he was *strong*, she reminded herself, as she wrapped her arms around his neck and pressed close to his warmth. "You are a stubborn, gallant idiot," she murmured, not worrying about wounding his feelings. Her dream man had a robust ego and was probably insane. He would recover from anything she said.

"Aye, but ye love me anyway." He shivered as she caressed his nape.

Love him? Did she?

Hexy didn't answer with words since she did not know what to say. Instead she kissed him again, absorbing more of the enchanting narcotic that he offered.

Rory allowed her to tempt him, but finally broke the kiss when his body began to be aroused. He buried his face in her hair. His hands were gentle as they traced down her back, kneading as they traveled.

"Come away, Hexy lass." Rory's voice was thick. "We'll take yer feast tae another isle and have a lay down in the sun. If yer a good lass, mayhap I'll sing ye a song about yer ancestors."

Hexy was more than amenable to this suggestion, but first there was something she needed to do. It was rank superstition, but somehow it felt right. She picked up a stray stick and wrote in the crusted sand: DCLXVI.

"What does this mean?" Rory asked, frowning at the Roman numerals.

"It's a warning to anyone who happens upon this island," Hexy answered, dropping the waterlogged branch back onto the beach. "I don't think that any of this nonsense is really true. But in case it is, they should know that this is the lair of the Beast."

"The Beast?"

Hexy quoted Yeats:

The darkness drops again; but now I know
That twenty centuries of stony sleep
Were vexed to nightmare by a rocking cradle,
And what rough beast, its hour come round at
    last,
Slouches towards Bethlehem to be born?

"I ken yer meaning," Rory said after a moment.

"If any of this is true, then I don't think the Beast is slouching toward Bethlehem anymore. We need to be very careful."

Rory nodded. "Aye, and I am thinking that I cannae leave until I am sure that my task here is done. We maun be assured of survival before I gae," he said softly.

For some reason, these words made her shiver.

Rory rubbed warm, smooth hands over her arms. His touch, though, was more arousing than soothing. She suspected that he intended it that way.

"I ken that ye did not mean the summoning, sae I'll not take ye against yer will, but ye'll come tae me soon, won't ye, lass?" he asked her, suddenly picking her up and walking toward their boat. His eyes were bright as they met hers. "It's been a hundred years since one of yer kind has made love tae one of us. Four hundred seasons."

Hexy closed her eyes, overcome with dizziness and a sort of thrilling terror. "I'm dreaming," she reassured herself. "There is no reason to be frightened."

"Certainly ye've nae reason tae be frightened of me here and now," Rory murmured. "But I tell ye true, Hexy lass, this is nae dream. I suspect ye'll realize it soon enough."

Chapter Six

Hexy rolled onto her back and watched carefully. The moonlight was bright against the wall, broken into distorted squares by the many panes of ancient rippled glass that made up the window she had left slightly ajar. The light seemed frozen in midundulation. There were thirty-six separate spots of hazy light. She had counted them several times as the uneven diamonds of brightness moved slowly over the wall, the shadows shifting lazily as the lunar path led the moon down into the vermilion sea. It was not as soporific as counting sheep.

The chill, still night brought plainly the sounds of the silver-painted breakers, coming closer every minute as they chased the cold moonlight up onto the barren landscape of broken gray stone. These were ancient rocks, sharp and savage and splintered, softened only by cotton grass and patches of stubborn heather that grew in the sand where the jutting stones stood.

Hexy rolled over and punched her pillow, trying to get comfortable. The down had a bad habit of gathering in the corners, where it welded itself into unbending bricks that tortured the body. No one could sleep under such conditions, not even with the sea whispering to them.

Rory would probably say that the storm kelpies were calm tonight, that there were no white horses riding the waves. The thought of Rory made Hexy smile even as she pushed the covers away from her face and rolled over onto her stomach, fitting her feet through the brass rails at the end of the bed.

It was a bit chilly with her bare feet sticking out where the eddies of cool air could tickle them, but she liked having the window open on the rare occasions when no rain threatened to disturb the coastal shores. The weather the last few days had actually been unseasonably delightful. She couldn't recall exactly when, but it seemed to her that she'd been here many nights when the sea roared as it was driven inland by a furious hand and there was nothing to do but take shelter in caves of stone.

Yet blustery spring, real or imagined, had to end eventually. That was the way of the seasons. The days were rapidly drawing in on the nights and had surpassed them in length. Soon it would be summer, the season of calmer seas and warmer days. Spring's lease might already be at an end, the old tenant being evicted for a newer, fairer one.

It was sad to think that she had wasted the season mooning over a lost love. However, there was still the summer to enjoy. Especially now that Rory was there.

Rory.

A shiver of awareness passed through her body, tightening her barely relaxed muscles. He was dangerous. Possibly even mad. He thought that he was . . .

A selkie.

It didn't matter. She was mad, too. Perhaps she could blame it on the spring air, which was very rare and fine.

Hexy sighed in resignation and finally left her bed. If she was not to sleep, then there was something else she could do, wanted to do.

Feeling oddly dreamy, a state of disjunctive thought that she had been in all too often since Rory's arrival, she walked to the armoire, vaguely glad for the rug that kept her bare feet from the floor's cold slate. She reached out with a pale hand and touched wood. It was real, cold and hard and not entirely smooth beneath her fingers because the sea air was destroying the varnish.

So, she wasn't dreaming; she was actually up and planning on giving in to the insane impulse she had had since her trip to the island.

Ye'll come tae me soon, won't ye, lass?

The panel door of the wardrobe, set with heavy mirrored glass, opened silently on Hexy's small and rarely visited world of silk and perfume. Hesitating for just a moment, she stripped off her practical flannel gown and slipped on her sheer combing robe. It was a lovely confection made of blue silk and sheer black lace by the flamboyant Espinasse. She could never have afforded such a gown on her own, but it had been bestowed upon her by Jillian in a fit of gratitude when Hexy had found the frantic Jillian's missing diamond pin. The fact that the gown was her employer's cast-off did not dim her pleasure in it. It draped over her in a soft caress that was almost like magic. In it she felt beautiful and strong, a person of value.

Hexy sat down at her vanity and, setting aside the sharper comb, which she used in the mornings, she selected a soft bristled brush set in a silver frame. Staring at her ghostly reflection, she resisted the compulsion to hurry, and once again measured carefully her sudden love for, or at least her attraction to, Rory.

Slowly counting strokes, she dragged the brush through her hair, considering as she primped whether she was wrong to do as he asked, to travel down the moonlit halls to where he slept. Or perhaps did not sleep. He might be awake, watching for her.

She felt far away and irresponsible but knew that she was thinking—and acting—in a far from aimless manner. And, of course, what she was planning was immoral. That went without saying.

Yet there was something about her seeking out Rory tonight that felt right, ordained, perhaps even holy. It didn't *seem* wrong to picture lying down with Rory under a blanket of stars and becoming lovers.

She had a rudimentary knowledge of what should follow such a surrender, having shared herself with a man once before, but she pushed the thought away. Somehow, whatever happened between the two of them would not be the same thing that other lovers experienced. It could not be the same because Rory was not like other men. His whole person was different, was built for graceful speed. He was elemental, powerful and . . .

And whatever happened would be glorious.

Simply considering it caused fire to bloom on her skin, and the heat to start percolating down into her depths, where it burned like a coke furnace. All other desires before this one had been superficial. This felt critical, unavoidable.

Hexy laid her brush aside and went to the window, delaying so that she might allow herself one last chance to change her mind.

She opened the window wide and leaned out into the night. Mist had enshrouded every strand of cotton grass and rendered them still and silver until a thin finger of wind approached. Yet she could tell the stray breeze's path because it carelessly flattened the slender stalks as it advanced and set the mist to eddying. She was alone in this part of the keep. No one would see her if she traveled Fintry's halls in search of Rory. There were not even the usual castle vermin about at night. Apparently they also favored living in warmer, drier climes.

Enough delay! She knew what she wanted. It was time to go.

With trembling fingers, she closed the window on the night. Though the sky was presently clear, she somehow knew that before the morning sun rose in the sky there would be a brief, violent rain. She always knew when it was going to rain.

The hall outside her bedroom was long and cut with bands of light that sharpened them-

126

selves on her susceptible eyes. The shadows became more solid as she neared Rory's room. The moonlight grew brighter, almost as abrasive to the eyes and skin as a fearsome sun, and in spite of the chill she began to perspire.

She stopped at the last door at the end of the hall and laid an unsteady hand upon the jamb. Through his open door she could see the fluttering of the curtains and smell the brackish air. The sea scent in his room was heavier than out on the beach, almost strong enough to be a taste on her tongue. She was very aware of the fabric of her gown clinging to her body in an unnatural layer of skin.

Ye came, lass.

"Yes."

She stepped over the threshold.

He was waiting for her, standing beside the bed, his body gleaming gently as if he had just stepped out of the water.

Without a word, he took her hand and helped her to shed her now unwanted silken gown. There were so many ribbons tied in so many tight knots, but he saw her free. The perspiration-damp fabric was untied and then rolled down off her shoulders, breasts, belly, hips and fell to the floor in a lacy heap. She was grateful for the end to the fabric's silken constriction. It had been like being caught in a net. But now she was finally as she was meant to be.

Face to face, eyes locked to eyes, Rory lowered her onto the down bed. The linens beneath her smelled faintly of the sea and something pleasantly musky. The scent was familiar and yet foreign.

He did not follow her immediately into the linen cradle but paused above her, lit by a stray silver streak as he examined her body with unblinking black eyes.

Hexy looked back.

Rory was naked: naked of clothing and naked of hair except for the sleek mane on his head and, in the moonlight, naked of the shading of tan that came from wearing clothing in the sun. All he wore was a beadless sheen, a silver gloss of what had to be sweat but gleamed like polished metal.

"Ye still fear me a bittock," he whispered.

"Yes. But only a little."

He seemed to reach some decision. He moved a knee onto the bed and caged her with his arms. Muscles rippled in a life of their own beneath his bronzed skin as he rolled onto his back and then pulled her over him. She clutched his arms as they came together breast to breast. The ligaments' patterns felt unfamiliar yet enthralling beneath her hands.

128

Rory was warm. Pulsing with life, with affection and desire.

Fear receded. He smelled wonderful, looked perfect. She wanted . . .

Hexy exhaled, and then, levering up onto an elbow, she leaned down, setting her lips to his chest, tasting him. Desire was so thick around her that she could float on it. Or drown in it. Her lips began to tingle.

"Lass! The brine . . ." he warned, but broke off speech to make a small noise that was neither sigh nor moan.

"You worry about tasting land salt, but you yourself taste of the sea. Why would you think this bad?" She licked her lips.

"Ye—ye daenna understand. It isnae bad, but there's power in the salt. Ye should nae have tae much tae soon."

She shook her head. "I don't understand half of what you say. If need be, you worry for us. I don't need to understand, Rory." And it was true. That night she didn't need to understand anything. He called it power, but it was passion that was crawling over her skin, occluding her mind and compelling an instinctive obedience to see this act to completion. "Truthfully, I don't want to understand. Not now."

Unable to resist, Hexy pressed her tongue against him, absorbing the peculiar, musky tang. He was as salty and elemental as the ocean, his taste drugging. A sensual lassitude slid over her, blurring her senses and making her already fluid thoughts further disconnect from one another.

Rory murmured something in a language she did not know.

Down his body she slid, moving frictionlessly over his glistening skin, and she tasted as she went, marveling at the satin texture of his uniformly tanned flesh. A part of her was astonished that even down here he was as smooth as silk and unvarying in color. And texture. Her lips snagged on nothing. He was smooth as glass, as tears. But hard, so very hard underneath! Muscle laid upon muscle, sinews crossing and recrossing. He was smooth and warm, but also like steel, like a wild animal without its muffling skin.

She raised her head to look up at his face. His eyes seemed to glow, golden lamps lit from within. They were fringed with a band of thick black lashes and were pupilless and as glossy as crystal or amber. It had to be the moonlight. It made for freakish optics.

But the way he felt? That wasn't the light. This taste and smell was so familiar, and she craved it like air. . . .

Intrigued, she bent her head to him again, but Rory's hand fisted in her hair.

"Nay. Enough. Ye maun stop or we'll be dangerously bespelled."

Unable to go any further with his hand in her hair, she finally retraced her path up the midline of his body, stopping only when she reached his mouth. Her own lips were feeling parched and seared, she noticed through her languor.

He stared into her eyes, pupils contracted to nonexistence, eyelids unblinking. No other gaze had ever been so intimate, or so certain. He touched a finger to her swelling lips.

"I dae nae ken entirely what ye are. Mac-Nicol, certainly. But whatever else is in ye, 'tis something wild and magical. I fear that we're in for it now, lass," he murmured, pulling her down to him, bringing their mouths together and inhaling deeply.

It was a strange kiss, she thought through her drowsiness. He wasn't taking her soul from her as he stole her breaths, but something was tapping her will, compelling her toward some only half-understood end.

Rory moaned. The sound was desirous, yet also stricken. She understood it, felt it herself. It seemed that they would not be able to slake this thirst for one another. All she could think to do was sink against him and try to make their bodies and breath one. She gripped him hard enough that her nails marked him and ground herself against him. She wished their skin would peel away and their bones would part so that they could touch heart to heart and soul to soul. Something in her wanted to transform, to escape out into the world and envelop them both. It wanted to create, to conjure.

Sweat spread, pouring off both of them. Fire ignited and etched her where they touched, exciting nerves that ran from breast to belly and then lower. His tongue flicked out as he tasted her briefly in return, his touch a light rasp that grazed over her neck, lapping at the pulse beneath her jaw.

It was like a cat's tongue—rough but exciting. It was doing something to her, making her dizzy, making her drown . . .

No. She wasn't drowning anymore. She was on fire!

Half-wakening from her daze, Hexy cried out and bowed off the bed as Rory turned her head and fastened his lips over the cords of her neck. He began to suckle.

Fire was everywhere, a strange blend of pleasure and pain spreading out from where he tasted her. Nerves were rioting everywhere on her body. Something was dispersing through her blood, driven into every cramping muscle by her hammering heart. She could hear it, roaring like the sea. It was ecstasy. It was torture. And it was everywhere!

It couldn't be real.

Her eyes were blurred by salty tears, but she looked carefully at herself and then at Rory. Between them they had but four hands, four arms and four legs. They were still two separate beings. Yet it seemed they shared a single skin and perhaps a single heart, for her every touch on Rory's baby-smooth skin set fire to her own and made her pulse hammer.

"Oh, God," she whispered, but no sound came forth from her seared lips and parched throat. She lifted her hands off Rory's body and stared at them. They were coated in a film of glistening silver that burned.

And suddenly she understood, fully and completely, that Rory was *not* human. He had told her the truth. He looked like a man, but he was not.

She stared, dazed. His slender build was so deceptive. The slim bones and muscles of his arms and legs, his very flesh were hiding places for unexpected, even frightening power. His ways, his very biology and physiology, were not hers. She could see it plainly in the silver on her hands.

And still she wanted him. She would, she thought, even die if she were not given an antidote for the fire running through her. She might die anyway. Sweat was pouring off her in briny rivulets, adding more scent to the linens as her body tried to purge itself of the flames of desire. Only the ocean seemed large enough to put out the conflagration, but she would never reach it in time.

"Rory?" she whispered, forcing her voice to work. "I think I'm dying. Please, if you can, help me. I need water."

Rory lifted his head from her neck where he had been laving the salt from her skin, his own eyes glazed and uncomprehending. Twin, gilded reflections looked down at her from the bronze mirrors of his eyes.

"Lass?" He touched a finger to her tears. His words were indistinct. "Ye've nae need of these. Ye already called me here."

"Rory, please. Wake up. I'm frightened. I need water. Look at my hands, my arms. They are dry. My skin is shriveling. I'm burning."

His eyes slowly focused. His breath sucked in sharply.

"There is nae call tae be frightened. I'll not let it hurt you. I ken what tae do."

"You knew this would happen?"

He shook his head, sending his hair to tumble down on her in a cool wave. "Nay. Believe me, I didnae ken all of this. They didnae tell me it would be sae strong." His voice was thick and drugged, and he seemed to have trouble shaping words. "But yer a MacNicol. And something else. Ye willnae die. Nae woman of yer

134

clan has ever died when she came tae the selkies. We shall finish it and the fire will end."

"I don't understand. But please, just finish it before it's too late."

"Aye."

He kissed her once, a meeting of lips that was both pain and pleasure, and then he rolled her onto her stomach. He reached for the carafe beside the bed and poured the cool water over her, from her head to the base of her spine. Her flesh seemed to drink it in, for none spilled onto the linens.

"It will be better this way," he said, lying between her trembling legs, forcing them apart. Somehow he was able to ignore the construction of human limbs and twined his legs about hers. His hands were laid over hers and he gripped her fingers. He set his lips to her nape and she felt his teeth.

If there was pain when he entered her, she could not discern it amid all the other sensations racing through her overstimulated body. She only knew that he began rocking, relentless as the tide at its peak, slamming into her with all the strength of his unhuman legs and hips and back. She buried her face in the sheets, biting the linen as she screamed, fighting for control of her body against the fire running through her.

He stiffened against her, exhaling in a low

growl, and an anodyne was suddenly there. It took several moments for the cooling sensations to spread, but slowly peace and calm lapped their way through her body, quieting scorched nerves.

Creation. It was done.

When the pain reached a manageable level and she relaxed tautened muscles, Rory let go of her neck and moved again, slowly and gently, this time taking her like the peaceful surf as it captures a flattened beach. In her ears she could even hear it, the ancient lullabye of the sea.

Pleasure rippled through her body, spreading out to encompass her.

"Rory!" she gasped as her inner muscles spasmed.

She was thrown into sensual release. The ocean seemed to pour through her, over her. She let go and drowned.

The bathtub on the second floor was vast, the length of a man, and a yard wide at least. It squatted inelegantly on thick legs, waiting patiently in the moonlight to be filled with hot water from a coal-driven water heater.

"It will take forever for the water to heat," Hexy said, staring at the cold metal monstrosity. "I am not even certain how to light the thing. Let's bathe in the morning."

Rory smiled and shook his head. "I think ye'll find that the water isnae sae cold and unpleasant as ye think," he said gently, reaching for the pump handle that would start the cold water's flow. "And we had best wash the salt off of ye. Fetch a cloth, lass, and I'll bathe ye."

Doubtful about the pleasure of a cold bath, even at Rory's hands, but unwilling to complain when she was so tired, Hexy went to the shaving table to gather up some soap and a washcloth.

A pace from the table, she recoiled, fighting the urge to sneeze. Usually she loved the scent of lavender soap, but for some reason, right then the perfume in the fine milled soap made her recoil. It smelled strong enough to be nauseating. Probably it had something to do with her allergies, though she noticed that for the first time in weeks her sinuses were clear and her eyes did not itch and tear.

Abandoning the cake of soap, she snatched up a washcloth and returned to the bathtub. Too tired to lift her legs over the high sides, she allowed Rory to take the cloth and help her into the iron basin.

It was a surprise, but he was correct that the cold water did not bother her, not even when she stretched out in it. It felt refreshing as it covered her now nerveless skin, though lacking in something important. She happily surrendered to the lethargy that Rory's slow sweeps with the cloth seemed to conjure as he cleansed her body of the glowing brine of their love-making.

"That's it, lass, close yer eyes," he murmured, urging her to lean back against him. The wash-cloth traveled slowly between her breasts and along her neck, then down the length of her arm. His voice came from far away: "Ye've had a dose and then some. Sleep now. We'll talk about what has happened and what it all means in the morning. It'll be hours yet before ye begin tae feel place-parted."

Obediently, Hexy closed her eyes. She should be asking Rory what he meant about her feeling extrinsic—could he mean this longing she had to go down to the sea and lie in the surf? It was important for her to understand, she knew that. But she had never been so exhausted. It was too much effort to ask him to explain.

A short while later, Rory lifted Hexy from the tub and carried her to bed. Holding her in one arm, he pulled the covers aside and tucked her in, kissing her a last time.

Hexy did not awaken.

Stretching out beside her on the bed, he stared at the scattering of fern tickles on her nose and cheeks, smiling at the tiny freckles even as he thought about what had happened between them, and what it might mean. If he was stunned, then she would be doubly so.

They would eventually need to discuss what had occurred, but after her journey back into her own senses. Perhaps by then he would have some words to explain their situation to her.

He also needed to return to the People and speak to his father about the oddities of the extraordinary coupling that had taken place between them, and what it meant. Hexy was more than she appeared to be, and apparently so was he.

They also needed to talk about what he had discovered on the islet where the strange chapel had been raised and then desecrated.

Yet what he needed most was the return of his skin. He had been too long without it. It was affecting his judgment, subjecting him to extremes of emotion. Without the sea and his skin, he would eventually grow feral and dangerous. Many selkies withered away and willed themselves to die, but it would not be so with King Lachlann's children.

Sighing, Rory turned his head and looked out toward the ocean that danced beneath the glittering stars. It was the fourteenth night, and both the sky and the sea called to him. But tonight he could not answer them. His place was with Hexy and with any new life that might be growing within her. He would know by the morning if his seed had quickened. If there was a babe, the new life would whisper to him.

139

It was strange to think that this beautiful creature sleeping beside him was the only credible human witness alive who knew who and what he was. The lasses before her who had lain with the selkies had all died or forgotten them when the blessing of amnesia was given. Secrecy was paramount to the People, but no one would question why he had revealed as much as he had to Hexy and taken her as soon as possible. She was the savior of their race.

Had he had his skin, he would have gone back to Avocamor and sought his father's blessing before bespelling her with the salt, before forcing the knowledge of what they were upon her.

But he did not have his skin, and Hexy of the MacNicol—and some other magical clan—was too precious to risk losing. Tying her to him was paramount.

He curled himself around her, feeling fiercely protective.

He only prayed that when she understood the desperate straits they were in, she would forgive him for what he had done.

She simply *had* to forgive him. He could not bear it else.

140

Chapter Seven

Hexy dreamed and was terrified.

"Good evening, Reverend," a deep, raspy voice said.

The man in the oilskin cape turned and peered into the darkness. The flask in his hand caught the light of the moon and redirected the lonely, silvery beam into the night. The same moonbeam danced over the rectangular lenses of his spectacles, making him appear eyeless and vulnerable—which he was.

"Who is there?" the old voice quavered, nearly carried off by the wind pouring in off the sea. He shoved the silver flask into a deep pocket and took a grip on his walking stick. His heavy shoes with their wooden soles were clumsy on the slimy rocks, littered with the

peculiar clots of rotting flotsom, he had climbed down to investigate.

"They call me Sevin, the guardian of the pool— when they call me anything. But then, you already knew that, didn't you?" A dark shape shambled out of the rocks. It was huge, misshapen, covered in decaying sea wrack where tiny white hermit crabs crawled. "Why do you trespass among the soul gatherers? Did you think to actually hunt us, meddlesome priest?"

The reverend stared in amazed horror, finally confronting the evil that the sin eater had warned him of. The evil he had long feared existed in his coastal parish, causing so many deaths, stealing so many souls. How could he have ever suspected that it was the selkies who were causing such harm? He should have heeded the words of the mad sin eater!

Phosphorescent mist followed the creature—and cold. There was a musky, rotten odor that filled the unnatural damp, and it drove chill and terror down into the marrow of the old man's fragile bones.

He wasn't prepared for this! He would never be prepared for this! His faith was not great enough to carry him through a war with true pre-Christian evil. He was a sinner, given to drink and other weaknesses of the flesh.

"Sevin! No, I do not seek you! Get thee behind me!" he gasped and turned to flee, but he could find no purchase on the lichen-covered stones, even when he *dropped his stick and scrabbled at the rocks with desperate hands.*

An impossibly long white arm reached out. It arced through the air like a whip. There was a violent blow to the old man's back that cracked bone, and he fell to his knees, crying out with pain when bits of broken shell were driven into his kneecaps.

Tentacles quickly enfolded him, lifting him into the air, spinning him about so he pointed head downward. A hole opened in the bloodless blue face of his attacker. He saw the needles of bone jutting out before the mouth closed over his nose. Then the world spun and he was flattened against the slimy rock, a horrible weight bearing down on his chest as it squeezed the air—and his soul—out of him.

The reverend screamed, but weakly. Blood and brine were running into his mouth, and the turning tide was lapping at his face, trying to snatch away his tears, his breath, his life.

And then it was too late for struggle. His soul was gone. He didn't even cry out when the blue-gray beast crawled off his chest and hoisted him back into the air.

"It's called faleste, priest. Your kind use it as capital punishment. It is less popular than burning, but I think that in this case it shall serve us best."

The reverend was thrown down hard, a flesh-and-bone stake driven into the ground. He heard the bones of his skull splinter and grate against one another when he was wedged headfirst into a crack in the slimy boulders. Agony filled his body as it was forced into the too small place, but the physical pain was no match for the horror of having his soul wrested from his body.

"You'll meddle with us no more, priest. Your soul belongs to Wrathdrum now, and it will feed my children."

There was a horrible noise, a gurgling rasp, and the reverend realized that the creature was laughing.

Waves closed over the reverend's head, closing out sound, and this time did not draw back from the pebbled strand. With his dying eyes stung by salt, he watched the retreating finman step into the sea and transform, his pale legs knitting together into a single black fin that cut the phosphorescent water like a whip.

The reverend wanted to pray, but for the first time in his life, conviction failed him. He had failed his test of faith, and he had been forsaken. Soulless creatures could not talk to God. They were an abomination in the Lord's sight. There was nothing he could do except bear silent witness to the transformation of the hideous beast who had eaten his soul and cheated him of a chance at Paradise.

He thought of the Eighty-fourth Psalm, understanding it in a way he had not before:

Incline your ear to me cry—adrift among the dead, like the slain who lie in a grave, whom you remember no more. Lord, why have you cast off my soul?

Only it wasn't the Lord who had cast off his soul. It was a monster who had stolen it away, robbed him of his most precious possession because he had been weak and careless, and vain about his strength of office. And he had been too curious about the dying Campbell girl's confession and why the family had sent for a sin eater, a man to consume the funeral meats with which they'd arrayed her body, and take on all the girl's sins on himself.

Finally alone, except for the darkening sea and his endless agony, Reverend Fraser accepted what had happened and willed himself to die. He opened his mouth and sucked the merciful black water down into his crushed lungs.

Hexy awoke with a gasp. She sucked air into her chest as if it was she, and not the man in her dream, who had drowned. It was several moments before she lost the sensation of rank water burning in her lungs.

A familiar shadow appeared at the foot of the bed, backlit by the waning moon.

"Rory?" she asked, sure of who it was but needing the reassurance of his voice.

"Aye, lass." His comforting weight settled onto the tick and he drew her into his arms.

Hexy suddenly realized that she was naked,

exposed to the chill night air, as was Rory. Vaguely embarrassed, she slipped out of his arms and wiggled down under the comforter, which still held the warmth of their lovemaking. She breathed deeply of the peculiar but reassuring smell of sex and sea that clung to the linens, and tried to calm her terror-wracked heart.

"I remember this time. Remember the monster who is always in my dreams."

"Hush now. Ye've been rovin' in yer mind, ramblin' in dark and strange places. It will seem more normal soon, these watery places that are now in yer mind."

"But I saw him," she whispered into Rory's smooth, hairless chest as he settled beside her. She fisted hands into his glossy hair.

"Who, lass?" he asked gently. "Whom did ye see?"

"*Sevin*," she whispered, her voice hardly louder than a breath. "The guardian of the cave sleepers, the monster of Wrathdrum."

Rory stiffened, his arms tightening. "What?" His voice held disbelief and displeasure, even as his hands continued to be soothing.

"The blue finman. I saw him. He was awful!" Hexy began to tremble. "I sometimes dream about him . . . and Rory Patrick."

"Ye actually saw him in a vision?"

"Yes, he . . ." Hexy swallowed and burrowed

deeper into Rory's arms. "He killed Reverend Fraser. He sucked his soul out with his horrible pointy teeth and then crammed him into some rocks to drown. He said he was taking it to Wrathdrum to feed to his children."

Unbelievably, she yawned on those horrible words. Her eyelids began to get heavy and her body slumped as though her bones had suddenly lost their rigidity. Her muscles ran like hot wax, pooling her on the sheets in a lazy *S*.

"I didn't believe it was true. But it is, isn't it? All of it."

"Aye, it is. But how is this? I ken that the Reverend Fraser did die on the rocks—at the time of the mellowing moon. But that was four hundred seasons back." Rory stroked her slowly, his voice distracted. "It is passing strange that ye should see this happening now. Father didnae tell me that this could happen when ye were disvirginaired. Have ye the sight by chance, lass? Is that the magic I sense in ye?"

"The sight?" Hexy asked, her voice slurring.

"Aye. Some humans hae the way of it and know when things hae happened, or will in the future."

She shook her head slowly, not in negation but with confusion. "Rory Patrick used to ask me that . . ."

"Your brother? Ye said he drowned? Was it

long ago? Was it here?" Rory's voice held concern and urgency.

"Yes—and no. They said he was looking for an island, a sort of paradise. But his ship went down—so many ships have sunk there."

"I know the place. The isle is lovely, but tides are treacherous, the waters as cold as they may be and not freeze, and the rocks deadly. Nae sane person would gae there."

"Rory Patrick did. He wasn't afraid of the ocean, and he was sure he would find plants there that would make new medicines. He wanted to help people," she told him, defending her brother.

"Aye? And mayhap that is so," Rory soothed. "But sleep now."

"Could that thing really still be alive and guarding the caves? Could a monster like that live this long?" she asked with ill-formed words, hoping Rory would assure her that whatever her dream had been, it was not proof of what he would have to face if he sought out the finmen in his quest for the drowned fisherman's soul.

Rory was a long time answering.

"I fear he could. Finmen, they say, dae nae die naturally. The only way they leave this warld is if they are parted from their sorcery by violence or magic." Rory slipped beneath the covers, urging her to turn on her side while he

148

wrapped his arms around her. He stroked her neck with gentle fingers. "But that is for the morrow. Ye must sleep now, lass. There isnae fighting the love sleep that comes after. It's amazin' that ye woke at all. And dinnae fear. I'll stay here and guard yer dreams. Ye'll not see that monster again, nor worry about yer brother."

As much as Hexy wanted to argue, to ask about her brother, she found that Rory was right. Sleep washed back up over her brain and drowned out both thought and memory before words of protest could form.

When she next woke it was to see the heavenly cresset flare with sunrise, which melted the after-storm mist in a rush of orange light. It bathed the room in morning glow and painted it bright gold.

"Good morning, Hexy love," Rory said gently, taking a seat at the side of the bed and brushing back her tangled hair. "Ye look less davered today. The dazed look is gone frae yer eyes."

"I feel well," Hexy answered, wondering when embarrassment would overwhelm her. "Just a slight headache, like I drank too much wine."

"Aye, the clamber skull is normal enough," he said gently. "And it shall pass away soon if ye lay still and don't gae clointering about. And if ye'd like it, I'd be honored to comb these elf locks while ye waken."

"Elf locks?"

Rory picked up a lock of tangled hair and dangled it before her eyes.

"Oh." Finally embarrassment began to dawn. She didn't so much mind being naked in Rory's presence, but to be slovenly was out of the question. "I should go to my own room and dress."

"Nay, ye must rest a bittock more or ye may harm the babe."

Hexy stared at him blankly. "The babe?"

Rory hesitated and then rose to his feet. "I'll fetch a comb and then we maun talk about last night."

"The babe?" she repeated. Then, still uncomprehending: "What babe?"

Rory returned to the bed with a comb, looking at it as though he had never seen such a thing before. He toyed with it idly, running long fingers over the teeth.

And maybe he hadn't seen one before.

"Lass . . . It is almost certain that ye are wi' child," Rory said, distracting her from the diversionary thought.

Hexy raised her gaze from Rory's hands. The eyes that looked at his face were wide, awe-filled and frightened.

"What?" She swallowed, started to deny the possibility, and then abandoned the idea as futile. She could be pregnant. Instead, she asked plaintively, "But—but how would you know?"

"The salt," he answered. "It would not hae come if ye were not ready tae conceive."

Hexy took a deep breath, and then another, trying to fight her way to some level of awareness where Rory's words meant something other than what he appeared to be saying.

"The *salt* . . . " She said the word, testing it to see if it had some other definition than the one she knew. "And because of this *salt*, you think that in nine months I will have a child."

Rory cleared his throat, looking uncomfortable.

"If ye carry a female, then it will be nine months. If it is a male, then it will be a bittock longer."

Hexy closed her eyes, convinced now that she was still dreaming.

After a moment, Rory began combing out her hair, being careful not to pull on the knotted tangles. She tried to relax and sink back into her comfortable dream state. If she were to hallucinate, she reasoned, then she might as well enjoy herself.

"How much longer?" she asked, curious about what her fevered imagination would reply.

"Six seasons," Rory answered.

"Six seasons!" Hexy's eyes popped open and

she sat up straight, uncaring when the covers fell away. "But—but that's . . ."

"Eighteen of your months." Rory nodded, looking both guilty and pleased. "But, lass, I am almost certain that ye are with a female child. Our coupling was sae odd that—please dae nae look sae distressed. 'Tis a gladsome thing tae be sure."

"Gladsome!" Hexy clapped a hand to her head, trying to hold the painful jumble of thoughts inside before they exploded her throbbing skull.

"Aye," he insisted doggedly. "A babe is cause for happiness."

"That is debatable," she muttered. Then: "Did you just say that our—that—that what we did was *odd?*"

"It didnae strike you as unusual?" he asked, surprise and a shade of disapproval in his tone. "Is it always thus for ye?"

It *had* been odd, she now recalled, *very odd.* But the strangeness of their lovemaking came in a distant second to the news that Rory thought she was with child.

She laid a hand against her belly. Of course, nothing moved, but she sensed that something—some spark of otherness—was there.

"The wages of sin," she murmured. Appalled, but unfortunately believing, Hexy fell back onto the bed and pulled the covers over her head. Her voice was muffled but still plain as she added, "Of course it isn't always thus. And now you probably see me as the whore of Babylon."

Rory drew the covers down again, searching her face. "Lass, please dinnae be distressed," he said, reaching for her neck. "I dae nae see thee as the whore of anything."

Hexy slapped his hand away. "No more of that! It does something to my brain. You've been drugging me, haven't you? You have something on you that's a narcotic, don't you?" She glared at him, wishing she wasn't so tired and fuzzy-headed. Or that he didn't look so sweetly concerned. "That wasn't sweat it was—was—"

"The salt."

"—an aphrodisiac. It's like opium or something!"

"Opium?"

"Yes, opium—from the poppy. Why didn't you tell me all this last night?"

Rory let his hand fall, obviously searching for words that would explain and soothe her. It was a hard search, for he was rather baffled himself.

"I didnae want tae distress ye. Sae many of the tales about us are frightening. I didnae want ye tae see me as a boggle afore ye knew me fer a good man. And last night ye said that ye didnae want to know."

153

Hexy ignored his telling point, considering that with the consequences being so grave he should have *made* her listen. "A boggle! More like a snake in the grass," she muttered.

Rory simply stared at her, his brows beetled in consternation. Apparently the reference to the snake had no meaning for him either.

"Lass, ye cannae hae been listening. I said I was a selkie, not a snake."

"A selkie." She said a bit helplessly, "You really, really aren't . . . a human." She's seen it last night, believed it. But it all seemed so impossible in the cold light of morning.

"I am of the People. I am of the silkie." His voice was definite.

Hexy nodded. "And I am . . . ?"

"*MacNicol. NicnanRon.* My *aroon.* My lover." Rory put the comb aside. He said matter-of-factly, "Hexy, lass, I maun leave you for a while today tae see my brother Keir. You maun promise that ye'll rest this morning and wait here tae receive my fur. Ye'll dae this thing for me?"

Her lover. Yes, for better or worse, he was that. And it had been her choice to join him in his bed. Her wrath deflated by several degrees, though not her worry.

"Yes, I suppose so." Her voice was cross in concession.

"Later I'll explain everything tae ye. This is a promise."

"Please don't," she answered peevishly. "You never say anything I want to hear."

Guilt stabbed her immediately when Rory looked hurt. Instantly penitent, Hexy held out her hand. "I'm sorry. That wasn't fair. I'm just upset." Taking a deep breath, she asked, "Tell me your name again. Your real name."

Rory looked at her and then nodded. She noted, with a trace of hysteria, that apparently it was satisfactory protocol to exchange names after you had conceived a child with a woman.

"I am Ruairidh O'Uruisg, great-grandson of the King of Lochlann, grandson of Ardagh, son of Cathair of *Clann Righ Lochlainn fo gheasaibh*."

She repeated it.

"That sounds very important," Hexy added, striving for a lightness she did not feel. "Are you an important selkie?"

"All the People are important," Ruairidh answered. "There are very few of us left. And as far as I know, you are the very last of the *NicnanRon*." Ruairidh reached out and put a hand over her belly. "Except for this babe—if it is a female. Sae guard both of ye well."

Then, with a quick kiss, he was gone.

Discombobulated, Hexy leaned back against the pillows and began to clean house in her ravaged brain. The first thing to do was to put the clutter into boxes and have some order. Simplification was the key. But step one was to get rid of outside distractions like . . . like everything else!

She could not send the repairmen away, but she could give the other servants a holiday. None of them were so devoted to Fintry that they would protest a fortnight's leave. Their only regret might be abandoning a source of gossip, but she would tell them that Rory was departing as soon as his fur arrived—which might well be the truth. Without the excuse of company, there would be no reason for them to stay.

Jillian would have a fit when she found out.

Hexy frowned, but refused to allow herself to worry. If she ever started down that path she'd arrive at panic as fast as the cat could lick its fur, and panic was not a luxury she could afford. Not if it was all true, Rory—*Ruairidh*—being a selkie, a soul-sucking monster attacking fishermen, her being with child . . .

Hexy slammed the door on that thought immediately. Perhaps she had her priorities confused, but of the three things she had just listed, the last seemed to her the greatest cause for hysteria.

Carefully, she pushed the covers aside and stood up on the cold floor. She reached for her puddled gown, shuddering in distaste at the smell of the perfume that lingered in its silken folds. Obviously everything in the wardrobe was going to need airing. Her allergies were getting worse.

First, though, she needed to eat. Nothing sounded particularly appetizing, but her body was crying out for food, so obviously it needed to be fed regardless of her rebelling tastebuds. Perhaps some plain scones without salt would do the trick.

Chapter Eight

As expected—and unwanted, at least by Hexy—
Ruairidh's fur arrived by special courier that afternoon. A uniformed guard with cravat and
white gloves, driven in a chauffeured automobile was a wholly melodramatic manner of returning the coat, but typically Jillian. Hexy
wished she could return the grand favor by
sending down her employer's sable, but that
coat was still nowhere to be found.

However, a suspicion of its whereabouts was
forming in Hexy's brain. If she had made the
mistake of confusing the two skins, so might
someone else who was out on the rocks looking

for selkie fur—someone like mad John of Crot Callow.

Compelled by guilt for her recent laxity, Hexy decided that she would pay a visit to the furrier the following day and see if he could not be persuaded to surrender the stolen coat.

If Ruairidh was mistaken, and the furrier was in residence.

Surely when John looked inside and saw the lining and Worth's label, he would know that it wasn't a real selkie skin and give it back. Indeed, she did not know how she had ever made the mistake of confusing one for the other. The magic of Ruairidh's fur when removed from Jillian's expensive garment bag all but danced along her skin, whispering to her that she should put the coat on and use it for some unknown purpose. It dazzled her, entreated her to hold it close while it wrapped itself about her like a lover. She could not leave it, could not imagine how she had ever found the will to pack it in the first place.

The longing had to be that much worse for Ruairidh, she realized with a pang of belated compassion.

Dazed, she carried the fur to the window, rubbing her cheek against its soft nap as she stared out at the gray waters in some vague hope that she would see Ruairidh there.

She wasn't so afraid of the sea now. It was open to her, welcoming of her. She was certain that its power would lift her, speed her, if she opened herself to it. It was a parent. It loved her. And it would return her lover to her if she waited patiently. Perhaps some day she would even see her brother again.

Lulled, she sat down quietly at the window, listening to the waves hushed beckoning.

Hexy was still waiting in his bedroom, the coat in her lap and sea-struck, when Ruairidh returned at dusk. His presence seemed to waken the thing, making its wild magic stronger. Every hair on her arms and nape erected itself. Impossibly, even the sea raised its voice in greeting, calling them to passionate union.

"*Aroon.*" He spoke no other word to her, instead taking her hand and throwing the fur out on the bed where he lowered them down upon it. Emotions chased one after the other across his face so swiftly that she couldn't read them all in the dim light. There was longing, lust, elation—and then something else that might have been awe or fear. Before she could decide, his beautiful dark eyes turned downward toward her body and were veiled by his long black lashes.

The buttons of her dress were quickly undone and he rubbed his cheek over the swell of her breasts where they escaped her chemise. His fingers touched her nape, moving lightly over her flesh as he gave a humming sigh. The fur nestled around them.

Hexy sighed, too. His skin was smooth, soft— the angled planes of his foreign-looking cheeks, his lips, his long-fingered hands, all were as smooth as the finest silk, for they possessed not the slightest hint of down. Yet, with fur or without, he was infinitely pettable. Her fingers could not resist him.

His own clothes were pushed away with hasty hands until he was naked and Hexy could feel the beating of his heart beneath her cheek, slow and deep like the crashing of the ocean. It caught her up, bespelled her more completely than the sea alone could. She would have resented the surrender of will had she been alone, but she knew that Ruairidh was likewise enthralled by the enchantment that happened between them.

There was no need for haste. The slivered bit of waning moon rose in silence as they kissed, and began its journey across the sky. It crept in the window, floating on stealthy wings. Its blue light danced over their skin until they glowed with lunar brilliance.

The warmth of Hexy's body grew even as it clenched in on itself, rolling tight like a fist before battle. The heat in her belly quested outward to her shivering skin and inward toward her loins, drawing muscles tight as it traveled. It was streams of lust, longing and love flowing into one another and making her nerves dance wildly when the combined emotions overflowed their normal capacity to feel and sought new channels of sensation. Fire was conducted immediately from nerve to nerve as it created new conduits of skin consciousness. Like Ruairidh's fur, her own skin came alive, and it hungered for something.

Perspiration sheened them both. This time she was careful, tasting only in moderation— just a small kiss of the salt to let the wild magic free.

And this time there was no pain. Their union was right, inevitable. He entered her, moved in her, and suddenly that clenched fist was flung open, pitching her toward the sky, hurtling her outward into a place so beautiful that it seemed unreal, perhaps even forbidden to mortals since they were driven from the first paradise.

She came back to herself in time to see Ruairidh arch back above her, moved by the same pleasure that was close kin to pain. His eyes in the moonlight were bright, a black obsidian being consumed by moon fire.

Then the moon winked out and soft darkness fell over them.

They collapsed, resting, letting their hearts

slow and their bodies cool. It was only after their respirations were even and calm that Hexy tried to speak.

"How lovely to see you again at the shank of the evening," she said, her voice polite. Inside, she was shaken by the blinding passion that had overtaken them. It was a sign—nearly proof— that something fundamental had altered in her world. He called it magic. She didn't know what it was.

Ruairidh rose up on an elbow and tried to smile. It was a lovely thing to be seen by star-light, but his bottomless dark eyes remained somber and serious.

"I am sorry, but I maun leave ye for a bittock, *aroon.* It is something I maun dae for the People. I shall try tae return before the dark of the moon, I swear. But I ken how ye think now. If I am longer away ye must have patience and not set out on yer own tae find me. There are other dangers than the sea, and I haven't time tae show them tae ye. Promise me that ye'll await me here."

Hexy's hands tightened involuntarily on Ruairidh's fur. She wanted to protest but was learning that Ruairidh could be as deaf as a gatepost—latch, hinges and all—when it came to matters of duty.

"Yer being stubborn, lass," he scolded, taking in her silence and her still face.

"You don't know me all that well," she said, speaking without giving the answer he wanted. "And you can't possibly read my mind. Right now, I'm certain I haven't got one."

"Ye hae a mind, Hexy lass." He grinned suddenly. "It is just a tad wee and a bittock lost."

Hexy punched him, though she did not truly feel playful. "Why must you go?" She swallowed, then asked fearfully, "Is it the finman you are going to see?"

"Nay. I am nae bound fer Sevin's lair just yet. But I maun speak tae my father and the others of the council about what I hae found. There is also something that maun be returned tae the People and placed in its proper site."

The merman from the circus.

"And, too," Ruairidh paused, and then added in a guilty rush, "I need tae speak tae him about my mother."

"Your mother?" Hexy blinked. Mother? Then she asked hopefully, "You know your mother?"

Ruairidh shook his head. He looked very uncomfortable and actually fidgeted by swinging a foot off the side of the bed, waving it to and fro.

"Nay. I always thought her some village lass, now long gone. But I suspected after our union that this isnae the truth."

"What do you mean, *long gone?* Are you saying she left you for the city, or to be with someone else?" Hexy blinked. She asked softly, "Or are you saying she died? That's it, isn't it? She died a long, long time ago. Lifetimes ago."

"Ye shouldnae be thinking on it." Ruairidh touched her gently.

"Don't think about it? Ruairidh, don't be ridiculous. How can one *not* think about this? She is your mother!"

And it would matter to them. What would happen to them in years to come? Would they stay together? Would she grow old while Ruairidh stayed as he was?

"Hush now." He touched a stray curl of her hair and smoothed it back from her face. Then he trailed a finger down her neck. "Ye'll distress yerself, and tae no good purpose."

Hexy knew that he was drugging her or bespelling her, but she didn't try to fight it. The fist about her heart was too painful and made it hard for her to breathe.

"It isnae the way of the People tae speak of our mothers or lovers, for there is naught but sad tales tae tell now that all the *NicnanRon* are gone, and none may come tae the sea tae be with their young. And it is a sad fact for our loves that we all live long past the short span of human years as well."

Hexy sorted through his reply. As always, there was so much she didn't understand. And a great deal that horrified her, though she was now relaxed enough that she couldn't give in to the incipient hysteria crowding her brain.

"How long *do* you live?" she asked, terrified of the answer but needing to know.

"Hundreds of seasons—often a thousand or more. If we are nae hunted."

Hexy digested this.

"But I'm *NicnanRon?* You said that before. I won't—"

"I believe ye tae be one of the People." Ruairidh laid a hand over her stomach. "And even if ye were tae be otherwise, I wouldnae leave ye and the bairn."

That was a wonderful promise, if true. Perhaps even enough. Maybe she didn't need white lace and promises of deathless love.

"You have a choice?" she asked, again surprised. Nothing in the legends she had heard suggested that the selkies had any alternatives in this matter.

"Aye, after a fashion." Again he attempted a smile.

"It must not be a very good choice," she answered, a sense of unhappiness and unease growing within her. "None of the legends ever talk about the . . ."

She stopped, still unable to say the word with ease.

"Selkies," he supplied.

"About the selkies staying on land."

"It isnae a good choice for a creature of the sea. Still, a selkie maun choose—his *aroon,* or the sea. If the female isnae *NicnanRon,* or some other *sidhe,* then the only way they can be together is if he casts off his skin forever." He added, "Most wha choose this also hae their memories bound and hidden sae they can never repine over what they hae lost. Otherwise they couldna bear the exile. Even with this precaution, many still pine away and die. Or they gae mad."

Hexy fought not to turn her face away and hide it in the covers. The darkness was a hindrance to her eyes, but she suspected that it did not handicap Ruairidh. He saw with something other than normal sight.

"Your mother wasn't *NicnanRon?* That's why she left?"

"She wasnae *NicnanRon.* Had she been, the People would hae eventually made a place for their daughter, even if she was from the outside."

Hope flared in Hexy, but it too was muted by whatever narcotic was clouding her blood. Before she could ask what he meant, Ruairidh went on.

"But she wasnae some village lass either. She maun be a *sidhe,* a faerie. What happens between us—" Ruairidh cleared his throat. He seemed embarrassed, though Hexy did not know if it was because of their lovemaking or the fact that he was breaking the taboo of speaking of his mother. "It isnae the usual way of things. I thought mayhap it was just you wha was touched by the *sidhe* blood. It seemed possible that long ago some ancestor of yers might hae been with a fae. Faerie blood is a hardy thing. It can dwell unnoticed for many generations, just biding its time until the right moment comes tae awaken."

"But it isn't my blood that does this . . . this *magic?*"

"Nay, not on its own. We both call the magic, and isnae something of the People. There maun be *sidhe* blood in my veins as well. Close blood." Color crept into his cheeks. "That means it is frae my mother."

"And so now you want to know about who your mother is?" Hexy asked, her voice soft and understanding. She could imagine how wonderful it would be for him to find that his mother was not, after all, dead and gone from the world—that for once the legends of abandonment and eternal separation need not hold true.

Ruairidh nodded, then shattered Hexy's nascent sentimental vision of reunion by saying briskly, "Aye, fer the blood may make a difference tae our child. Perhaps it shallnae be necessary tae take our babe tae the sea. It may also be that I hae other strengths, other magic, I can use when we gae tae see the finman." He paused. "Of course, this maun be thought on carefully. There is always a price for using magic for violent purposes. And the People are very wary of it. Some would even fear me if they kenned I was part *sidhe.*"

"Oh."

Hexy thought about this. It seemed that danger was everywhere. Her first impulse was to beg Ruairidh to stay with her and avoid all of it.

Her second was to ask him to let her come with him. It frightened her to think of meeting more of Ruairidh's kind, especially if they were prejudiced against anyone with fae blood. But it frightened her more to think that he would leave and perhaps be prevented from coming back.

She throttled both thoughts before they could leave her lips. This was a personal quest for Ruairidh, and an emotional one—though what the emotions were, she could hardly guess. He deserved the right to explore this without embarrassment and hindrance.

"You'll only be gone a night?" she asked instead.

"Mayhap two. It shouldnae be any longer, sae ye'll wait patiently for me here. I'll worry else." He stared at her, braced for argument.

Hexy swallowed; her mouth was parched and she was very thirsty, but she didn't want to leave this conversation unfinished.

"If I didn't know about my mother . . ." she began, and then stopped when Ruairidh flinched.

Ruairidh said that they did not speak of the women who bore them. The fact that he was willing to violate this tradition had to be taken as a hopeful sign, however practical his stated reasons. She repeated to herself that she would not stand in the way of his going, or mortify him with further discussion of this painful topic. This was something that would have to be brought up gradually.

"Well, I think that you must go—but I shall miss you terribly!" She buried her face in the curve of his neck. Against her hair she could feel Ruairidh finally smile and his muscles relax.

The pleasure and relief were also in his voice when he answered. "I shall miss ye tae, *aroon.*"

"And you have to promise to be careful! That you won't go near that finman without telling me first. Nor go off to find any faes. Swear it!"

"Ye worry overmuch," Ruairidh soothed. "I'll come tae nae harm in the sea. There isnae a finman yet born wha can catch a selkie in the water. And there isnae any need for me tae talk to the faes. I wouldna ken where tae start my

170

quest. The *sidhe* are everywhere but live inland and underground these day."

"You better *not* get hurt or go looking for faeries. You have other responsibilities now." Hexy twined her arms about Ruairidh's waist even as she scolded. "Anyway, they are all very dangerous. The stories about them are terrible."

"Aye, *aroon*. I dae ken my responsibilities, and I promise that I shall protect ye and the babe with my life. Naught shall harm ye while I live. Now dinnae fret any more. Gae on tae sleep. I shall be back almost afore ye know I'm gone." Rory reached for the carafe of water on the bedside table and poured a glass. He held it to her lips. "Have a drink now, and then close yer eyes. I can see that ye are very tired."

"I am tired," she answered, taking the glass and drinking it down in a few large swallows. "But that is all your fault. You drugged me again. It isn't fair that you aren't sleepy, too."

"Aye," he agreed, not quite smiling. "It is unfair. But the salt doesnae take selkies that way. Instead it gives us strength and speed. Yer gift shall be my shield, *aroon*, and I will return all the faster for it."

Gently, he tucked her under the covers, and then lifted his skin off the bed. Hexy didn't protest, but she felt the loss keenly. It was hard to lose both Ruairidh and the comforting fur.

"There is one last thing: Ye maun stay away frae haunted places. With yer blood awake now, it may be that ye'll feel spirits keenly. I was wrong tae take ye tae the fisherman's island. Ye must not distress yerself this way again."

"I won't go anywhere haunted," she promised sleepily.

"Good. Ye dwell in happiness until I return," he instructed, his tone formal, the words nearly ritualistic. "The sea shall send ye some lovely dreams."

Exhausted, she nodded once.

"Sleep and I'll return after moonrise on the morrow. Or on the night that follows." Then he whispered something in that strange language he sometimes used and kissed her eyelids.

Chapter Nine

Hexy awoke the next morning to the sound of distant singing and a strange play of color upon the clouds outside Ruairidh's opened window. She watched, half-asleep, as the thin strings of wispy vapor wove themselves into a sheer blanket that slowly pulled itself over the sun.

Unbidden, part of a poem from childhood came to mind. "The Little Sea Horse" was a favorite of Rory Patrick's written by a Missus A. S. Hardy:

> *Did the little mermaids ride*
> *Through the ocean's foamy tide . . .*

Do the little mermaids weep
In their sea caves, fathoms deep . . .

The poem's unhappy question brought her
awake. She scolded herself. This wasn't the moment to be wondering about mermaids. Details
about the previous night were somewhat hazy,
but she knew that she had important things to
do that day that might be of help to Ruairidh,
as well as making Jillian happy—though making Jillian happy was seeming less and less important every day.

Hexy climbed quickly from bed, scooping up
clothing and hurrying to her own room. She
had no wish to linger in the bed now that Ruairidh was gone from it, taking all warmth and
happiness with him.

She did not pause to ask herself, as she
bathed away the traces of his salt, whether a visit
to mad John's cottage was an impulse best left
unpursued; she was not interested in hearing
dissenting answers. She *had* to help somehow,
and it seemed that she must go to the furrier's
cottage and discover what she could of all
skins—selkie, seal or sable.

It did not take her long to dress, for she did
little more than brush her hair and fasten it
with a comb before venturing into the dimming
day.

Though hungry, she did not take the time to

visit the kitchen in search of food. She knew there would be nothing there that she wanted, and the effects of Ruairidh's presence were still with her, protecting her from hunger.

She took in a deep breath and set off for Crot Callow. The world these days seemed different to her, fresher. She was looking at it with new eyes that saw strange sights and yet perceived them as something vaguely familiar. And wonderful.

The world was rougher here. It had not had the edges taken off and been smoothed into civilized blandness. And there were many dangers here, too, but at the moment she felt confident of facing them—eager, even. Her blood thrummed with excitement, pounding like waves on a stony shore. She felt everything more deeply. Her hungers were stronger, her energy greater, her need for sleep an undeniable compulsion. That morning she welcomed all of it.

The hazy day welcomed her back. Velvety bees hummed in the furze, their song a lovely drone that underscored the sea's soft voice, and she watched with intense interest as her fluttering shadow strolled before her, growing more pale with every step, seeming to rub itself away as it was pushed over the stony path until it disappeared altogether as she entered the shade of the horse chestnut. The ancient tree spread its limbs above her, a thin parasol of waxy cream-colored blossoms that whispered softly as the wind moved through it.

Hexy glanced up at the darkening sky through the lacy branches, hoping that it would not rain until afternoon but unwilling to turn back even if it did. Urgency dogged her, pushing her to a hurried pace.

It was a long walk to Crot Callow, made only a little shorter by cutting through MacKenzie's Rath and using the tiny bridge over the moat, which forded the sea-bound stream that ran there through the early blooming heather. It was there that the mallow trees grew, and Hexy decided that she would stop another day and gather sap to make marshmallow candy. Her grandmother had always sworn that sweet mallow could heal wounds, cure coughs and prevent illness of all kinds. It was a good precaution for her to take for the babe's sake as well as her own, but it also sounded like something she would like to eat. Lemonade was wonderful, but she could not afford to go on drinking it even if the grocer got more lemons.

She had somehow forgotten that taking this route through the all but forgotten rath also meant that she had to pass through the eerie shell dunes. It was not so much a midden as a graveyard, a place of many birds, where the bank of abandoned mussels and oysters rose up to nearly three times her height and hid her completely from the sea.

The way through the bleached shell hills was slippery and the sharp-edged shells grabbed at her shoes. In spite of her best efforts, Hexy often found herself off balance and on the verge of falling.

Disaster was avoided until she emerged on the sea side of the dunes, but then the solid earth gave way to slippery sand. The soil beneath her boot-shod feet became untenable, her weight shifting the fragile crust, and she suddenly found the shell-strewn earth rushing at her with upthrust blades of white and gray.

Birds screamed and scattered as she toppled, arms stretched before her. The impact was hard, and it forced painful shards of broken shell into her hands and knees with enough force to slice through her skirt and draw blood.

Tears started to her eyes as the pain pierced her nerves, but Hexy did not cry out. Before her lay a quaking skua with a bent leg trapped in the joint of a mussel. The bird was hiding its tiny face in terror as her ragged breath washed over it, ruffling its delicate feathers.

Moved by a new compassion for this creature—for all creatures, but especially those of the shore—she took out her handkerchief from its temporary place in her chemise and, using her teeth, tore off the ancient cotton lace that edged it.

"It's all right," she cooed softly, pitching her voice so it was as gentle as a sigh. "I'm sorry I frightened you. We'll fix that leg and then I'll find you something to eat. Please don't be frightened."

Slowly, she folded her own bleeding hand around the small body and carefully freed the bird's leg, which did not seem broken but was badly scraped and bloodied. With infinite care, she bound up the tiny wound. The bird did not fight her. It seemed frozen with fear, its trembling and the thud of its tiny heart the only sign that it still lived.

"There now," she said gently to the terror-stricken avian as she returned it to the ground. "We are all done. You can be off now, if that's what you want."

The skua slowly untucked its head and looked first from its leg and then to her. Its eyes were wide and black and unblinking. It ceased shivering. Making a small noise, which Hexy chose to think of as thanks, it opened its lovely gray wings and flew away toward the sea to be with its kin.

Abandoned by the bird and feeling suddenly lonely, Hexy scrambled to her feet and inspected the damage to her own person. Fortunately, it turned out to be minimal. She had apparently imagined the wounds to be more serious than they actually were, hallucinating the white knives piercing her hands. The shells *had* cut her, but only shallowly, and the wounds were already closed and had stopped stinging. A few dabs of the ruined handkerchief removed the last of the damp blood from her right palm, which was the worst afflicted.

With extra caution, she worked her way slowly to the edge of the shell dunes where the alarmed birds impatiently awaited her departure from their feeding grounds.

Hexy muttered an apology for disturbing them and continued on her way.

Because of the malodorous occupation pursued by the furrier, he had bought a cottage well outside the village, located on a bluff in lonely solitude where it would be cleansed by the wind. She had not heard the particulars of Crot Callow's history—other than that it had once belonged to a shark fisherman who had chosen it for the same reason as the furrier—but she was still absolutely certain that she knew this place. She had a clear image of the path from the dunes, which had in years past been well-beaten down by travelers. Once the flensing shed had been set up and the sharks' blood had leached into the ground, it had become unpopular. The narrow way had grown steadily more ill-tended as fewer and fewer people came to visit the sharkman, and then John and his son.

Hexy's feet slowed, hesitating for the first time. An image of the old Crot Callow swam before her eyes, the past dissolving into the present and then reasserting itself.

"Stop." Her voice was feeble. She put a hand to her eyes and shivered.

The deterioration of Crot Callow continued to unfold in her mind as her feet walked on of their own accord. Weeds were shoving their way up between loosened stones until it looked as it was today. The thick hedge that encircled the cottage turned gnarled and brown, reminding Hexy of the dead grapevines she had once seen in a vineyard after a root blight had killed the crop. All the vegetation on the bluff looked as though it had been recently hit with a killing frost.

Perhaps that was from the salt leaching through the soil. Perhaps it was some other thing. The furrier and sharkman had both traded in death. Maybe it was this that had poisoned the land.

"Enough," she muttered, putting some force behind her words, and happily the vision died. "This isn't the day for an imagination run amok!"

Rounding the dying hedge, Hexy stopped abruptly, her lingering wisps of dreamy hallucination banished by shock. Just as she had imagined, the small stone cottage's gray door was opened to the cleansing breeze.

What she had not seen in her waking dream was that the way would be blocked by a nasty snarl of fishing nets and rotting sea grass that still ran with water. Rivulets of misplaced sea ran along the stones' joints and into the dead ground, adding salt to whatever poison was already there.

Was there something caught in the net?

Her breathing grew shallow, and dread awoke in the pit of her stomach. It uncurled slowly, trying to reach her brain. Without the lingering aid of Ruairidh's calming salt in her blood, she would have panicked completely.

"No," she assured herself. "Nothing's there. It's just a net."

The opened door should have suggested that mad John was at home, but this thought never entered her mind. All she kept seeing was the thick mesh from the fisherman's chapel, the one that Ruairidh had said was a shroud, and she wondered what might have dragged it to the cottage. And for what purpose.

Hexy stood still, listening, watching. There was nothing moving but the shadows of clouds before the sun, no one muttering except the wind and sea.

She wished passionately that she had a telescope, so that she could see what was in the cottage without venturing any nearer. She wondered for a wild moment if anyone in the village would have such an exotic instrument that she might borrow, but reality was swift with its unpleasant answer.

And if wishes were horses then beggars might ride. But she had neither horse nor telescope. She would have to go on alone, or else abandon her quest to find Jillian's missing fur, and to help Ruairidh.

Don't be a coward. There's nothing there.

Taking a shallow breath, she stepped off the path and chose a less direct route to the opened door. She promised herself that she would look inside the cottage, but under no circumstances could she touch that horrible net.

She did not call out.

She also thought suddenly of the old legend that said you could escape faerie enchantment by turning your pockets inside out. Unfortunately, she had no pockets that would invert, and it was unlikely that such a counterspell would be effective against sea monsters anyway.

"Sea monsters! What rot!" she whispered.

Striving for common sense and normalcy, she told herself that it was not unusual for people to open their doors on a fine day and let in the sun and sea air.

But this rationalization was short-lived, for it

182

was increasingly obvious with every step she took toward the cottage that the day was not particularly nice. And the ugly jumble of out-of-place fishing nets grew more alarming with every step that brought her nearer their dripping, gnarled strands.

What if it was John's son, or his ghost, come home from the sea? Ruairidh said that the body had returned, but maybe it was not at rest because it was searching for its soul. . . .

Hexy stopped just outside the door, breathing rapidly, reluctant to cross the narrow stone threshold that opened into the room beyond, which was long and low and eerily bare.

Except that was not entirely true. The room was not really all that long, the ceiling no lower than any other cottage's, and there were furnishings that filled the room: tables, chairs, an oil lamp whose chimney was badly smoked, and a cot made up with woolen blankets. There was peat neatly stacked by the inglenook, waiting to be put on the fire.

Still, the place had about it a feeling of desolation—of desecration—that reminded her of the poisonous air that had enwrapped the fishermen's chapel, and the illusion of barrenness persisted in spite of her eye's testimony to the contrary.

Do you go back, or go on?

Onward. She had to.

Doing as Ruairidh had, she closed her eyes and took a deep breath and tried to open herself up to the place so that she could *feel* who had been there.

Shadows pressed against the threshold but wouldn't venture outside the door. She would have to go to them.

When she felt ready, her eyes opened and they slowly adjusted to the dark interior. It was suggestive that there were dirty cobwebs on the shutters, and the beginnings of construction of a swallow's nest high up in the corner of the room. They would not be there if the door had not stood open, the cottage unoccupied, for a long while. This was evidence for the eyes of what her other senses already told her.

She looked back once more at the wet net, and then in at the empty room. No one was there that she could see—not a bird or a spider or a ghost. She had to go inside and find out what *unseen* things might be there. Since there was nothing and no one about to hurt her, there was no logical reason not to do so. It was simply a matter of conquering distaste and fear.

"I must."

Slowly, cautiously, and with breath held tight, she stepped over the stone threshold.

Immediately, there was a change in atmosphere. The light took on a metallic gleam, and the sea sounded distant and immeasurably dreary as it sang its ancient dirge.

She understood immediately why the swallows had abandoned their building site. No creature of air and light could stand this place, which reeked of death. It looked like a cottage, but it was a grave.

A sudden cold wind invaded the room. Hexy swung about and grabbed at the cottage door, which was swinging shut behind her in stealthy silence. The wood beneath her fingers was warped and split and covered in some sticky brine. Reluctant to touch anything, she nevertheless dragged one of the chairs over to the door and propped it open so it would not shut upon her.

Feeling dizzy and knowing that it was because she had exhausted the oxygen from the breath she held in her lungs, Hexy stepped back outside and allowed herself a few moments to calm her nerves, her heart and her breathing.

The net hadn't moved.

While she waited, she scolded herself for being too imaginative. She reminded herself that it was her job to find Jillian's coat. She also reminded herself of the risk Ruairidh would have to take if they could not find out what had happened to mad John and his son.

The last argument was the most persuasive, for she would do anything to keep Ruairidh away from the evil creature she had seen in her dreams.

The wind had been picking up while she dallied. It played slyly with her skirts, trying to wrap them about her legs so she would be hobbled, and it vexed her hair with its cold fingers. It would rain soon. She could smell the storm coming.

And something worse than rain might come back for that shroud.

She needed to hurry.

Taking a last deep breath, Hexy reentered the cottage and picked her way with nervous precision through the room's furnishings. It was irrational, but she would not breathe for fear of encountering some contagion. Nor would she touch anything, for the entire room felt like a trap waiting to be sprung, an alarm that would summon the hunters to see what they had netted.

She walked steadily toward the door at the back of the gloomy space. That would be the place where John had done his work, where he kept his furs. She folded her lips firmly against the increasingly thick atmosphere. She did not need her nose to know that she was nearing an abattoir. It was as though she was in a maw and walking down the throat toward the beast's belly and all that rotted there.

Death! Death was everywhere. It pressed in on

her, stinging her eyes. She was overwhelmed by all the lives that had been ended so cruelly in this place, the poor trapped animals that had had their skins ripped from them before their souls had escaped their tiny bodies.

Two steps from the back door, the air congealed around her. It was like pushing her way through tar to reach out and touch the door latch.

The metallic snap of the bolt was loud, a report that could be heard even above the ringing in her ears. Straining her muscles, she pulled the door open.

She had a brief glimpse of empty cages. She supposed that the prisoners they had once held were either dead or had fled.

Hexy took one more step and then it burst over her, a wave of fright and repulsion so strong that she began to gag. Turning about immediately, she ran for the propped-open door and the clean air, stumbling against furniture and overturning it, but no longer caring about whether she sprang a trap around her and alerted *it* to her presence. Escape from the site of slaughter was now her only thought.

Outside, the cloud bowl inverted itself in a dizzying swoop and poured icy water down upon her bent head and shaking shoulders. Hexy didn't feel it. She knelt on the cracked stone that covered the dying earth and retched up the poison and despair she had swallowed during her crazed flight.

The spasms were violent but finally passed. Gulping down clean air between slowing belly heaves, she laid a protective hand over her abdomen and tried to make sense of what had just happened.

Had she truly just encountered a jumble of terrified animal souls? Or was it her imagination, being fed by all the new and confusing senses that had awakened in her and her terror of those double damned dreams?

She shuddered. The only way to know for certain was to go back into the cottage, which was something she would not do.

If Jillian's coat was in there, then it would remain in the furrier's abandoned hovel until the building tumbled to the earth, or until someone else brought it to the castle. Hexy doubted that she could bear to handle the thing now anyway. She had touched Ruairidh's skin and knew the difference between a fur that was living and one that was dead. Dead fur would never have contact with her body again.

Hexy struggled to her feet, looking back at the open door. The gaping darkness made her shudder.

Only one thing would have forced her back into that place of death, and that was if Ruairidh was there. For him, she would brave the cottage.

Fortunately, she had had no sense of him in that ghastly place and had seen no place where he might be imprisoned. The relief of this knowledge nearly made her weep with the black, leaking sky.

Starting out slowly on legs that trembled, Hexy began her journey back to Fintry by taking the longer sea route, which ran through the village. She was very careful as she picked her way through the loose stones on the path, for the rain had made them slippery and treacherous, and she did not want to be injured and immobile anywhere in the vicinity of the furrier's home in case the net's evil owner returned for it.

Her intuition—her *sight*—had been wrong this time. There was nothing useful for her to learn about mad John or the monstrous Sevin at the cottage. Perhaps the finmen had been there and left that net, but she would never know, for the aura of animal death was so strong that it blotted out everything else. She had failed in this task. She would have to seek knowledge somewhere else.

But where? And how, if she couldn't trust her intuition? Would she even recognize a clue if she saw it? And what if the place of enlightenment was somewhere at sea? She would be of no help at all then.

Feeling suddenly adrift and useless, Hexy realized that she would need a new rudder to pilot herself by. Everything about her world had changed, been reshaped—every rule, every law, every sense—and would likely never be the same again.

The thought was terrifying. She prayed that Ruairidh was right in his guess that he would be back before nightfall. She wanted desperately to talk to him, to touch him, to reassure herself that he was well and that all would be well between them. In that instant, she felt that she hadn't a friend in the world and did not know how she would protect herself and the baby she was carrying from the horrible evil if he were lost to her.

Chapter Ten

Ruairidh and Cathair brushed noses and then stepped back the length of an arm to look at each other in the soft blue light that ruled in Avocamor. Both had shed their skins and were in human form. Ruairidh had requested this and some privacy because he felt that their conversation was to be most unselkie-like, and it seemed difficult to attempt it while in their sea form, or with any witnesses.

They sat down on the flat stones at the side of the tarn where the luminescent blue water danced. They took a moment to dispose of their unaccustomed clothing, tucking their robes up out of the water.

The son looked at his father and said in a neutral voice that belied his growing embarrassment, "Da, I think ye best tell me a wee bit about my mother."

Cathair started, clearly shocked at the request, but Ruairidh went on anyway:

"The others ne'er questioned ye about yer lover—nor have I, for I ken well that ye may still miss her. But Irial wasnae just some village lass in Cornwall, was she?" Ruairidh paused. "And that, as much as tradition, is why ye never spoke of her tae us."

Cathair continued to stare at his son for a long moment and then sighed in resignation. "Nay, she wasnae some simple village girl," he confessed. He drew a slow, deep breath and then added, "Irial was *sidhe*, one of the Twlwyth Teg of Pendeen."

"I thought she must hae been," Ruairidh answered lightly.

Cathair looked at his son. "You guessed? It is true, then. Keir thought that ye'd found a mate while ashore."

"Aye, and *she* isnae a village lass either." Ruairidh smiled slightly at his father's further shock.

"She is *sidhe?*"

"After a fashion. I am certain that she is MacFie and MacNicol."

Cathair whistled through his nose. "Then she

may well be *NicnanRon*. If this is true, then ye must have a care at the first mating and limit the salt that passes between yerselves. *Sidhe* can easily become poisoned, and strange things happen—" he began excitedly, rising to his feet.

"So I already discovered," Ruairidh interrupted. His expression was slightly rueful as he said reproachfully, "Da, I know it is embarrassing to hae been with a *sidhe*, but ye should hae warned me. Hexy and I well nigh poisoned ourselves at the first joining. And she is definitely wi' child, which I didnae intend to happen sae soon."

Cathair laughed softly and sat down again on the glassy stone of pristine black that edged the tarn. "I am sorry, Ruairidh. I shouldnae laugh when ye are sae distressed, but this is delightful news—the best we've had in four hundred seasons. And I didnae look for any glad tidings until the Beltane eve. I shall go at once and see about procuring a skin for her and arranging a celebration. Samhain surrendered his when he had his memories bound and he went to live with his mortal, so we've one tae spare."

"Thanks, Da, but there is nae need for haste. Hexy has not yet accepted who and what she is. Her family told her nothing of their ties tae the People. I believe that the grandsire and brother knew, but they didnae explain anything to

Hexy." He added sadly, "She cannae even say the word *selkie* without stumbling over it."

Cathair shook his head, baffled. "Not know that she is MacFie and MacNicol! But if ye have mated, then she maun ken now that ye are of the People. And if she is *NicnanRon,* then she maun be feeling the call of the sea. She could nae live on the coast and not feel it. And if she kens there is a babe . . ."

"Aye, she does feel the sea. And she knows that she is wi' child because I told her." Ruairidh sighed. "She was also bloody angry wi' me and does not speak of the babe at all."

"It shall pass. Yer mother—" Cathair cleared his throat. "She was much the same in the beginning when she found that the pregnancy would be sae long. But eventually the babe will start sharing the salt wi' her, just as ye and yer brother did wi' your mother, and she will mellow then. Especially if the babe is male. Females, when we were blessed wi' them, were always trickier."

"Aye?"

"Aye! Females! Well do I ken the feeling of being in disgrace." Cathair smiled slightly and began an unheard of reminiscence. "It was a tearful summoning that had me leaving Avocamor and swimming down the coast. Yer Hexy summoned ye this way, did she not?"

"Aye, but not with intention. Her tears came

frae the yews. They vex her terribly. *Allergies,* she calls it."

"Ah. Well, yer mother did not weep by mischance. In fact, tae this day, I dinnae ken whether she weeps at all. I think perhaps she stole her sister's tears. The feys who milk the roses maun be able tae cry, ye ken. But many others dinnae have the gift."

"My mother cannae weep?" For some reason, this news disturbed Ruairidh.

Cathair shook his head briskly. "I think not. There is a price for using magic, and I think her tears were taken at an early age. In any event, what is important tae know is that it wasnae a usual summoning that brought me south."

"I ken. Gae on."

"No, it wasnae a normal summoning. This I kenned from the first. The compulsion was tae strong." Cathair's voice slowed, grew softer. "Tears wept frae so far away should not have had this power. And there was a maddening song in the air every day and every night that I traveled that I couldnae quite catch, no matter how hard I listened. And there was a beauty tae the shoreline—a kind of color—that I had never seen."

"Had ye been elf struck?"

Cathair's hands clenched in his white robe and he stopped smiling. "Aye, I was, though I didnae ken this at the time. Naebody warned me that we were vulnerable to the *sidhe*." Cathair's voice was almost inaudible, the pitch momentarily low and angry. "On the third night I came tae the place of summons and climbed out of the water—still having enough sense left tae hide my skin well. I walked inland farther than I ever had, until I came tae the Field of the Hollow beside the Pool of Stars. It was there I saw her. She was sae different from any woman I had ever seen, a child of two fey clans, one of Wales and one of Cornwall, and she glowed like the moon. Though it was night, I swear a rainbow held out a shining hand and pointed to her, saying 'This is for ye and ye alone.'"

Ruairidh smiled at this rare poetic flight. He understood completely, though, for he felt much the same way about Hexy even without *sidhe* magic.

"She was bonny, then?"

"Aye, that she was. There is none like her." Cathair did another fast shake of his head. "She was also a perverse wench. She waited until I was close and then skipped away. I called tae her, but she ran. The harder I chased, the more hedges she set between us—and all the while that maddening *sidhe* song was filling the air." Cathair cleared his throat, as though again embarrassed. "She finally halted beneath a blossoming hawthorn where they were many Druid wrens. Ye ken what a portent this was? What it betokened?"

Ruairidh grunted.

"It was a Dyad tree?"

"Aye, but the dyad had fled, leaving it tae whomever wished tae use it. I think the wench thought to entrap me in it. She might hae succeeded if I hadnae hidden my skin." His nose wrinkled, showing his lingering irritation. "Whatever her intent, the magic turned on her then, and she was soon as bespelled as I. We lay down in the velvet moss."

Cathair stared into the distance, recalling a moment that was clearly filled with many powerful emotions. Finally he went on.

"Those _sidhe_ birds were beautiful, their feathers glistening under the moon. I ken that ye've seen them, for they followed ye and Keir both when ye were pups, a gift frae yer mother. Any road, 'twas they who sang sae sweetly of desire that I saw the stars themselves lean down out of the sky tae listen, and then drown themselves in that pool when they couldnae have her."

Cathair again stopped speaking.

"What happened?" Ruairidh asked quietly, as his father's silence lengthened. He was having trouble imagining this woman as his mother.

Cathair shook himself.

"What could happen but disaster? She was a

novice filled wi' strong magic she couldnae control. Until then, she had known nae enemy save the inclement weather of the inundation—and I nae enemy save a rough sea. We were nae prepared for what happened. The power overran her will and swallowed us both up. Had she nae been *sidhe* she would hae died. I—I went mad for a bittock. I didnae know where I was or what was happening."

Ruairidh grunted again. He was sympathetic. His union with Hexy had taken him the same way.

"I didnae return tae my senses until a bird of the rainbow appeared and dropped a sprig of fiery yew upon us. Of course, by then the deed was done and she was wi' child. Two of ye, in fact. Ye and yer brother Keir."

Cathair stopped, His jaw was clenched tight, apparently unable or unwilling to go on with the story.

"And sae she came here for the birth?" Ruairidh prompted.

"Nay." The word was harsh.

"Nay? But I dinnae understand. If she was *sidhe*, why could she nae come? The People wouldnae hae been pleased, but they would hae given her shelter until the birth—" Ruairidh stopped at his father's sorrowful expression. "She didnae *love* ye? Even after the mating?"

"Nay. She wasnae like a human, son. Some

fey cannae love. And the King of Wonders wouldnae force her tae come tae me here in the north until the time was upon her. This was at the time of the bad winters, when we built the great cofferdam to save Avocamor from the changed tide. Every able-bodied selkie was needed here. I couldna stray frae my home until the season of the golden moons when ye were born, sae we separated." He looked closely at his son and then went on. "I knew when it was time fer yer birth and returned then. After ye and yer brother had fed once frae her breast—a mistake that was, for the milk made ye both ill—I took ye both away with me. She sent ye both north with her blessing, saying she didnae want to see us ever again, as she couldnae bear to look upon us and recall her arrogance and shame. And frae that day onward, we were tae be as the dead tae her and her kin. I thought that she didnae mean this, that she said this because she was young. But she hasnae relented."

"I wish . . ." Ruairidh looked down for a moment, uncertain if he was glad or sorry to have heard this tale. For the first time in his life, he had an urge to see and know his mother. It had been easier not to think of her when he had imagined her long dead and beyond his reach.

"Yer Hexy shall mellow wi' time, though," Cathair consoled him. "She isnae pure *sidhe*. The babe shall see tae her surrender. It is always that way with the MacNicol."

"Aye? Even if she should have a girl babe?"

"Assuredly, my son. It will just take a bittock longer. In any case, ye'll need tae take some fruit back wi' ye. If she is MacFie and MacNicol, the craving for it will be strong. Ye'll need tae bring it tae her until she is ready tae come here herself. And ye'll have tae persuade her by the season of inundation. Once the storms begin, the tide will be tae strong for one in a delicate condition."

Cathair rose. Ruairidh could see him setting sentimental memories aside.

"But that is for later. We've more immediate troubles. Come along, now. Ye need tae talk tae the others. And we need tae talk wi' ye as well. There has been another attack on the pups."

Ruairidh nodded soberly. "Aye. And I've news about that as well. It is as ye feared, Da. The finmen are behind those who hae gone missing. And it was they what gave the ancestor's body tae the circus. I fear that Sevin is attempting some new and evil necromancy. There is a new pall over Wrathdrum. And we ken from the past that once a finman begins a conquest, he'll nae be content until he has dominion over all the sea. I am also worried, fer Hexy dreams of him."

Cathair looked grim at this news. "Has she the sight?"

"She doesnae ken. Mayhap it is only bad dreams."

"And mayhap not. I'll send swimmers for the council. The People must be warned."

"Why are they nae here?" Ruairidh asked with surprise. "Surely they kenned why I went ashore."

"My son, 'tis nearly Beltane. They are abroad, as they maun be. Since this last war of men consumed the land, it has made males scarce. There has been a greater welcome for the People frae the lasses in the villages." He said practically, "They and we must repopulate. Let us hope that some of them are fertile unions."

"That is fair news, of course," Ruairidh answered after a moment. "But I cannae stay fer long. Ye'll have tae explain it tae the council wi'out me. I dare nae leave Hexy tae long on her own. She likely tae gae wandering."

"I trust that we shallnae be long in gathering. This news is eagerly awaited. But the council must hear yer words firsthand. We've had twelve hundred seasons of peace with the finfolk. There are many who will be reluctant to act against the finmen unless they are convinced beyond all doubt that they are responsible for recent events."

Ruairidh sighed and gave a reluctant nod.

"There is one other thing, Da, which I want tae know before we leave the subject of my mother."

"Aye?" Cathair looked wary.

"What happened tae Irial? Where is she? I know that she said tae never come near her again, but ye must have looked in upon her a time or twa. We always dae look over the women even if we never touch them again."

Cathair rubbed his nose. "I saw her once, perhaps twice. Be assured that nothing bad happened tae her. You are thinking of the women who have hard labors and then hae children nae more? That didnae happen in this case. All went well at the birthing. She gave ye and yer brother up tae me, not because she was ill but because ye needed the sea. And the Pendeen feys wouldnae accept ye—though I believe the Twlwyth Teg would hae welcomed ye both had ye not needed the sea tae live. Their numbers hae dwindled tae." Cathair spread his arms wide, then slapped his hands together. He added briskly, "After yer birth she went back tae practicing her magic, only this time she set about vexing the mortals of Pendeen."

Ruairidh stared at his father in consternation.

"And ye never saw her again?"

Cathair smiled sadly at his son, his dark eyes as bleak as Ruairidh had ever seen them.

"After that first season, nay, I didnae. Why would I? I was mistaken in her. It was all magic. She wasnae my true *aroon*, Ruairidh. And she didnae love me either." Cathair touched his son's arm. "I believe she loved ye and Keir, though, as much as she could, poor heartless, tearless creature. Sometimes Fate decides these things—and often she knows best."

Ruairidh shook his head, for the first time uncomprehending of his father's sentiments and the way of the People. He could not imagine ever being willingly parted from Hexy or any child they had. Surely his heart would shrivel and die if he tried. He could never accept the exile that had been his father's lot.

Seeing his expression, Cathair added, "If ye feel otherwise for this woman, then she is your true *aroon*, Ruairidh, and ye've been doubly blessed. 'Tis a' the more reason to bring her safe tae the sea."

Chapter Eleven

Ruairidh was gone and Hexy had to find him.
The compulsion was unnatural and infuriating,
but she had no choice. He'd become an addic-
tion, and whether waking or sleeping, she
craved him. His presence was necessary for her
happiness—maybe even critical for the survival
of their child. Something inside her was crying
out for nourishment, and no food she ate
seemed to answer the need.

She wanted a reasonable, socially under-
standable explanation for what she was feeling—
but her previous life experience and logic had
abandoned her. All that was offered in its place,
all that made sense—however nonsensical—

were the wild legends and what she thought of as some sort of biological magic.

At first, she had been unhappy, but not alarmed by his absence. Ruairidh had said that he would be gone for a day. She had not been pleased when the day stretched into two, but had not allowed more than normal concern to color her thoughts.

But then the dreams returned, terrible dreams about Sevin and two others attacking seals and fishing boats, and they grew worse during the dark of the moon. Some of them were so real that she could have sworn that she had been an eyewitness to a real event. There were other dreams, too, dreams where ranks of selkies sat as a hostile jury and condemned her for luring Ruairidh away from them.

The current that carried her thoughts, waking or dreaming, was running fast and deep. There was no resisting the direction in which it was taking her, fight it as she might.

She vexed herself with questions. Was this relationship with Ruairidh and all the discomfort it entailed a good thing? A bad one? She knew what society's jurists would say. Yet she was coming to believe that some things were amoral, that some things could only be assigned meaning because of their effects on oneself and others. Religion and its narrow rules of human morality—or even science, the new religion—

didn't yet admit the existence of the reality she faced. It did not know of selkies and their culture. Neither science nor religion had an adequate framework for judging her actions.

Hexy couldn't bear the waiting anymore. She walked through the days and too many of the nights frightened by her thoughts, her always growing inner anxiety over the possible reasons for Ruairidh's failure to return outweighing external fears of her pregnancy and alienation from her previous life. And poured over the top of all this was a growing fright of this evil creature that haunted her dreams in an increasingly personal manner. It seemed that he now sensed her there, for sometimes he would turn and scan his surroundings as though searching for a hidden watcher.

Something inside her was amiss as well. The babes—for she no longer doubted that Ruairidh was correct about her being with child, and she suspected there might be two—were crying out for something in tiny voices that hurt her head. And she did not know what it was the children needed. She had tried every fruit available in the village and even taking mallow sap, but nothing helped for long.

Given this feeling of near certainty of disaster if Ruairidh did not return soon, the question was not if she should begin a quest to find him, but simply where she should start.

In this she was stumped. In spite of their intimacy and the feelings flooding through her body in heated surges that told her to act—*now*—she knew almost nothing about who and what Ruairidh was.

He was a selkie. But that was just a word. What did that mean? Where did he live? Where had he gone? What could be keeping him away? His father? Heaven forbid, could it be his mother? Had he learned something so awful about his past—or his mother—that he was unwilling to return to her?

The whole of their relationship she had wandered through some dreamy mental twilight, and only now was her brain beginning to awaken. Part of her was afraid—afraid of kicking over a wasp's nest of new realities that would forever change her perceptions of the world. Once this mental veiling was pulled away, she would have to face the truth about what Ruairidh was. And the truth about what she was, too. Was she ready to face it?

Did she have a choice?

Though she knew in her heart that it would be a pointless exercise, she had searched Ruairidh's room, hoping for some clue of where he might have gone. Though she had not expected any obvious answers, the blankness of the chamber's somber interior was frustrating. There was nothing there to suggest that Ruairidh had ever been there—not even clothing. There were only the shadows of shivering leaves against the window's half-drawn curtain and an empty carafe with silvery smudges at its neck.

Hexy paced in front of the sooted hearth in the library, hating the smell of the cold damp ashes but having no desire to kindle a new fire. Fire was one more thing that was anathema to her now. It was one more sign that she was withdrawing from the world. And where it would end, she could not guess. There was only a distant hope that it would finish in some happy manner.

Certainly there was no going back, whatever the eventual outcome. The life stream, like time, only flowed one way, and that wasn't backward.

She had to think. Logic and intuition were her only weapons. What did she know with certainty? She knew that Ruairidh had gone into the ocean and headed south and west. But the ocean was a huge place, and with the finmen involved, possibly an unnaturally hostile one. And she did not know where to begin her search after that. She needed guidance. But from where or whom? It was insane to think that she could go down to the seals who slept on the rocks offshore and ask them where Ruairidh was. They were likely just seals.

And if they weren't, what if they could also

tell that she was part faerie and they hated her and her children? They apparently hadn't accepted Ruairidh's mother.

Her inquiries among the natives near Fintry had not been helpful. The only one who would talk to her at all about legends was Mr. Campbell, and he had not offered her anything useful beyond the advice to read a few of his old books. She had necessarily needed to be somewhat discreet in her questions, approaching him with queries that any curious visitor might ask. It was a shame, because she was certain he knew more, and could eventually be coaxed into speaking if she had the time to persuade him in stages.

She had been so distracted by the babes' hunger when they spoke, but now that she thought back on it, there had been something in his demeanor—or maybe his speech . . .

Hexy closed her eyes on the dark room and, murmuring softly, she reconstructed their conversation.

"I've heard these songs, about sealmen becoming women's lovers, entrancing them and then stealing their children from them." Hexy had swallowed and *forced herself to go on. "And others about women killing selkies by rubbing their necks with Orkney grass—"*

"Or yew," Mr. Campbell had supplied, his face

oddly serious. "Yew is poison tae all magical beasties, seelie or not. But mind, ye must rub it on their necks or in their mouths or it'll do ye nae good. That's the only place for the magic tae get intae the blood."

His expression was supposed to be indulgent, but his eyes had remained curious and watchful.

The vulnerability to the neck she already knew about from firsthand experience. Rory could touch her there and make her weak, or lustful, or able to ignore pain. But the news about the yew was something she didn't know. She would remember that. It might work to deter finmen, if she could bear to have it near her for any time.

Hexy forced her mind back to her meeting with Mr. Campbell.

"But what are the selkies, Mr. Campbell?" she had finally asked. "Does anyone really know about them? Where are they supposed to live?"

"I think none but the selkies can say for certain. Some people think that they are fallen angels, and that when the rebel angelic horde was cast from heaven, some went tae hell with Lucifer, some fell tae land and became faeries and others fell intae the sea and became the slioche nan Ron."

"Slee-ock non Rone?" she'd repeated.

"The children of the seals, aye. But others say they are the souls of the drowned given another chance to

live through means of sorcery. And there are others still who will swear that they are the Clann Righ Lochlainn fo gheasaibh—*the sons of the King of Lochlann who were bespelled by their jealous step-mother and condemned tae live in the sea for all eternity. But that's the fanciful Irish for you." Mr. Campbell had shrugged then, suggesting that fathoming the Irish mind was impossible. "What you need tae do, mistress, is tae go down to the beach and weep seven tears into the water. That'll bring a selkie for certain. Or find one of their cast-off skins and hide it from him. Then ye may ask him any number of questions and be certain tae get some answers. Then come and tell me about it, for I'd dearly love tae know more about them myself."*

Hexy had smiled blindly at what she thought was the postmaster's attempt at humor and nodded her head. She didn't tell Mr. Campbell that she had already wept into the sea and brought forth one of its legends, or that she had accidentally hidden his skin and still failed to gain any answers or even understanding about what he truly was. All it had done was drive her into Ruairidh's arms and give him some power over her—and the children she now carried.

"I need to go."

"Lass." Mr. Campbell had stopped her as she turned to leave. His voice was hesitant as he asked, "You are not a MacFie, are you?"

"My last name is Garrow, you know that," she

211

answered. "But why do you ask, Mr. Campbell? What's wrong with the MacFies?"

"Nothing. 'Tis just that there are stories about them and the silkies of Sule Skerry."

"Stories?" The fine hairs on Hexy's arms had begun to rise, erecting themselves with incipient alarm. MacFie had been her maternal grandmother's maiden name.

"Well, the name MacFie comes from MacDuffie—which is an Anglicization of MacDubhsithe. That means son of the black faerie. Some of the clan was supposed to be descended from the Irish sithe—the unseelie ones."

"How interesting." Hexy marveled at the sound of calm interest her voice achieved even with her heart in her throat.

"The only clan I know of more tied tae the selkie are the MacNicols. That name means both son and daughter. It is thought that they can bear both male and female children tae the selkies." Mr. Campbell had sounded suddenly uneasy. "Are you well, lass? You look a wee bit pale."

"I'm fine, Mr. Campbell. About the MacNicols? Why does this make them unique?" she'd prompted, saying her paternal grandmother's maiden name casually, giving it the American accent because it comforted her with its normalcy. Campbell's rendition imbued it with too much power.

"Your pronunciation is all abroad, lass. Mac is for son and Nic is for daughter. They are long gone *from these parts, all moved away a century ago. It was thought by the natives that the MacNicol women were the special choice of the selkies for mates because they were the only ones who could bear live selkie females. Ye even look like a MacNicol lass with that red hair and those green eyes. But if ye were a MacFie or a MacNicol, ye'd would know it." Mr. Campbell had laughed suddenly, sounding relieved.*

"I would? How?" Hexy had forced her lips to smile.

"All MacFie children are said tae be born with scales between their fingers—"

Not scales, Hexy thought; webbing. She had been born with webbing between the first joints of her fingers and still had the slight scars from where the perplexed doctor had cut it away. Her grandmother had had this defect, too.

She pressed her fingers together and listened carefully while Mr. Campbell went on.

"Supposedly, the MacNicol women were all horribly allergic to yew," Mr. Campbell continued. "With all the trees leafing out up by Fintry, you would be weeping your eyes out day and night if you were of that clan."

"How strange. Well, thank you again for the books. I shall read them soon."

"You dae that, lassie. It'll dae ye some good, I'm thinking."

Hexy had managed another smile before she turned and stepped out into the day.

*   *   *

213

Hexy opened her eyes onto the library and re-
sumed pacing. Her visit had been helpful in
some ways, she supposed, but it still hadn't told
her where to start her search for Ruairidh.

Hexy paused in her perambulation and
rubbed her tired eyes.

Mr. Campbell was right about the allergies.
Her allergic reactions weren't bad yet, but her
sensitivity increased with every passing hour
that she was divided from Ruairidh and whatever shielding affect his presence had on her.

She had to decide what to do. And she had
to leave Fintry before the people noticed the
change in her—her inability to eat anything
with salt in it, to stand strong smells—especially
fire—her craving for shellfish in the raw, her
need to bathe in the sea. Her appetites and
compulsions were growing unruly, perhaps
even dangerous.

It was ridiculous—mad, even—but perhaps it
was time for her to go down to the rocks and
talk to those seals, or whoever else was waiting
there. And if that didn't work, then maybe she
would cry seven more tears into the ocean and
see whom it brought this time.

But first she would finish reading Mr. Campbell's books. They had seemed to be nothing
but a collection of strange and irrelevant fairy
tales written by superstitious people, but he had
been insistent that she read them. It was pos-

sible that they would tell her something if studied carefully.

Determined upon a course, Hexy seated herself at the small desk and forced herself to blot out all cravings and to focus on the task at hand.

She began with Mr. Campbell's last book, the only one completely unexamined. The tome was water-stained and worn, but still in a remarkable state of preservation. It was also a work of strange beauty. The worn cover was illustrated. When opened, the book revealed pages that were bordered with peculiar decorations that were similar and yet different from the illuminations of the kind seen in the *Book of the Kells*. Instead of the usual Celtic knots, there were intricate intertwinings of sea grass and creatures like a half-snake/half-woman wreathed in seaweed until it almost disguised the undulations of her coiled body.

Hexy turned another page and saw merrows. On another one she finally found the selkies.

"Ruairidh?" she whispered, staring at the achingly familiar face. Its gaze, unlike the merrow's, was not sterile and blank. Fringed with those eyelashes, it should have seemed effeminate. But though unearthly in beauty, it was nothing other than masculine.

The whole design was one of wondrous loveliness even though someone had scraped the gold gilding away from the art. She peered at the minute text but could not read it. The writing wasn't the expected Latin but appeared to be some stylized form of Gaelic. She turned another page, searching for some readable text, and found something penned in the narrow margin in what looked like a careless gloss done in inferior ink.

I pray for Thy blessedness, O Father, O Word, O Holy Spirit, that whosoever shall take this book into his hand may remember the fallen who unwilling inhabit the deep waters, and that they be liberated and called home on the Day of Judgment.

I have read of the monk's experiments with peas and believe that these examples of persistent traits may explain the NicnanRon. It is my belief that if she mates with a normal man, her children will appear normal but still carry the hidden curse of their mothers. This is a terrible enough burden, as I can attest. But if she is seduced by a water demon, then she will surely conceive and give birth to another demon, or else another full-blooded NicnanRon.

The shame of my family is so great that I cannot bear it. I place this book into the

sea and will suffer it to rest there, incom-
plete, until I return to a state of grace.

By my own hand, Ferdomnach Meic Maor

"*Meic Maor.* MacMoyre," she muttered, beginning to understand Gaelic spelling and pronunciation. "But what does this mean? It is all just
more riddles! I need something plain."

She turned the old vellum pages quickly. As
she had feared, the rest of the book was blank.
It had never been finished by the poor Mac-
Moyre, and it explained nothing.

However, on further examination of the
book she discovered in the back of the folio a
sort of pocket, and there was a piece of parch-
ment tucked between the last page and the
cover. Inside the brittle vellum there was a lock
of hair. It was short and sleek and glossy brown,
and it looked all too familiar.

She clenched the hair between her fingers,
her heart suddenly thrumming as the lock
seemed to curl about her fingers with a life of
its own. Shaking, Hexy read the blurred words
scribbled on the paper. It had been penned by
an unsteady hand.

'Tis all I have, this hank of hair, and all
he'll allow me to keep as token of our love.
And it is not enough to sustain me in my

loneliness and disgrace. They do not know him, so what care they for his own tender heart's wounds, his beauty, his purity, his fidelity to his people? They only see that his fidelity, in the end, belongs to the sea, and it is there that he has taken our son so that he might live on as he was meant to. They see this as pitiless abandonment of me, the woman whose innocence he destroyed by leaving her with a bastard son. But what else could he do? Ardagh, our beloved son, would die if he remained here. Much as I dreamed that we would be spared and my son could live a life as Kenneth Campbell, it was not to be. It was the sea, or death. How could I let my son die?

But now I am likewise stricken, grievously wounded by my loneliness. This is true, and soon I shall pass out of this life where all hope of love has been forever deferred. But I tell you all that this is not Donagh's fault, or his decision. I inflicted my own wounds when I went to the sea to ask for a lover, and I am without remorse for what we have done, or for the life we created.

I am not MacNicol, so I cannot ever live with my love and my son, and they in turn, without evil enchantment, can never return to me. So I choose not to live. I have foolishly confessed some of my thoughts to Reverend Fraser, and he says if I choose not to live, then I am surely damned. Well, so be it. They'll have to call the sin eater after I'm gone. If he eats enough of the funeral meats, mayhap that will help save my soul.

My love! Perhaps they are wrong. You must have a soul! And perhaps God is not pitiless and we may someday see each other in heaven.

Morag Boyne Campbell

Horrified, Hexy wiped tears from her cheeks. Her hands shook as she refolded the page about the lock of hair and replaced it in the book. She closed the cover on the bit of old tragedy and then rested a hand over her abdomen.

Her emotions were tangled, but one thing she was certain of—this tragedy wouldn't happen to her! Disaster happened when people were weak. It was about the failure of certain personalities in times of crisis. Circumstances that doomed one couple would not necessarily damn another, if they had enough fortitude to face adversity and master it.

Look at Ahab! He had eventually found Moby Dick, and he had to search an entire ocean to do it. All Hexy herself had to do was go and look at a couple of islands where some sea monsters lived. She even knew where one of those islands was. Ruairidh had warned her away from it, but that was before. He surely had not known that they would be separated this long.

Though inner doubts still plagued her about other possible reasons for Ruairidh's absence, her nightmares of the monster Sevin collecting selkie souls were even stronger.

Hexy straightened and pushed back from the desk. She tried not to notice that her hands were less than stable, and she quickly looked away from her reflection in the glass-fronted bookcase. She wouldn't admit it, but she was a little afraid of the undermining effect of the appearance of the woman in the glass. She was too pale, too thin, too hollow around the eyes. What she didn't need to see at this moment was her own fragility.

This was about spiritual and mental courage, not muscles, she lectured herself. She was MacNicol and MacFie—and very angry. No one, not humans or monsters, would keep her from Ruairidh—and no one would take her babies away either! She'd see them dead first.

And thanks to this poor, doomed Campbell

woman, she had her starting place at last. It was time to go to the old hooded man who lived somewhere beyond the village, the one who had been pointed out to her some time ago as the sin eater. The thought of confronting this legendary creature, who was supposedly the vessel for all the sins of the people he had been called upon to save from hell was frightening. But if there was anyone still alive who would know more about the history of this poor Morag Campbell and her selkie lover, it would be he.

Chapter Twelve

Ruairidh looked out over the assembly, waiting for the last echoes of noisy greeting to die out in the hall. It had taken longer than anticipated to call all the People home, but they were there now. All their dark, thoughtful eyes in their furred faces were upon him—some concerned, some wary, some eager for news. Some were resentful of being taken from their human lovers.

It was time to speak of the danger that faced them, to put into words what he feared was happening.

Ruairidh cleared his throat and moved to the edge of the stone ledge and leaned out over the assembly. He began speaking in the slow, liquid vowels that made up selkie speech.

"Welcome, children of Lochlann; draw near and hear me, for I have news of the world." His words were formal and put an end to the few remaining smiles in the room. "A dark cloud has moved over the sun and cast a shadow on the sea. Though we have had peace for over four hundred seasons, war is again coming to Avocamor. And this time it is not of the land dwellers' making."

There was a shocked murmuring that rippled through the room. Some of them had heard of the stolen bones, but they had incorrectly assumed that it was mad John who had taken them.

Ruairidh spoke over the dazed voices.

"We have long known that the finman, Sevin, had given himself over to darker alchemies, but there is proof now that he is stealing souls and ancient bones to create more power for his dark arts."

"What care we if he steals land dweller souls?" one angry voice asked. All heads turned Eleth's way. "We should never have aided the humans. Look what the pact has done to us! I care not if he steals their dead. Let him turn his sorcery loose upon them. It is only what they deserve for their eternal war-mongering."

"Do you care if he steals *our* dead? Do you

care if he steals *our* souls to gain power?" Ruairidh asked. "For that is what he has done. It was our ancestors' bones that were taken from the *last grotto.* It is our pups who have been attacked."

There was a long moment of shocked silence, and then the hall erupted into speech.

Ruairidh turned from the babble and spoke softly to Cathair.

"They shall argue for moons about what this means. Eleth and his ilk will never believe that there is a serious threat against us unless they are personally attacked by the finman."

"Perhaps this is so, but ye must stay here and convince the rest of them. If we delay now and let the finman and his followers grow any more powerful, we may be unable to stop him later."

Ruairidh nodded, acknowledging the truth, but he looked unhappy. He had a growing uneasiness about how Hexy was faring in his absence. It was typical for a selkie's lover to be placid once she was with child. Many times they were even unaware of the passage of time—an excellent thing when the pregnancy with a male selkie could go on for so many more months than a human gestation. But Hexy had not been typical in any of her reactions, and he placed only dubious faith in the notion that her pregnancy would keep her pacified and accepting of his nonattendance.

And the other side effect of pregnancy was that it could, in rare instances, drive some abandoned females to acts of desperation. The watchers he had posted on the shore had seen nothing in the days past, but he had had to call them home for this meeting. No one was there to look out for Hexy now.

Frustrated, he turned back to the assembly and raised his voice in impassioned argument.

The ancient, rheumatic creature that had been born Padraig Gordon was now known almost exclusively by his professional title of sin eater. Sin eating was a gruesome custom that had fallen out of favor in many parts of Scotland, but the man's occupation was not so forgotten and disused that he and his tainted soul were welcomed into village society. Unlike the selkies, sin eaters were known to the church and their status was firm.

Though he was not welcome in town, everyone knew where his isolated cottage was located, and Hexy had no trouble discovering from the now very curious carpenters at Fintry where to find the outcast man. She regretted the necessity of calling attention to herself by asking so many questions, but with the servants gone there was no one else she could seek out for information. Certainly she would not go back to Mr. Campbell, who—though kind to her so far—already knew far too much about the selkies, and had every reason to fear and dislike them, since a relative of his had been driven to suicide over one.

Hexy stepped out into the day, relieved to be away from Fintry and the noise of construction. The workmen there seemed to believe that it was their duty to raise as much din as possible while they worked, perhaps as proof that they were struggling diligently for their wages.

Hexy did not understand them. Had she been working at converting the cesses, it would have been with her face muffled and drawing as few breaths as possible. That certainly let out stringing together long, creative curses that managed to combine both scatological and sexual references. So uncharacteristic was this swearing to the usually courteous Scotsmen that she had to wonder if it was not some corruption brought home from the war.

She sighed, rubbing her head. Every day she felt more alienated from the world. At least she would not be there at elevenses to hear the workmen slurp down their tea in repulsive, noisy gulps.

As she hurried down the long drive, she took time to appreciate that the weather was fair for her quest. Though not previously a superstitious person, she had recently begun to believe in omens, and was glad to find the signs fortuitous. It also meant that she need not bring the rain cape whose oiled hide smelled foul to her.

Armed with the gift of a plug of tobacco taken from Mr. MacKenzie's smoking room—an offering that one of the older workmen warned her to bring—and also the proper greeting in Gaelic, Hexy started out for the sin eater's cottage.

The sin eater's home was located several hundred yards past the end of the village in a stand of ancient yew, which ringed the small farmstead and all but obscured the cottage at its center. The ancient trees were so adept at blotting out the light that a person could easily mistake the gloom beneath them for the fall of twilight. She had to wonder if the choice was not a deliberate one.

Hexy had a bad moment when she first tried to approach the cottage and was overcome by a wave of gut sickness so strong that it brought tears to her eyes. But she found that after a moment, if she breathed shallowly and did not look up, her body calmed and she was able to approach the pitted stone building, and the man who sat quietly smoking out in the only patch of fractured sunlight the woods afforded.

Hexy was nervous, both at her task and at facing a man that so many feared because of his knowledge of the wickedness of mankind.

But she found, instead of a wrathful, towering Old Testament prophet, with a piercing gaze and a staff of lightning clutched in a steel fist, that old Padraig was actually very small, and that his eyes were bandaged in cataracts, his hands too knotted by arthritis to wield staffs. Strange subdermal lumps also misshaped his beardless face and made him both a frightening and pathetic creature to behold.

His voice was fine, though, smooth and soft and as soothing as a lullabye. Nor did he seem at all surprised by Hexy paying him a visit.

"Forgive me for not wearing a veil, but I am taking my ease today and so left off the uniform of office while I enjoy the rare sun," he said gently in the voice of an educated man, marred only by the smallest country burr. "I hope that the sight of me does not distress you. It has been some years since I saw my own image clearly—which is a blessing in a way, as I was none tae fond of it anyway."

"I am sorry to disturb you on your afternoon of ease," Hexy began.

"Nonsense. *Ciamar a tha sibh?* Take a chair, mistress, and speak tae me of what is troubling you." The old man waved a brown hand at the empty stool that sat beside his own.

"Thank you." Hexy seated herself carefully, praying the stool was not made of yew. Relieved that the wood did not burn her or make her

228

itch, she asked politely in return: *"Ciamar a tha sibh fhein?"*

"I am as well as it is possible for a man like me tae be," Padraig replied with a hint of a smile as he put the stem of his pipe between his lips and puffed gently. He was obviously accustomed to speaking around the stem, for he was able to add clearly, "But tell me, what brings you here? Is it the selkie?"

Hexy started so hard that she nearly unseated herself. "What?" she whispered.

"There is little else that would bring one sae young and healthy tae me. And it is drawing toward the season of the hunt. With sae many men dead in the war, they'll be abroad by Beltane, if not before. Ah, well, it means more work for me."

Hexy stared at the nearly blind eyes and shivered. He might not be sighted, but it seemed that he had the sight. Still, he was the first person she had met who actually knew about the selkies and was apparently willing to talk about them. She needed to find her voice and ask sensible questions.

"You are nervous, mistress? Do you seek someone tae take away your carnal sins? Is that why you have come? If so, I should warn ye that sin eating works best with corpses. Of course, I should be glad tae make an appointment for some future date," the old man said softly, smiling at his small jest, as a pale gray wreath of smoke encircled his head.

"No! I don't need a sin eater!" Hexy was surprised at how emphatic she sounded when her words finally burst free. The tone was nearly rude, but it only made the old man's smile widen.

"I didn't think sae. The lassies never do repent. It's just as well. I do believe that I shall predecease you, anyway. A body can only hold sae much woe before it collapses." He shook his head. "If it isnae the selkies, what then troubles you, mistress?"

Feeling a catch at the back of her throat, Hexy reminded herself to keep her breathing slow and shallow.

She was also not entirely without gifts, and reached out with what she was beginning to think of as her inner eyes to probe at Padraig's intentions. She could read very little about the man, for he seemed able to cloak himself, but what little she sensed was entirely benign.

Afraid of frightening him away with a spill of wild words, she began hesitantly: "I have been reading an old book—a diary of sorts—and I ran across a letter from a woman who died. She killed herself, actually. Did you by any chance know a Morag Campbell?"

Padraig thought for a moment and then said carefully, "I know of her. She died before my time of calling, but the sin eater before me was summoned tae her deathbed, and having his memories inside me now, I know of her, too. And all the lassies before her as well. Of course, I cannot speak of their sins or hers. In that, mistress, I am rather like a priest."

Hexy shivered, considering how it was that the sin eater might have acquired his knowledge. She wanted to reject the notion that a sin eater could actually have absorbed the experiences of his predecessor by consuming the baked meats laid out on the corpse's body, but she couldn't dismiss the notion as easily and as entirely as she might have a month earlier.

"I don't want to know anything personal about Morag Campbell. I need some help locating someone else. I need to know—" Hexy swallowed, and then said bluntly, "I need to find a creature, a finman called Sevin who lives in a place called Wrathdrum. I thought that perhaps Morag had known someone who was familiar with this place."

It was the sin eater's turn to be unbalanced. His smoldering pipe fell to the ground, scattering red embers as it landed awkwardly on the packed earth.

"Och! Why dae you seek the sorcerous monster Sevin?" he asked harshly, bending to retrieve his pipe. The burning embers touched his withered flesh as he groped for the bowl, but he didn't seem to feel them. "No good can come of it, mistress, I warn thee."

She agreed with the old man, but her options were all but gone. She was certain now that it was not family matters that detained Ruairidh. And this man seemed the only person who knew anything concrete about the other, invisible society that lived on the outskirts of the land. She didn't want to risk endangering Ruairidh or herself by admitting to what would be seen by many as a blasphemous union, but she didn't feel that she had much choice. She reminded herself that the sin eater had said he was like a priest, and that he had probably seen so much wickedness that he would not be shocked by anything she said. Besides that, he *felt* safe.

But even with these rationalizations, it took Hexy a moment to answer. Admitting out loud, to a witness, what she believed was happening made it all real. After this there was no turning back, no possible denial of what she believed. She could not someday tell herself that she had had a brain fever that made her imagine wild things, for there would be another person who knew that she was not in the clutches of illness when she said them.

Ruairidh had teased her that she was probably bad at sums and plussages, and it was true. So she calculated everything again, slowly and carefully. But no matter how she totaled up the facts, she still came up short of needed knowledge. Frankness, at least to a degree, was called for on both sides if she was to learn what she needed to know.

Throwing away more caution, Hexy answered plainly.

"I believe that this monster of Wrathdrum has stolen the soul of someone this friend of mine knows, and I fear that my friend—this person I love—has gone to retrieve it." She stopped then, refusing to voice any more of her fears of what might have happened to Ruairidh. "Do you know where I could find the finman? Do you know where this place called Wrathdrum is?"

"I don't know Wrathdrum. It isn't the concern of men, sae I do not search for knowledge of it. There's wickedness enough in our world." The reply was instant and emphatic.

"Please. Help me. I sense that I have very little time." Involuntarily, her hand settled on her stomach. "You must know something that can help me. I *have* to find my friend."

Padraig considered this, his blind eyes moving over her and settling on her shielding hand as though he could actually see inside her.

"You are with twins? Children of a selkie?"

Hexy swallowed.

"I . . . Yes. I believe so. And I am afraid for

them. They need something I can't give them."

Padraig sighed and then relented. "I know nothing personally. But the sin eater before me met this Sevin once, long ago." Padraig closed his eyes, his brows knitting as though he searched his memory for something obscure. His voice grew thin and light. "It was in the time of the harvest moon, when the sky was shadowed with smoke. Iain was walking by the shore one night when a blue horror rose out of the rocks and tried tae suck out his soul."

Padraig laughed suddenly. The sound was pleasant even if his words were not.

"There are few benefits tae being what we are. The priests hate us for taking work from them, and the devil surely hates us for keeping true sinners from his toils. Aye, there are many dangers, not the least of which being that we shall not find a new sin eater tae take away our wickedness when it is our time tae die. But Iain's tainted soul saved him that night. That horrid creature put his spiked teeth over Iain's nose and tried tae suck the spirit out of him. But the meal was tae large, bloated by all those years of collecting sins, and he could not get it all down in one breath. The nasty creature started tae choke and vomited the soul back up—minus a particularly bad sin or twa—and while he was felled in a heaving heap, Iain was able tae flee him, his own burden of wickedness much lighter thereafter."

Padraig stopped smiling. When he spoke again his voice had returned to normal. "I should not make light of this. Sevin is an evil and dangerous creature, mistress, and doubtless grown more powerful over the years as he has consumed sinful soul after sinful soul. Look at me! Look at my face! And the body is the same. The wages of sin are terrible. And I am not malevolent by nature, nor do I traffic in evil magic." He asked gently, "Are you certain that you must seek him out? You are an innocent, mistress. He'll want your soul badly. He'll want the babes' souls even more. Is there no one else tae go tae Wrathdrum for you?"

Hexy stroked her hand down her belly. "I don't know if there is anyone else seeking him. No one may know that he has been called away." She shook her head. "Perhaps his family *is* searching, but I don't know where to find them and am certain that I must go regardless. If Ruairidh is in danger, then I must be there. We are tied together now and share the same fate. And I *know* that without me something dreadful will happen when he meets this monster."

Padraig again closed his eyes and communed with some internal voice or memory. After a moment, he nodded in agreement.

"Very well, then; so mote it be." He laid his pipe aside and sat up straight. Suddenly he seemed tall and strong. "There has been an accident. I was called last night tae the home of some lads who were bringing in some liquor from France. It is not uncommon in these parts. Duties are outrageous, and free trade without Sassenach interference is considered the right of every Scotsman," he added blandly.

He meant smuggling. Hexy was surprised that it still happened, now that the war was over, but merely nodded and said, "Go on."

"Well, the accident came about near the isle of the chapel of the fishermen. Do you know the place?"

"Yes."

"A deal of cargo was left behind. Be there tomorrow morning as early as you may and watch the rocks on the north side of the isle carefully. It often happens that there are seafolk who visit these sad sites for a bit of looting. It may be that one of them can direct you to this monster's home." The blind eyes again turned her way. "Now, you have brought me a gift?"

"Yes." Hexy withdrew the pouch of tobacco from her shawl and placed it in Padraig's lap. A brown hand quickly covered it, the fingers caressing.

"The MacKenzie always did have the finest of

smoke weed," Padraig said happily. "Well, then, since this is such a fine gift, I will tell you something else. The creature you are likely to meet is called a merrow. He's a sort of merman. Be careful not to ask his name. Be polite. And above all, do not let him think that you want his drink, for they do not at all care to share their liquor."

The old man cleared his throat and began a weak coughing. He seemed to shrink in upon himself, returning to his former, diminished stature.

"Get along now, before you make yourself ill with yew poisoning. Eat some fish without salt before the babe sickens. Then go bathe in the sea. And if you can bear it, go later tae the kirk and say a prayer. I don't cotton to the kirk myself, but you shall need as many blessings as you may get."

Hexy stood up. Her knees were weak, frightened by what she had set in motion, but they bore her because there was no choice. "Thank you for talking to me. It was kind of you to let me invade your privacy."

"I need no thanks for this day's work—and shall take none. If you survive, mistress, come see me again and we'll talk of other, better things."

He didn't offer a second time to cleanse her soul. Probably because he knew that if the finman captured her, there might be a body to lay out but there would be no soul in it to look after.

Hexy straightened her spine against that thought.

If that was to be the case then, as Padraig had said: *so mote it be.*

She did not allow herself to think about the babies she was carrying. That would weaken her as surely as her own fears and doubts. The time for fear was past. Her course was resolved upon. Tomorrow she would go to the fisherman's island.

"*Slainte mhath,*" Hexy said, turning to leave, completing the ritual with wishes for Padraig's health. She wouldn't have worried about such niceties in the past, but now she did. Never again would she disdain rituals.

"*Slainte mhor,*" Padraig answered, his returned wishes sounding like a blessing. "And may the hand of God shelter you on your journey, mistress."

Chapter Thirteen

She was getting stronger and her sense of direction better. It was as though muscles and bones and senses were all finally being put to proper use after a long sleep. Hexy had no difficulty rowing the boat over to the fishermen's deserted island and past the reef where she could now plainly see the jagged upthrusts of gray stone that lurked just below the surface. Nor was it any great effort to pull the water-saturated boat up on shore above the tidal line, though attempting such an act would not have been considered even the week before.

There was a new acuity to her other senses as well that was sometimes actually painful.

239

Sight, hearing and especially her sense of smell were all now particularly keen. The repairs continued at Fintry, but Hexy avoided the workmen as much as possible. Their curious gazes annoyed her. Also, her sense of smell had grown so profound that to be near them and their perspiration-soaked woolens was a battery on her olfactory nerves.

The only thing worse than the smell of the workmen's unwashed bodies was the open cesses being converted to modern sanitation systems. Since that was the case, Hexy wished the workmen all good speed and hoped that native bashfulness would continue to win out over curiosity, and that they would leave her unquestioned. It would be agony if she had to send them away before the conversion was done, but if she had to, she would dismiss them as well, and worry about explaining her actions to Jillian later.

The other unpleasant thing about her situation was that she—or perhaps it was the babes inside her—were hungry all the time, and they filled her mind with clamoring. She found that drinking lemonade and eating uncooked fish somewhat appeased the cravings but knew that there had to be something else—something less dear to the purse than the precious lemons and something less repellent than raw fish— that would better suit their needs. Unfortunately, she had yet to find out what it was. Many of the shellfish she saw on the rocks were appealing, but she knew that some species were poisonous. In an act of madness, she had even tried eating seaweed, but that had been so disgusting that she had been unable to swallow it even after it was boiled into submission. The hunger was left ravening, eating up her reserves of strength and peace of mind.

Her poor mind! It, like her belly, was oddly empty now. Fear had been banished. Occasional thoughts of the outside world and its worries would enter her brain, but perhaps these cares felt lonely with no other thought or worldly ambition to cling to, for they did not stay long.

Perhaps it would be different if any of her family still lived. Then she would have some reason to cling to her old life and resist the course that she was taking. But she was quite alone in the world except for Ruairidh and her unborn children. She had no ambition now save to see Ruairidh again. And that ambition was with her day and night.

Ruairidh cocked his head and tried to listen for something that most confoundedly could not be heard with the ear. It was a futile gesture, a ridiculous one, but there had been several times in the last four tides that he had been fairly certain that Hexy was speaking to him.

It was ridiculous fancy, of course, but that morning he could almost hear her breaths of exertion as she performed some task—perhaps rowing a boat.

But that was simply his own impatience and worry talking. Short of being magicked, Hexy would never willing take a boat out onto the sea. She was still nervous about being in the deep water, and possibly would be all of her life.

He felt badly for being away so long, for as the child grew she would begin having cravings for fruit, and Hexy would start being uncomfortable without it. But a single, female babe would not truly require any special food for another moon's phase. It was different in the cases where women bore twins, but those babes were always male. It made sense that their cravings would be stronger.

It was fortunate for both of them that she was pregnant with a girl child. If it were otherwise, Ruairidh would have to choose between staying in Avocamor and persuading his people to preparedness for war with the finmen, and returning to Hexy and their babe.

He would have been loath to leave now because the tide of argument had turned; he was sure the People were prepared now to defend themselves if given a plan and a leader to guide them.

Ruairidh smiled. It had partially been his inspired argument that the finman's magic could be used against the young selkie's new human partners that had turned the battle in his favor. Enough of the young men were in the throes of mating protectiveness that they had been inspired to agree to go to the sometimes hated land dwellers' defense.

The People did not make war on women—any women—nor would they allow others to do so. They were too precious and too necessary for the selkies' survival.

It took Hexy no more than half an hour to walk the edge of the tiny islet to the windward side of the stony dome. She simply followed the sky trail of the rasp-voiced skuas, one of which trailed a bit of lace like a kite as it called her on. Like the avian messengers in the fairy tales of old, they led her directly to the creature the sin eater had told her to look for.

The merrow sat atop a rock on the far side of the island, a safe distance out from the shore. Beside him was a broken crate filled with bottles, and the smell of brandy was thick in the air. It was a local lad's smuggled cargo, no doubt.

No longer surprised by the existence of

things she had previously doubted, Hexy waded out into the surf and forced herself to smile up at the green-haired man fish.

"*Latha math*, good merrow," she said politely, suspecting that it was useless to rush things when dealing with magical creatures. Padraig and Ruairidh had both told her that most of the sea's fae were very shy and apt to disappear if annoyed. Her brother's faerie stories had all emphasized this point as well. It seemed odd to be relying upon the advice of fairy tales and people whom society would consider outcasts or insane, but those were all the reference points she had.

As the merrow turned his large head to look down at her, she wished passionately that she had paid more attention to what she'd thought were her brother's whimsical discussions of folklore. She couldn't recall if he had ever said whether merrows were dangerous, even if you didn't try to steal their drink. Their large green teeth and hair were certainly alarming.

"And a *slainte mhath* tae ye, mistress," the merrow finally answered, doffing his red cap of seaweed and revealing his eyes, which were black and obliquely set, and looked like they belonged on a giant pig. Not actually interested, he still asked politely, "What are ye about on this fine morning, *NicnanRon?*"

NicnanRon meant daughter of a seal; she

knew that much now. Hexy was uncertain if this was a completely accurate description of what she was, but she did not correct him.

"I am seeking my love. He is a great-grandson of the King of Lochlann, grandson of Ardagh, son of Cathair," she related, giving Rory's selkie title in English because she still could not say *Clann Righ Lochlainn fo gheasaibh* without stuttering. Hoping that the ritual was nearly complete, she asked in return, "And what are you doing this fine morning to bring joy into your world?"

"Why, I am doing what I maun dae on every morning, mistress. I am drinking my joy." To illustrate his words, the merrow raised a bottle in his webbed hand and drank deeply. His already red nose flushed a shade darker. When he smiled she could see his sharp green teeth glinting in the sun.

Knowing she shouldn't do it, Hexy nevertheless asked, "And why must you drink in the morning, good merrow?"

"Why, I maun drink in the morning for there'll be nae drinkin' when I am dead! And who know when this shall be?" The merrow began to laugh, beating his speckled tail against the rock.

"Very true," Hexy admitted.

The merrow sobered suddenly and looked at her with a suspicious eye. "What do you want with me here on the eve of war?" he asked bluntly, pulling his bottle back as though he feared she might try to reach across the space between them and snatch it from him.

War? Hexy almost asked what he meant, but, recalling from her stories that conversations with magical beings rarely lasted long and were apt to wander onto unrelated topics, she stayed firmly with the task at hand.

"I need a guide, someone to show me how to reach Wrathdrum." Her answer was equally blunt. She was careful not to look at the bottle, and tensed her legs in case she had to run back up the shore.

The merrow's black, pupilless eyes widened. "You'll nae need a guide if you gae searching for the finmen, for they will surely find you if you speak loudly enough, daft one. Don't ye ken that these are their hunting grounds, and the wind can drag your words across the sea directly tae their evil ears?"

"That may be true, good merrow, but I still seek a guide." Hexy forced herself to meet his eyes. "Can you help me?"

His tail twitched. "You *are* daft, mistress, bespelled by yer selkie. And I'll not help ye to yer doom, or my own. Ye'd best seek out another who has lost her wits." He jerked his head toward another rock. "Talk to the finwoman yonder. She's got the finman's blackhand upon her anyway. Mayhap she'll help ye to yer death if ye truly seek it."

With a violent smack of his tail, he flipped himself backward into the sea, taking his crate and bottle with him.

Not certain if she was ready to face an insane finwoman, but feeling she had little choice, Hexy turned slowly toward the nearby granite upthrust the merrow had indicated and tried again to smile welcomingly.

Before Ruairidh had awakened her magic, Hexy was certain she would not have seen the finwoman. The mermaid was sitting quietly on her rock with her tail in the water, blending in with the sea wrack on the stone. Once Hexy managed to discern her outline, she could see that the mermaid was pretty in a way no human could be. Hexy could not even find fault with the silvery scales that covered the thin web between her long fingers, or the scent of the red and purple seaweed she wore as a gown and twined through her dark hair, for both were lovely on her.

The only disconcerting thing about her was her gaze. Eyes as black as the merrow's, but far wiser and prettier, studied Hexy with unblinking attention.

"You seek Ruairidh O'Uruisg?" the musical voice asked softly, barely audible over the shushing sea. Hexy had a feeling that this was

247

a talismanic question and once again answered formally.

"I do."

"Because you love him?"

Hexy nodded, not trusting her voice to avoid a quavering pitch when she spoke of Ruairidh. She sent her inner eye to look over the pretty creature, but it couldn't *see* anything. It was as though she wasn't even there. The sensation was dizzying, and for a moment Hexy wondered if her desperate mind had conjured a hallucination.

"And you know where he has gone?"

Hexy nodded again, though with less certainly. "To Sevin's lair, I believe. He was seeking a lost soul when last I heard from him."

The mermaid shivered, and for a moment it seemed as if the sun blurred above them.

"Do not say that name again. Do not say any name. Not yours, not mine. He listens. And every time you speak his name, you give him power over you. Already he is large with it and ready to attack the selkie."

It was Hexy's turn to shudder. Though she had misgivings about this alternate guide, she still asked, "I won't speak of him again. But I need help. If you cannot take me to—to that place, can you take me to the selkies?"

"Nay. It is said this morning that the selkies and the finfolk are to go to war because of wizardry practiced on the People's dead. Being of the finfolk, I dare not approach them at this time."

"There is to be war? But what can I do?" Hexy asked, allowing herself to plead as the dread inside her grew. "He said that he would be gone only for a day and it has been seven."

."He was gone for the dark of the moon?"

"Yes, and I thought perhaps that this was what delayed him, but there is a new moon now and he still hasn't come. And I—I *dream.*"

"Selkies leave women," the mermaid said gently. "It is their nature, their way."

"Not without their babes," Hexy said flatly.

"You are with child?"

Hexy nodded.

"And so it is something more. I pity you. Truly I do. Seeker, I lost my love once. A fin-man drowned him in the sea and stole his soul away." The mermaid did not weep, but Hexy thought she wanted to.

"I'm sorry," Hexy answered, and meant it. Tears filled her own eyes.

The mermaid nodded. "Thank you for your words—and for the tears I cannot weep. No one else has cared." She bobbed her head and hummed something sad beneath her breath. After a moment, she stopped singing and said reluctantly, "I can take you to *his* hateful promontory if that is where you want to go." The mermaid's gaze was unhappy as she offered to do this.

"Yes?" Hexy prompted.

"But that is all I can do, for he has power over me as well. And we must use every caution. You do not understand, perhaps you cannot understand, what you are asking yourself to do. Everything about the finman's domain is dangerous and ravening, and it eats women." The merwoman rolled off her rock and disappeared into the water. After a moment she reappeared, carrying several red blobs in her arms as she swam toward shore. "Come here to me, seeker, for I cannot go to you. The king of sorcery has enchanted my limbs and pierced them with cold iron so I can no longer walk about on two legs."

Hexy swallowed and waded out into the cold water, which was chilly but not unpleasantly so. As she got closer, she could see that what she had taken for decorative scales on the half-submerged tail was nothing of the sort. The mermaid's fin was punctured in several places with wicked iron hooks.

Hexy looked at the raw wounds and was filled with compassion, but before she could speak the mermaid said briskly, "Take off your dress. The wool of sheep is too heavy to swim in. And then tie these sponges into your hair. Most sea creatures cannot abide the taste of them, and perhaps if I swim fast enough we will arrive un-molested."

"But—" Hexy protested, a hand going to her bosom. She hadn't thought that she would actually be going to confront the monster this day, and had never considered that there could be other things in the ocean that would try to kill her. Her worry had all been for the evil Sevin. The thought of swimming in the deep without even the protection of clothing was unnerving.

"Keep your shoes, but leave your dress up on that rock. It will be safe from the tide there."

"My underclothes?" she asked hopefully. "I can keep them?"

"If they are heavy they will only slow us. I am already weakened by the weight of iron. If I tire before we reach shore, you shall surely drown and I will be captured. If he finds me again, he will not stop with torture." The mermaid frowned and said harshly, "Be honest, seeker, before we risk our lives—and your soul. Do you wish to find your lover or not? Have you the resolve to face great evil without flinching? Decide now if you cannot, and spare us both this journey."

Hexy swallowed and abandoned modesty and her fear of the unknown deep. "Of course I want to find him. But my lantern?" she asked. "I'll need at least that."

"I'll put it in a bag and keep it dry, but you shall have to hold it while I swim," the mermaid said impatiently. "We must hurry. The merrow is indiscreet. The drunkard will find someone to talk to. And if *he* knows that you are coming, *he* shall lay a trap—and I tell you now, seeker, I will not let him catch me again."

"I understand," Hexy said softly, wishing that she had thought to bring one of Mr. Mac-Kenzie's ancient pistols. Chances were that the old gunpowder would not have worked, but a firearm would have been comforting. At the very least, she wished she had a knife.

Hexy began to strip, feeling more than merely naked when she peeled her dress and chemise away. For the first time in her life, sun and wind were able to thrust themselves upon her bare skin and touch her at will. Under other circumstances, it might have been enjoyable. As it was, it merely reminded her of how tender was human flesh.

The bag in which the lantern—and her silk chemise—was stowed looked a bit like a sheep's stomach, but Hexy did not ask from which creature the bladder came or how it sealed up so tightly.

The nameless mermaid had to help Hexy bind up the sponges to her hair and limbs with strips of fish skin, but as soon as they had the sponges tied, the mermaid seized Hexy by the

252

arm and towed her out into the deep water. Her fingers felt like a giant snake coiled about Hexy's limb. The mermaid's strength was terrifying as she forced them both out into the sea in opposition to the tide, but Hexy did not struggle against it. If what the legends said was true, then this woman was risking more than her life to take Hexy to the lair of her nemesis.

In what seemed a very short while they arrived at a gray peninsula, which was guarded by an unwelcome offshore wind that caused discord among the waves and did its best to push them away. The breeze's unhappy susurrations increased the closer they came to the island, and it finally became necessary to swim under the water to escape it.

Hexy did not close her eyes, since the water did not seem to bother them at first, and she felt the need to watch for danger. It was difficult to judge from beneath the waves what was happening above the surface, but it seemed that Hexy and the mermaid passed under a band of pure black clouds, which suddenly dropped an unpleasant sousing rain upon the water's surface. It was a painful rain that did not dissolve when it hit the sea, and though she did not breathe, Hexy could still tell that it smelled strongly of sulfur. So bitter and caustic was this water that it forced Hexy to close her eyes against it. After a moment, her skin began to sting. The hand on her arm tightened and jerked her deeper into the ocean.

Finally, when she thought she must cry out from the pain and lack of air, they moved into a place of eerie calm and clean water, and their pace slowed to one less frantic. They came back to the surface and, realizing that she had not inhaled for some impossibly long time, Hexy took a great gasp of air. Beside her, the fin-woman's breathing was also fast and labored.

Hexy treaded water and looked up at the sky. It was quite impossible, as it was full day and the skies were again clear, but it seemed as though something had swooped over the face of the sun and blotted out its healthy light. An evil veil separated them from the real world. There was illumination in this strange mono-chromatic land, but no heat. Around them, the water was completely clear, but it was also dead—as sterile as water boiled for tea.

As they drew into the shallows and Hexy found her feet, she was able to see that it was not simply the rock of the peninsula that was the unhealthy gray of blotched accumulations of seagull lime. There was also some scabrous and diseased seaweed that thrived there, grow-ing all over the steep-sided banks, all but mask-ing the narrow entrance to a cave.

"Beware the crabs," the mermaid said softly, her tired voice hardly louder than the breeze.

"They pinch viciously and will eat you if they get a chance, for they are trapped here and always hungry."

Hexy stared at the rock. The hermit crabs, if that was what these creatures were, were scuttling along under scorched pans and cracked jars and other human-made castoffs. The brief flashes of their pale corpulence when their borrowed shells wobbled were revolting.

"What's wrong with them?" she asked, grateful that she had chosen to keep her shoes. "Why do they use those things instead of shells?"

"They have gotten ferocious and fat off the finmen's poisoned leavings. They don't fit in their own shells any more." The mermaid met Hexy's eyes. "Now, listen carefully. You must go quickly to the cave and get out of sight of spying eyes. The crabs probably will not follow you inside, for even they fear the finmen."

Hexy glanced at the scuttling monsters and then looked back at the nameless finwoman. Her face was paler than it had been when they first met, her skin completely without color in spite of her exertions. Hexy wondered if she herself wore the same shade of ghastly white, or whether the finwoman was ill.

"Thank you for bringing me," she said softly.

"I'll take no thanks for this," the mermaid answered, reminding her of Padraig. She took the bag from Hexy and, opening the bladder, showed Hexy the dry lantern and her chemise. "I'd not go in here even to save my love. Howbeit, the decision is yours."

Hexy nodded.

"Here," the mermaid said. "I leave you with this gift. This is fresh water from one of your people's holy fountains that I have been using on my wounds, hoping that it would help heal them. It is supposed to banish evil and cure disease." She reached down and detached a vial from one of the hooks that marred her tail. She paused a moment before handing it to Hexy.

Hexy hesitated before accepting it.

"What will happen to you without this?" she asked. "Will your wounds get worse?"

"If you have the chance, kill him," the mermaid advised, not answering her question. Her eyes burned with a mixture of hatred and pain. "You'll not get more than one chance with that soul-sucker. Good luck, seeker. Kill him and you'll set us both free."

The mermaid melted back into the clear, dead water and was suddenly gone.

Chapter Fourteen

Ruairidh looked closely at the pearl mussels clustered on the rock. Millions of them abutted one another, fighting for space on the ocher stone. The tiny crevices between their shells hissed as the foaming waters pushed through them, bringing them their almost invisible prey.

He knew by smell which of them had the pretty bits of layered grit that the lasses liked. It would only take a moment for him to retrieve an appealing gift for Hexy, which perhaps would help sweeten his apology. His long absence caused by the dark of the moon and the slow deliberations of the council would perhaps be forgotten in the shimmer of pearls. The meat from the mussels would be good for their babe, too. Her craving for flesh from the sea had to be strong now.

He had plucked open several mussels and was harvesting their treasures when he noticed a wounded skua sitting atop the rock staring at him with small black eyes. It had a tiny lace bandage wound about one leg. The bird trilled at him as soon as he looked up.

Ruairidh dropped the mussel and started forward. The bird grew alarmed at his approach but did not flee. Slowly, Ruairidh bent over the trembling body and drew in a breath. The bandage had come from Hexy and bore both her and the bird's own blood.

Suddenly anxious, he nevertheless spoke softly to the little bird. "Where is she, winged one? Where has she gone?"

After a moment the bird blinked and then answered in the way of its kind.

Its words made Ruairidh's heart leap into his throat. With the greatest haste he had ever used, he reached for his skin, shoving his arms into it even as he ran.

"Keir!" he called, his voice echoing over the water like a lighthouse's alarm. "The finman has the *NicnanRon!*"

Hexy pulled the sponges from their moorings, dropping them into the water, then ran up onto the beach, picking a hasty path among snapping crustaceans until she reached the mouth of the cave. Once inside its empty shadow, she paused to catch her breath and light her lantern. The smell of the kerosene was awful enough to upset her stomach, but less awful than going into the darkness without it.

As she dressed in her tiny bit of useless silk, she looked about, trying to orient herself to the strange and horrible place. She was surrounded by confusing disorder, which reminded her of the fisherman's chapel. Heaps of rotting grasses were tumbled together with shattered boards and what looked like bones. Every inch of putrescent flotsam abounded with pale, misshapen crabs as yet too small to compete with their husked brethren in the open stretches of the beach. It was like being inside a stomach.

And the finman now lodging there was a maggot, a cancer, growing inside the stony island and eating it away bit by bit.

The thought sickened and terrified her. Every particle of Hexy's nearly unclothed being wanted to cry out for Ruairidh to come to her, because she sensed that he was nearer than he had been in days. But she also recalled what the mermaid had said about Sevin listening, and kept silent. The soft patter of water from her sodden hair followed her as she walked and a thought came to her: It could be that Ruairidh was nearby because he was a prisoner, and it was she who would have to free him.

Hexy didn't allow herself to consider the idea that she might already be too late to save him.

She noticed a small pile of red rocks shoved to the corner of the cave. They looked almost molten in the trembling light of her lantern, so different from the other stone of the island. Dimly recalling Ruairidh saying something about the red rocks being weapons against sea monsters, she opened the bladder bag and dropped seven fist-sized stones inside. Her fingers were burning by the time the last had been added. Apparently iron ore was now anathema to her as well.

No obvious path presented itself, but she kept searching. After several minutes, Hexy began to fear that there was no exit from this insane cave and that she would have to return to the beach to search for another entrance. She might also have to go out into the water and look for an entrance from under the waves.

This thought made her shudder and renew her efforts to find some entrance, and she finally did discover a tunnel concealed behind the fractured prow of a shattered rowboat. It was low and dark and sloped downhill at a steep angle. The odor that floated up from below was a miasma of terrible smells.

Repulsed, she nevertheless started inside. It

seemed for an instant as she bent her head nearer to the ground that over the sobbing of the tide she could hear the distant barking of seals, but when she stilled her breath and listened, there was nothing left in the air except the sound of waves and hermit crabs' clicking claws.

A green darkness clutched at her as she descended into the earth. The tide had cleft out a passage from the heart of the stone by millenniums of torrent, and the channel she was traveling was not made for those who went about on two legs. Hexy was soon forced to her hands and knees, her burdened fingers and bare limbs making reluctant contact with the green phosphorescence of the walls that was her only light aside from her lantern. The near darkness was Plutonian and cold as death itself, and the tunnel soon wound back on its own length and headed away from the land and down toward the dead sea.

She was deep in the cave now, and the weight above her was oppressive and the green darkness was horrid and dank. She had to fight off paralyzing claustrophobia as the tunnel continued to shrink in diameter.

The silence around her was as profound as the grave, and why shouldn't it be? If she were correct in her suspicions, and this was Wrathdrum, then she was venturing among the dead—or at least among souls that belonged no more to the living.

Unbidden, some lines of poetry from the legend of Kathleen and St. Kevin came to mind:

> *Fearless she had tracked his feet*
> *To this rocky wild retreat*
> *And with a rude repulsive shock*
> *He hurled her from the beetling rock.*

Only Kathleen had likely worn clothes when she went to her death; Hexy had nothing to protect her save a pair of sodden shoes and a bit of damp silk that did nothing to preserve her modesty.

At last, the horrible constriction of the tunnel ended, and she was able to stand erect again inside a broad chamber. The air was less breathable than ever, and the foulness of the now familiar stench was beginning to make her dizzy.

The room she entered was circular, with a flat pool embosomed in the rock floor where there arose a column of still white vapor. Its dimensions were unguessable, but it felt large.

There was a second half-round antechamber off to the right, with an apsidal ledge spiraling up its glowing chimney. In its walls were cut a series of niches, chipped rudely out of the stone, and in each of these, save two, there rested overturned pots.

Avoiding the flat pool and its mist, which was somehow terrifying in its unnatural stillness, Hexy hurried for the antechamber, her lantern held high.

Terrified but resolved, she paused at the first urn. She set down her sack of stones and took a slow breath before she turned the pot upright. Her nervous exhalation condensed into vapor and refused to dissipate until it attached itself to the pot surrounding it in a light fog. Her lungs told her that they were drowning, even though she was above the high-water mark of the chamber. Except for her ghostly breath she was alone.

Hexy tried to convince herself that this meant that she was safe.

She tipped the first pot upright. The moment the seal broke, something rushed out, an entity formless but vaguely visible and warm. It blew by her in a short hot stream with a sigh that was like a mournful bird's call. *Chyrme,* Rory Patrick had called the bird's death songs, the ones they sang when their nests were raided of their young.

A soul! she thought, tears starting in her eyes as she watched the faint, silver trail that marked its passing. *But not Ruairidh's. Ian, the fisherman, son of John of Crot Callow.*

Crying silently at the horrible proof that this nightmare was real, Hexy hurried to the next pot, turning it over quickly. And then another and another, searching frantically for her lover and praying that he was still recognizable and sane.

But each soul she freed was weaker and paler than the last, and none were Ruairidh. Seaumus, John, Coelph, Cennfailad, Sihtric—some human, some not quite—she knew their names and histories for an instant as they fled past her, searching for the freedom of the open air. The contact weakened her, part of their fear and sorrow clinging to her when they touched her mind and stole a little more warmth from her body.

It was a horrible and draining assault, but she did not blame the lost and sometimes insane souls for their unthinking panic, and forced herself on.

Midway up the ledge, she laid her hands upon an urn and received a ghastly shock. It was not a stranger she touched; it was a soul she knew well.

"Rory Patrick?" she whispered, horror taking her voice and all but paralyzing her. It wasn't her lover beneath her hands, but her brother. *Her brother!* The thought made her feel sick and dizzy. She had never suspected that he might be here.

The pot under her hand quaked and grew warm, as if the soul inside knew she was there and wanted desperately to be freed.

"Rory?" she whispered again. Gently, fearfully, she lifted it, waiting for the familiar spirit to brush by her unheeding, as the others had.

Hexy, beware. Sevin comes. Flee! The soft zephyr that had been her brother touched her gently on her face. Instead of draining her of heat, the touch was warm.

Behind her, she heard water lap against rock and a wave of sulfurous gas climbed up the cave walls, partly obscuring the green light in it noxious veil.

Hexy looked longingly at the remaining dozen or so inverted jars and then at the pool below, where the mist had begun to writhe and the water shiver. She was exhausted, but escape for herself and freedom for the caged souls were both equally necessary tasks.

"I can't leave them with this monster. I just can't! Rory, can you help me?"

No. I have no form, no strength. Run, Hexy! He'll take you, too. You cannot save them. His shade shimmered violently as he warned her.

"But the others—I can't leave them—"

Before Hexy could decide what to do, the pool exploded in what looked like an aquatic inferno of limbs and sea wrack.

She looked with eyes that strained madly to

see and comprehend but could not at first understand what the creature was. In fact, she thought that perhaps it was more than one type of animal wrapped about each other like some host and parasite. But the mass had only one set of eyes, which were yellow and set in a familiar blue face. They glowed like baleful candles, their tiny, internal fires flickering with fury as they looked upon her.

WHAT HAVE YOU DONE? a voice screamed in her head, concussing her brain with its vicious din.

Hexy gasped in pain as the thing in the water boiled toward her, heaving itself out of the pool and moving swiftly toward the stony ledge.

Sevin. It was the creature of her dreams but, like everything in his domain, grown infinitely more hideous and warped in the last century. The thing that came toward her was no longer human-appearing at all, but rather a conglomeration of the sea's dead horrors.

Its head was large and bloated, and covered in gray-green patches of mold or scaled flesh, which had replaced most of its hair. It had an animal's mouth, though Hexy could not think of any animal that had such needlelike teeth in its maw. Indeed, it looked as if the individual teeth were covered in coarse bristles. Or perhaps the juts were made of more bone.

Its legs, such as they were, were short and

powerful, but it was its arms that made it into a nightmare. They were not arms at all, but rather boneless appendages of an impossible length, covered in large suckers that belonged to a squid.

Its ferocity and spiritual miasma was beyond anything she had dreamed.

Hexy, run! Rory Patrick urged her again, refusing to leave her, though she could feel his fear and helplessness as the creature approached. *Don't look at him. He's an eye biter. He'll hypnotize you.*

A tentacle reached for her, elongating until it squirmed over the edge of the path and touched her shoe. The tip scorched the leather as he tried to drive in his hooks and drag her down to him.

Another tentacle touched her leg, searing away the thin silk and burning her thigh as it tore at her flesh with wicked hooks. Unable to help herself, Hexy screamed and scrambled farther up the ledge, shoving pots over on the creature as she went.

Souls rioted, bouncing off one another in their confusion. She recognized Reverend Fraser when he was freed, and for a moment, it seemed he would stay with her, huddled around her heart. But then he seemed to gather himself and flew at the scaly horror clambering up the ledge toward her.

Flee, my child! He said to her. *Save your soul!*

Horrified but unable to move, Hexy watched and listened as the old clergyman attacked the monster. For an instant, she thought that perhaps he would be able to force Sevin off the ledge and open her escape route. But Sevin never moved. Reverend Fraser's soul blundered into him at full speed and began screaming as it encountered the beast's mouth. Sevin breathed it in, his massive chest expanding as his jaws gaped wide. He gulped it down in one swallow.

"Rory Patrick! Leave me," she breathed, horror blanking out her mind. "I have nowhere to run, but you can escape."

I will not.

She had known fear before—dread, like her fear for Ruairidh, which grew slowly over hours and days. She knew plain startlement, which made the heart race and lent her needed speed when action was called for. And she had learned to fear the helplessness of dreams.

But this was different. It was terror of something beyond her world. Terror of the unexplainable paralyzed her. Despairing souls gibbered at her, as frightened as she.

How could she fight such a monster? How could she save them all?

Then she remembered the mermaid's gift, still clutched in her left hand. Hexy pulled open the vial with shaking hands and hurled the tiny contents at the monster.

The water hit him in the face and spattered over his shoulders. Sevin screeched, dislodging rotten seaweed and loose shale from the ledge and knocking Hexy to her knees with the noisy percussion. Thick smoke rose from his body where the water had seared him. So piercing was Sevin's voice upon her brain that Hexy put her hands over her ears and screamed, calling for Ruairidh.

"I will feed your soul to the kraken," Sevin screeched, catching hold of the ledge for a second time and heaving himself upward. His smoldering body oozed toward her.

For a second time, terror froze her mind and flesh. All she could do was wait, helpless as he came for her.

Then a second form burst from the water behind the beast, half-shedding fur even as it broke the air.

"Hexy, run!" Ruairidh's voice filled the cavern.

"You! Come, selkie! I'll take your soul, too." Without any hesitation, the finman spun about and hurled himself down upon Ruairidh. The two bodies met in violence and fell to the floor, where they began tearing at one another with teeth and claws. Blood, both black and red, flowed.

"Ruairidh!" Hexy cried, trying to regain her feet.

Behind Hexy came the sound of stone grating on stone and then two phlegm-choked roars.

She remembered the other monsters in her dreams.

Reacting without conscious thought, her only impulse to keep any more horrors from touching her, she turned and hurled her lantern at the two finmen who pushed their boneless forms onto the ledge from the impossible tightness of a narrow crevice between the last two wall niches.

Flaming oil and shards of glass spattered over the two eely forms, making them writhe in agony. Trapped in their stony prison either by their size or by Sevin's call, they were compelled to try to kill her even as they burned.

Hexy heard more creatures heaving themselves out of the pool and entering the fray, but she could not turn to see what was happening. One of the finmen—*Turpin*—had entoiled her.

Hexy. You're eye bitten! Wake up! Rory Patrick cried at her.

But she couldn't. Though the creature was crisping, burning to nothing as she watched, he still held her in thrall, his power unbreakable. Almost he made her believe that the battle between her lover and the sorcerer was something unimportant, a longueur through which to sleep. She should just lie down and have a rest until Ruairidh could come to her and take her worry away.

Against her will, Hexy began to slump.

Then Rory Patrick was in her eyes, abrading them and obscuring her sight for the one moment she needed to take back her own mind.

Iron, Hexy. We need iron. An ax, a knife, a needle—anything.

Iron! That was what Ruairidh had said was in those burning red rocks. Turning, Hexy scrambled back down the ledge toward her bag of stones. She prayed that Ruairidh hadn't been teasing her about the stones' efficacy.

Her hands trembled as she unsealed the bag and reached in for a rock. Again it burned her hand as an ember would, and she had to hold back a scream of pain.

Behind her, she heard and smelled Turpin's slow approach.

Praying for a true aim, she turned and fired a stone in his direction. Evil, get thee behind me! she thought, hurling her thoughts at him too.

Panic lent her strength and accuracy. The red rock flew from her hand and hit the creature between the eyes. As David's slung missile had done for Goliath, the stone felled the finman where he stood.

Behind Turpin, the second finman, Brodir, tried to retreat into his niche, leaving behind strips of burnt flesh and a trail of black blood. His gaze was malevolent but unable to bespell her now that she had iron in her hand.

Hexy hesitated and then let him go. Instead of chasing him, she turned to look down at the confusion of bodies below her. There were a number of cast-off skins on the floor and a half-dozen pale, blood-smeared bodies grappling with Sevin. Ruairidh was there, too, still half cloaked in fur and more ichor-stained than the others. Long welts cut his skin, plain even in the green light, which made blood look more black than red.

The selkies had Sevin pinned on his back, but even with their vast strength and superior numbers, they seemed unable to deliver a killing blow to the amorphous blob.

The rocks. They are poison—put them in his mouth, Rory Patrick instructed her.

Hexy stumbled down the ledge. Touching the creature with her bare flesh would be horrible beyond words, but she didn't hesitate to push her way between startled selkies and throw herself on Sevin's scaled chest.

"Hexy!" Ruairidh gasped. "What are ye doing?"

"Killing him!" she answered.

"Then hurry."

The monster's mouth and eyes were open, pulled wide by Ruairidh's grip on his bony brow ridge, which forced his neck into an arch. Her lover's long hands had pierced the scaly skin, swallowing Ruairidh's finger past the first joint as he grabbed bone in a punishing grip.

Sevin's flesh was cold and abrading between her legs, scraping skin as he thrashed, but with a strength she did not know she possessed, she was able to stay atop him, in spite of the pain and revulsion.

Having learned her lesson, she did not look into Sevin's eyes. Hexy quickly opened the bag and emptied it into the monster's gaping mouth, cramming the bladder in after it for good measure. Teeth cut her hands even through the thickness of the sack, but she trusted Ruairidh to keep him from snapping his jaws shut upon her arm as she rammed the stones home.

For a heartbeat, nothing happened. Then the finman gasped, and something pale and green boiled out of Sevin's mouth. Right behind the bile came the Reverend Fraser, bursting out of the maw and racing for the top of the cave with an audible howl of one driven mad.

Hexy fell back, trying to escape the green ooze that she knew would burn worse than the iron had.

Spurred by rage and pain, the creature gave a titanic convulsion of his chest and limbs, throwing off Hexy and the selkies as he heaved himself toward the pool and freedom.

Ruairidh was the only one who did not let go when the burning acid hit him. He was pulled toward the water as well, riding the monster's shoulders as it tried to flee into the deep.

Hexy saw that much before she landed against the wall of the cave, striking her head on the smooth rock. She didn't lose consciousness from the blow, but the world dimmed and spun on it axis, and she found that she could do no more than lie on the floor until the dizziness stopped.

You did it, Hexy girl, Rory Patrick said, his voice faraway and much weaker than it had been in the beginning. *You've set us all free, love. Hang on now. Your man will be with you soon.*

"Is Ruairidh all right?"

Her brother hesitated a moment before answering.

He is alive. Don't worry about that now.

"I'd have come sooner, Rory Patrick, but I didn't know you were here," Hexy murmured.

That's all right. You came in the end.

"I love you, Rory Patrick," she whispered, her voice barely audible above the snarls and barks that filled the air. The selkies were chasing Sevin into the pool. This time, she was certain that they would be able to kill the monster. The iron had weakened him into vulnerability.

And I love you, Hexy. Rest now, or you will harm the babes.

"I will." Having no choice with exhaustion upon her, Hexy let her eyes close on the horror and pain of Wrathdrum.

Chapter Fifteen

Hexy was relieved to waken and find herself clothed in the sensible woolen dress she had abandoned on the fishermen's isle. It made her return to reality in a foreign situation nearly bearable.

The world she woke to *was* foreign. It was a place she had never seen or imagined, except perhaps in long-forgotten dreams.

Her memories of how she came to this place were hazy. Two bloodied Ruairidhs had come to her after the battle in the finman's cave. Kneeling down, one of them had taken her in his arms. The other had gathered up a cast-off skin, examining it with a worried frown.

At the edge of the frightening pool where the finman had gone, the nearer Ruairidh had leaned over and whispered, "I shall breathe for ye, *aroon,* until ye can manage on yer own. Hae no fear of the sea."

Then he had fastened his mouth on hers and plunged them both into the blue water. After the first shock of the cold water, and seeing a phalanx of seals close in around them with elongated flippers extended, she recalled nothing.

There was a movement beside her and Hexy turned her head, expecting to see Ruairidh sitting beside the bed as he had been so many times when she awakened. But it was not her lover who sat beside her, keeping a vigil. It was an older man who had Ruairidh's hair and eyes, and another who might have been Ruairidh's twin.

Her brain was sufficiently awake now to understand that she probably hadn't been seeing double back in the finman's cave. Ruairidh actually did have a twin, or at least a brother.

The older man intoned formally, "I am Cathair—son of Ardagh and brother of Colm; first son of Lachlann; father of Keir and Ruairidh. This is Avocamor, home of the People. The ground whereon ye rest is sacred, consecrated by the passage of our ancestors and great progenitor whom are now but foam upon the ocean. Enter our home wi' veneration, and welcome, daughter."

The two men stood looking at her, waiting for some response.

Ardagh. She knew that name.

"Um—thank you for the welcome."

Dazed, and unable to think of a better reply, though she felt that there was something formal that she was supposed to say, Hexy sat up slowly and looked around at Ruairidh's father, brother and home.

They were in a grand chamber that had a cathedrallike atmosphere, though it more closely resembled an exotic pleasure garden than any church. Bizarre treelike plants grew from the glassy ceiling downward, their succulent, strangely hued leaves hanging protectively around the reddish fruits that clustered there like grapes. The plants glittered where the pale light caught in their dewy leaves. Their roots ran along the walls in tangled bundles and trailed down into the numerous pools of blue, phosphorescent water, which sent up silver veiling into the air.

She stared at the water, momentarily transfixed. Whatever it was that lived in the water and made it sparkle must have gorged itself on moonlight, swallowing it until it overflowed with silvered illumination. It was liquid moonlight; there were no other words for it.

She turned slowly. There were any number of beautiful crystals growing in the walls' niches, clusters of calcite that looked like sparkling spider mums from some faerie's autumnal garden.

Her eyes traveled upward. Through the narrow chimney that opened to the sky, Hexy could see the horned moon, as white as hoarfrost on a wintry night. But something about the image was distorted, as if she were looking into a mirror, or perhaps through an imperfect lens.

Hexy struggled to her feet. Her head throbbed once, and she raised a hand to the back of her skull. She didn't feel any knots, but the skin was tender, as though pain lurked just beneath the surface.

"What are those marks?" she asked, pointing at a violent zigzag that marred the chimney's flue. "It looks like lightning."

Ruairidh's brother looked at her oddly, but Cathair answered easily.

"And sae it is. These caves are made of sandstone. When lightning hits the ground it melts the sand intae glass and is frozen forever, braided intae the earth. Yer people have a name for this. I am told it is called *fullgerite.* Such an ugly word for something sae miraculous and beautiful." Cathair's voice was slow and deep.

It was a strange thing for her to talk about with Ruairidh's father, but so was everything in her life these days. Like Alice, she had wandered into some land on the other side of the looking glass.

"Sandstone? But the entire cave seems to be made of glass." She added politely, "It is very pretty."

She didn't add that it also looked a bit hard and cold, and seemed to reverberate with some odd harmonics that distorted both voice and sight. Too, the proportions were subtly wrong now that she was standing upright.

It was also plain that no women lived here.

"It is glass, after a fashion," Cathair answered. "Back when men first came tae this part of the isle they showed the *sidhe* how to make glass from sand. As a tribute tae one of the great feys, a wall was built tae hold back the tide, and then a huge magical fire was kindled inside this cave. After it burned for nine days the wall was taken down and the tide allowed inside tae carry away the ash and tae cool the crystal."

Cathair paused, giving her a chance to speak, but again Hexy was at a loss. There were important thing to ask and know, but her brain seemed unable to recall them. It was as though she had a sort of logic amnesia.

After a moment, Cathair nodded and continued the lecture. "Unfortunately, the sea disturbed the *sidhes'* power, which comes from the living land, and they could not abide here. It was given to us in exchange for the shells and pearls they wanted tae decorate their inland castle. It wasnae long after that that the fruit began tae grow in here. It became our new home when the places south were overrun by men who hunted us for our furs—and simply because they love tae hunt."

Unprepared to discuss either faeries or hunters, Hexy looked for some other topic.

Her eyes turned to a row of bladders similar to the one leant to her by the mermaid. She realized that the reason she was still feeling dazed was that she was likely under the influence of a familiar narcotic.

"Ruairidh drugged me, didn't he, before he left?" she asked suddenly.

Cathair frowned. "Why dae ye say that?"

"Because I know this feeling, this disconnection of thought. Why did he do that?" she asked. "Did he think I would be afraid of you if he wasn't here when I woke up?"

Cathair hesitated, then said, "The babe was disturbed when ye arrived. He thought it best that ye be calmed so the babe could rest."

"Babes," Hexy corrected. "There are two. And they aren't disturbed. They are hungry. They've been hungry for days now, poor things. I haven't known what to feed them."

Cathair turned and looked at Keir. No words were exchanged, but Hexy sensed that they had marked something significant in what she had said.

"What is in those bags?" she asked quickly, to distract them, recalling belatedly what Ruairidh had said about the difficulty of being part *sidhe,* and fearing that perhaps she had said too much. "The finwoman gave me one. I do hope that she is all right now."

"Aye, ye put yer iron rocks in it. That was most clever of ye. But these arenae for stones. They are for making cheese." Cathair smiled at her stunned look, as though knowing that she had not expected so prosaic an answer. The smile made him appear a great deal more welcoming. "But I must tell ye, daughter, it isnae the cheese frae sheep or cows that you are used tae eating."

"Cheese," she repeated. "For what? Do seals eat cheese?"

"Nay. It is for the People—the selkies. Though the seals help, of course. The bags of seal milk are mixed wi' brine and fruit and then taken out at high tide and anchored in the kelp. The sea stirs them. After, the whey is taken out and fed to the young ones who are tae old tae nurse any longer." He added, "We eat the curd ourselves sometimes when we tire of fruit and fish."

Hexy tried to envision babies nursing from seal nannies, but a low humming filled the air for the space of a long breath. The dark glass resonated around them, shivering like a tuning fork and making her mind go blank as the noise erased her thoughts.

"What is that noise?" she asked as the vibration passed and the ability to speak returned. "It sounds almost like a horn."

"A rip current races through the underground passages. It would be dangerous to us, but we have a sea gate that holds back the worst of the tide and storms. At the turning of the riptide the cave sings tae us. If ye like, later I'll take ye to the gate sae ye may hear the music clearly."

"Thank you, I—" Hexy's eyes began to blur. Fatigue was abruptly overwhelming, and some unpleasant message began tapping out a distress signal in the back of her brain. Her body also began to ache.

"I'm sorry, Cathair," Hexy began, putting a hand to her heart, where it seemed her energy was draining from her. "But I am suddenly very tired. Can you fetch Ruairidh?"

Instantly a strong arm was about her waist, lending her support.

"Come, *NicnanRon*. You maun eat and then rest. Ye have a task ahead of ye yet and will need a steady hand."

"A task?" A low pain began in her chest and spread outward as her brain and body began to truly awaken.

"Aye, now that we are certain ye are truly *NicnanRon*. But it can wait until ye are rested and have eaten," he assured her.

Sudden alarm shafted through her, making her stiffen against Cathair's grasp. "Where *is* Ruairidh? Why isn't he here? He hasn't gone to look for Sevin, has he? Not alone?"

"Nay. Ruairidh is resting, and the abomination is dead, sae ye have nothing tae fear now," Cathair said soothingly.

But Hexy had been watching Keir and saw him cast a worried glance down a dark corridor. A hand pushed hard against her heart, as though holding blood back from a gaping hole where it wished to flood. Hexy said, "He isn't *resting*. He's hurt and I want to see him. Now."

Cathair looked at her assessingly and then, perhaps seeing that she was going to hunt for Ruairidh no matter what he said or how much it hurt her, he nodded assent.

"Very well. Ye may see him. But ye maun eat before ye work. We cannae risk either yer health or the babes'. Ruairidh can wait a while yet."

"Fine, I'll eat. Just take me to Ruairidh."

The corridor was darker than the grand chamber, but still not black, since small lighted rooms opened off it. It was in one of these that Ruairidh was found sleeping on a bed of long grass with his skin half peeled off.

Seeing her surprise at his semi-naked state,

284

Cathair explained, "We had tae dress Ruairidh in his skin as soon as we arrived or he would hae bled to death and the skin would hae died."

"He used his last bit of strength to bring ye here where ye may be safe," Ruairidh's brother said, his voice sharp. "It nearly killed him."

Hexy looked at her beloved's pale chest, seeking signs of injury. There were none visible to the eye, yet she was sure that she had seen him cut and bleeding.

"Where is he wounded?" she asked, worried that they might have laid his wounds on the bed of sea grass.

"It was a blow tae the heart, as ye plainly feel now that yer awakening."

"But I don't see anything."

"Ye wouldnae. The flesh heals quickly in the People. But the wound is there all the same. His fur is torn clean through and some terrible magic was used tae inflict it. Because he is part *sidhe*, it didnae kill him straightaway. But if he is tae be saved, ye must bind his wounds with yon needle of bone and a thread of yer hair."

"But why me?" Hexy asked, sinking to her knees beside Ruairidh and touching his pale face with trembling fingers. His usually animated features were still and waxy, almost deathlike. "Why haven't one of you stitched him up? He is suffering. I can feel it."

"He doesnae suffer greatly," Cathair assured

her. "The sleep protects him frae the worst of the pain."

"But he maun be healed soon. And only the hand of his *aroon*, his true love, may seal the wounds of the sorcerer," Keir answered, speaking for the second time. His face was nearly as pale as his brother's. He held out a long needle to her.

Hexy wanted to protest against the task, because she knew his skin lived and would feel the piercings of the needle even if Ruairidh did not, but she did not speak aloud.

Nevertheless, Keir seemed to be able to read her mind. His tone was almost contemptuous as he added, "Had ye not been here, I would hae done it, since I am also part *sidhe*. But I doubt that it would save him, for a brother's love isnae enough now that ye have bespelled him. Sew well, *NicnanRon*. Use yer *sidhe* magic to undo what ye wrought by going to that evil place. Yer sewing will determine the scars he bears for the rest of his life, or if he shall even have one."

"Keir!" Cathair's voice was sharp, but Keir did not retract his harsh words.

"I'll bring ye some food," Cathair said gently to Hexy. "Eat, and then if ye feel strong enough ye may start. Save my son, *NicnanRon*, if ye can. Save the father of yer children."

Shaken by sudden guilt, Hexy accepted the needle and the responsibility of saving Ruairidh's life.

Chapter Sixteen

She sewed for an eternity, pausing in her minute stitches only to pluck another hair from her
head when the previous one ran out. Her eyes
teared, protesting the strain of work that she
did by the shimmering light of a clear glass jar
of the phosphorescent water. But she did not
stop working. Her heart ached with Ruairidh's,
perhaps because of the air they had shared
while he carried her through the sea, perhaps
because of the salt exchanged, perhaps because
of their *sidhe* blood. She knew not why, but she
felt his pain as if it were her own.

Periodically, Cathair or Keir would bring her
something to eat or drink, and she would pause

to gulp it down, but always she returned to her work on Ruairidh's skin. Every stitch was set with a prayer of hope or an utterance of love; an overhand seam chained one hair to another, prayed over like a rosary, until, when she was finally finished, it almost felt as though part of her soul had been stitched up in the skin with him.

When the final stitch was set and the hair tied off in a minuscule knot, Cathair and Keir returned to the room to help ease Ruairidh's fur back over his body. No outward sign of mending was visible as the fur was smoothed over his heart, but he began an immediate transformation.

Hexy had feared that perhaps watching Ruairidh change would seem an unnatural or repellant thing. Yet watching him shift to fill the skin, seeing the way the fur rejoined his body until it was not *on* him, but *of* him, she was not moved by disgust or fright, but rather a sense of awe. And she knew that she had done her job well when the pain in her heart finally eased and no blood seeped from his wound.

"Well done, daughter," Cathair said. "Now you must rest."

Hexy didn't answer. Her eyes remained fixed on Ruairidh's face, hoping that he would waken and speak to her. But other than an easing of posture, he gave no sign that he was aware of the change she had wrought.

She succumbed to exhaustion, but lying down she slept only lightly. She curled up beside Ruairidh, a hand resting over his heart where she could feel its beat and listen to his breathing. Life pulsed there, weak at first but growing stronger with every hour. Whatever spell the finman had used on Ruairidh, she had undone it. He would live. Her relief was overwhelming and mitigated some of her feelings of guilt.

For a while, she lay in a semi-trance listening to the distant waves that made the cave whisper. The sea had no concept of time, and at the moment, neither did she. Along the shore, it knew the moon and tides because of the intrusion of the land, but it did not divide itself into hours, only into light and dark. It was timeless. It made Avocamor, and those in it, also seem disconnected from the passage of time.

Oddly, when she finally slipped into her deepest rest, it was not Ruairidh she dreamed of, but her brother, Rory Patrick. They were trying to find each other as they wandered through a dense fog where ominous shapes loomed. She knew that he was trying to warn her about something, but the wind and mist always caught his words and hurled them away before she could actually hear them. With every passing moment, she grew more upset, her mind so agitated that it made her body twitch.

This wasn't right. She should not be dreaming of Rory Patrick anymore.

"Hexy, lass." A quiet voice interrupted her nightmare, and something stroked along her neck. "Ye dream, lass. Awaken. We have a present for ye."

Hexy opened her eyes at once and found herself back in Avocamor, curled on a bed of sea grass and snuggled up with a half-furred Ruairidh. Standing on the other side of the low bed were Keir and Cathair. They were completely furless and dressed in kilts, and Hexy realized that this was probably in deference to her and her inability to speak with them when they were in selkie form.

She sat up quickly, shoving her hair back from her face, where it had dried in a dreadful tangle. "Is something wrong?" she asked, though she was certain nothing was amiss, because all three men smiled—though Keir's expression was somewhat forced.

"Nay, lass," Ruairidh answered, his voice normal and sweet though still rather faint. "We hae brought ye a gift—a skin of yer very own. Because ye truly are of the *NicnanRon*, ye may wear this skin now and swim with the People."

"It belonged tae Samhain, who chose tae leave the People and live out his life on the land with his human lover," Keir told her. His tone suggested that this was a terrible fate, and she supposed that he blamed the woman for it. "But it is yours now, brother's mate. Use it wisely."

"You mean that I can put this on and become a selkie?" she asked, awed. She turned to look at Ruairidh with wonder in her eyes.

"Nay," Keir denied. "A seal is what ye shall be."

" 'Tis true that ye shall never be a selkie," Ruairidh answered gently. Seeing her disappointment, he added, "But ye may be wi' us in the sea and borrow some of our strength and skills for a time. It is a gift none other of yer kind can have. Take it, lass. 'Tis an honor and a blessing."

"You are certain? I'll be able to swim like a seal and everything?" she asked, reaching out nervously for the pelt Cathair held out, somewhat fearful that it would not react the way Ruairidh's fur did when she touched it.

"Ye carry twa babes. Only a *NicnanRon* can dae that. The skin shall work for ye," he assured her.

"Oh, it likes me." She sighed when she touched the skin and felt it shiver beneath her hands. Cathair carefully laid it in her arms, transferring it as he might a baby. Hexy gathered it close, rubbing her cheek against it and then offering it to Ruairidh, so that he could feel it, too.

"Guard it well, daughter," Cathair's voice was

warm. "Ye may not be magiced by a fur thief as one of the People would, but if ye lose it, ye shall feel its loss forever more. And ye are vulnerable tae other things that ye maun learn about before ye gae out into the sea. And always remember that ye may be hunted by yer own kind."

"Da, ye'll frighten her," Ruairidh protested, leaving off touching the skin to stroke Hexy's tangled hair. "There is time enough for all that later."

"Can we try it now?" Hexy asked, not allowing Cathair's concern or Keir's aloofness to dampen her spirits.

"Ruairidh shall teach ye the ways of the sea when he is well," Keir said. As always, his voice was a little sharp and disapproving. "Ye maun wait until then. And practice some patience this time."

Hexy barely resisted the urge to stick out her tongue at Keir. Instead, she turned back to Ruairidh. He was still smiling happily, his eyes shining brightly in his too pale face.

"And, speaking of patience, come, Keir." Cathair's voice was still calm, but Hexy guessed he was annoyed with his son.

"Soon, lass," Ruairidh promised as Cathair and Keir quietly left the room.

"Your brother doesn't like me," she told him. "He thinks it is my fault that you were hurt."

"My brother is jealous and doesnae understand why I am now bonded tae ye as much as tae the People. He'll realize why in time, if he finds his own *aroon*. And it was the beast, Sevin, that wounded me. I place nae blame on ye."

"Thank you."

"Though I am a wee bit disappointed in ye myself, lass," Ruairidh said. Was his soft voice teasing?

"By what?" she asked, staring into his dark eyes.

"I can feel ye here inside my skin right against my heart." He touched the area she had mended. "And yet ye hae nae kissed me now that I am wakeful. Perhaps all yer affection went intae yer sewing."

"Ha!" Hexy rose to her knees and leaned over Ruairidh. "I am not certain that kissing you is a wise thing to do," she murmured. "You are still recovering from a near-fatal wound and should be resting."

"Sae I should, and sae I shall. But a wee kiss willnae hurt me," he coaxed. "And we've been apart a long, lonely while."

"Hm." Being careful that no other part of their skin touched, Hexy leaned over and brushed her lips over Ruairidh's. The contact was fleeting, but still enough to make her heart beat faster and put a slight flush in his white skin.

Hexy moved back immediately. "No more of that until you're well," she told him, concern plain in her voice. "We've risked enough already."

"Aye, that we hae done, lass." Ruairidh paused, and Hexy wondered if he was going to scold her after all for going to the finman's lair. But all he said was, "Yer a reckless lass. If we hadnae managed tae kill that monster there in the cave, or had he killed ye, we should hae been forced tae bloody war with the finfolk before we were ready."

"I thought the finman had taken you," she explained, trying to make him understand. "Something was calling me to that cave. I dreamed about it every night. And when you didn't come and didn't come . . ."

"It wasnae me that called ye there," Ruairidh said, his eyes instantly concerned. "Are ye sure that it wasnae yer imagination? How did ye find the place?"

"No, it wasn't my imagination. It was my brother, Rory Patrick," she told him. "I didn't realize it until I started freeing those souls, but the finman had him trapped in there, along with mad John's son and the Reverend Fraser— and lots of other people."

Ruairidh took her hand.

"I think some of them were selkies, too. They . . ." She tried to think of a way of describing how the souls had felt. "They felt different to me, but familiar, too."

Ruairidh continued to look concerned. "But how did ye find the place, lass? It was concealed by magic nae person could see—not even one with the sight."

"Well, as to how I got there, a finwoman brought me."

"A finwoman!" He sounded dumbfounded.

Hexy nodded. "Sevin had done something bad to her—put iron hooks in her body so she couldn't turn into a regular woman and walk on land." Hexy's brow knitted, showing her perturbation. "I hope that she is better now. She said she would be if I killed him."

"Then she should be well, for the monster is well and truly dead," Ruairidh assured her. "But how did ye find the finwoman?"

"The merrow told me where she was."

"The merrow?" He sighed. "This is a long tale then, is it?"

"Yes, and it can wait. You need to rest," she answered, unhappy at the weakening of his voice.

"Maybe so, but maybe no. Lass, this is important. Yer certain that it was yer brother that called ye there? It wasnae the monster himself, perhaps pretending tae be yer brother? He could have made the finwoman and merrow dae his bidding. He had many of his own people enslaved."

"I am sure it was Rory Patrick," she said instantly, wanting to smooth away the worried look from Ruairidh's brow, but not daring to physically touch him and risk a transference of the salt. "My brother and I were very close, probably like you and Keir. It was natural that I should feel his presence even if I didn't understand what it was at first. And anyway, I only found the merrow because of some old books Mr. Campbell gave me, which gave me the idea to go see the sin eater. It was all just a string of coincidences. And you said that Sevin is dead now. He can't hurt us anymore."

Ruairidh nodded, looking relieved. "That is true. And ye would hae no choice but tae answer if yer brother called. Even Keir should understand that," he said, as much to himself as to her. He smiled then, but it was with less brilliance than before. "I've another gift for ye, lass, but it can never compete with the skin yer cuddling, sae I shall save it for another day. Perhaps I'll give it tae ye on the day we are wed."

"Wed?" Hexy asked, her mind going blank. "You mean when we get married?"

"Aye." Ruairidh's head cocked. "Would ye not wish tae be wed in the ways of yer kind? We've nae such customs here, as ye know, and I thought perhaps ye'd wish it."

296

"I . . ." She thought about it for a long moment, imagining marrying in the kirk, perhaps with Jillian in attendance. Somehow, the image would not hold together. "I don't know. It never occurred to me to do it. I mean, we are already wed in all but name."

Ruairidh smiled again. His eyes began to drift shut. He pulled his fur back up over his shoulders. "Think on it, then. We shall talk when I wake. We also maun decide where ye would like tae live. We've a cottage on a coastal island that might suit ye and the babes."

Hexy was disturbed by Ruairidh's choice of words. "We won't live together?" she asked.

"Aye, much of the time, but t'would nae be healthy fer ye always tae be in Avocamor—and sometimes I maun be here." Ruairidh settled back into sleep, his fur tucking itself about him, though stopping at his face.

In her own lap, her new gift waited patiently. Hexy stroked it once in consolation, and then laid down beside Ruairidh, pulling the fur side of the skin over her.

She tried to go back to sleep, hoping that Rory Patrick and the fog were not still waiting for her. She needed to put the nightmare of Wrathdrum behind her.

After all, it was as she had said to Ruairidh; Sevin was dead and he couldn't hurt them anymore.

Chapter Seventeen

Hexy roused from sleep, called to wakefulness and longing by she knew not what—a voice, a song, a thought. Perhaps it was her new fur telling her that it was lonely. She thought for a moment that she could hear Rory Patrick's voice calling to her, but it faded even as she opened her eyes.

After a quick glance down at Ruairidh, to reassure herself that he was sleeping peacefully and unlikely to awaken, Hexy padded from their bed, taking her skin with her.

Her very own skin! She still could not believe that this miracle was possible. How she longed to put it on and go out into the beautiful sea.

It was time. She had slept enough. Of course she had needed to rest, the same as anyone would after a terrible ordeal. But she was awake now and wanted to be out in the open. In the water—not here, where she was kept deaf and blind and all but dead to the world.

Without realizing what she was doing, Hexy began to disrobe.

It seemed odd now that she had ever feared the deep waters. But she *had* feared the ocean, as all supposedly sensible land dwellers did. It had appeared to her as a voracious thing, which swallowed up ships and men and brought terrible storms. It had even taken her brother from her.

But she had learned to ignore that fear when a sort of suprarational knowledge of her true self came to her. Of course, later, when she had no longer actively dreaded it, the sea had still seemed a lonely place—a vast and empty desert of dreary color, only different from the ones on land because it was covered in water.

But then the sea gave her Ruairidh, and she now knew that it was not lonely at all. She had met others who lived in the ocean, and they were kind. And now that she had her own skin, she had no reason for silly fears.

Hexy stood naked in the doorway, holding the skin to her face, rubbing her cheek against it while it caressed her back.

She was not supposed to venture into the water without Ruairidh, and she understood everyone's concern that she not go out alone for the first time in case she had difficulties or got lost. But the long wait chaffed at her. Who knew how many days it would be before Ruairidh awakened and was able to join her for a swim?

Still . . .

Hexy paced and sang softly, and tried any number of things to keep herself from answering the skin's siren call. But it was useless. The allure was too strong. Something powerful, magical, was telling her to put on the skin and go into the sea. Everyone was worrying needlessly. What could possibly hurt her? There was nothing dangerous out there.

Unable to resist the strange compulsion any longer, she took her fur out to the deserted great room and tried on her borrowed pelt. She hoped that a quick wearing would be sufficient to end the wild longing.

There was no awkwardness to this first dressing. The fur slipped in place as if it had always belonged on her, like drawing on a velvet glove. Without any help, it sealed itself along her breastbone, snugging close.

The transformation of her body was amazing. She could feel her limbs foreshorten and her fingers fuse, and her spine grow long and flexible. There should have been pain, but she felt nothing but the slide of velvet over naked skin.

She laughed softly, and her voice changed.

Her world shifted from a vertical orientation to a horizontal one, and she grew heavy and graceless and slid to the floor.

She found at once that prone movement was difficult without proper legs and put pressure on her belly. To escape from her painful land wallow she would have to go into the water, where her new shape belonged. There she could move the way the water flowed. She would be strong and graceful.

Just into the pool. She wouldn't go beyond the cave, she promised herself as she sank beneath the surface of the lovely blue water of moonlight. *There were no riptides running right now. No reason that she couldn't just play in the pool right there inside the cave. No one would ever know.*

The first thing she noticed as she dove down into the tarn was that the pressure on her ears wasn't half what it had been before, and then that it was easier to float than it had been in her human body. She turned about a couple of times, rolling and spiraling, delighting in her flexible spine. How easy it was to move! She knew that out in the open she would be fast and elegant. This was what she had always dreamed of when she was a child.

What could it possibly hurt to venture just outside of the pool? To only go out as far as the shore and look at the land for a moment or two? Didn't she want to know what it was like to bob on the surface of the sea, to ride the wind and waves as they rolled toward the land, to have her nose tickled by foamy spray?

She hesitated a moment, trying to recall why this might be a foolish thing to do. But when no answer occurred to her, she arched her body into a steep dive and swam for the open water. Thrusting downward with her tail, she moved quickly for the mouth of the cave.

Once there, she hesitated again. Water surged over her and crashed as it smashed itself against the sheltering stone, many currents braiding one into the other and making the sand swirl.

It should have seemed cold but didn't because her beautiful fur insulated her from the chill. She looked out shyly through the jungle of kelp, swaying in time with surges that breathed in and out of the cave.

Next she looked up at the surface. It was bright with light and sparkles like crushed glass. It had to be near noon for the waves to be so bright.

There was nobody about. No one to notice if she went up to the surface for a quick peek.

Smiling with glee at her newly found freedom, she stroked upward for the glistening surface, allowing the current to help carry her toward the shore.

She shoved her head up through the storm-wracked flotsam and looked around with her new eyes.

How different everything was! She saw now not just with her eyes that had amazing peripheral vision, but with her nose. She felt like a bloodhound, able to scent everything and everyone who had paused near her that morning. She knew that a rowboat with two men had gone by near dawn, and recently some seals had passed to bask on the rocks, and there were many birds that had floated in the water here.

The rocks that made up the shoreline looked bigger now that she was in the water, but also inviting, and she had a strong inclination to climb out onto them and enjoy the glorious sun while it gilded her fur with golden light. She didn't even mind the northern wind that sang mournfully of a coming storm, because its cold could not touch her.

But there was an even stronger compulsion whispering in her brain, urging her away from the shore and toward the islands.

What she really wanted to do was go back to the island of the fishermen's chapel and see if all traces of the monster had been washed away by the violent storm. It would be so good to know that not only was Sevin dead, but that all traces of his taint had been washed away, too. Without his ghostly traces, the island would be an ideal place for sunning.

She shouldn't do that, part of her mind argued back. Ruairidh could wake up at any moment, and he would be worried about her. He would probably even be angry that she had not waited to share this moment with him. And hadn't Cathair warned her that people might mistake her for a seal and try to hunt her?

But the islet was deserted. There were no people there now. And she really wanted to go to the island. She needed to go. And it wasn't far. No, not far at all. She could go and be back in almost no time. And wouldn't it be good to know that that awful chapel was truly purified?

Hexy shivered even though she was not cold.

But what about rip currents and deadly undertows? Cathair had told her that there was one right outside the cave—one so strong it made the stones vibrate like a horn once the tide had turned.

That was only at the turn of tide and in narrow places where the tide ran fast. That didn't happen in the open sea. And as for undertows—they didn't affect her when she wore her skin. With her fur in place she was fast and strong and had nothing to fear. She could cavort all day in the strongest current and never tire. She should come to the island . . . come at once . . .

Hexy twitched, her muscles wanting to be off, in spite of her mind's hesitation.

What about sharks? The mermaid has made

her wear those red sponges to keep hungry predators away. There must be something large and dangerous lurking in the water.

Nonsense, the inner voice answered impatiently. *The wicked finwoman had worn nothing herself, had she? Obviously she did not fear the slashing bite of the shark. That was because she knew that sharks did not come near the shoreline of the islands. They did not like the turbulence of the sea when it met land. And they did not like the People, or water when it was hot and bright. She would only be in open water for a very few minutes anyway. If she left right now, she would have bright sun for her entire journey and be able to see any warning fins if they should come her way . . .*

Hexy looked over the delicate wavelets toward the fishermen's island. Its pale outline was reassuringly close. She could swim very fast and be there in only a moment's time. She would have a quick look to be sure that all was well, and then she would come right back. No one would ever know.

She pivoted to look at the shore behind her, reassuring herself that there were no witnesses to see her misbehavior. Then, turning back and taking a last look at the island to check her direction, she dropped beneath the surface and, putting on a burst of ecstatic speed, raced toward the gray islet.

* * *

Ruairidh fought his way up from the fog of sleep, disturbed by a voice that claimed to be Hexy's brother. The healing sleep did not have dreams, and this intrusion was enough to rouse him from slumber.

"Hexy?" he called, rolling onto his side and reaching for her.

She was gone, her place cold.

Her fur was gone, too.

Alarmed, he rolled from the bed.

The attack came without warning. The finman who rushed at her, eyes in his burnt face held wide in some form of religious ecstasy, was not as powerful in body or mind as Sevin had been. But he was fast, and Hexy realized immediately that he was far stronger than she, even with the aid of her new skin.

She tried to dodge him, but he snagged her in those long ropey arms and spun her around in his coils. She managed to avoid his eyes, so he could not paralyze her with his gaze, but she felt his presence prying at her mind in the mental wound her earlier overshadowing had given him. Before he had whispered sweetly to her, acting as a lure. Now he roared. And the thoughts he battered her with were not his own; they belonged to the dead Sevin. The finman, Brodir, was carrying out his master's last orders. As revenge on the People, the *NicnanRon* was to die.

Her horrified thrall ended as the finman's attention wavered. He searched the nearby stones and then began towing her toward the rocks. She knew he planned to thrust her head-first into a narrow crack after he had sucked out her soul.

Recalling Reverend Fraser's fate, Hexy bent double and, planting her flippered feet on the nearest outcropping, thrust back with all her might. At the same time she ducked her head, getting as far away from the finman's mouth as she could.

With all her will she cried out to Ruairidh, praying she could reach him in his healing sleep and he would understand what was happening. The internal scream was loud enough to shake her brain. Hurt followed hurt. Sharp pain stung her right shoulder and left hip as the finman tried to subdue her struggles and turn her about for an easy mouth hold. He could not trick his way back into her mind and so he spent all his effort in trying to squeeze the air from her body and latch his teeth over her nose. They fought all the way to the sea floor, where their thrashing sent up a mushrooming cloud of sand.

Hexy soon realized that there were many limitations to her borrowed skin's abilities. Perhaps selkies had the knack for breathing underwater, but she did not. Her lungs were beginning to cry out for a clean breath. And though her neck was stronger than before, it was no match for the power of the finman's tentacled arms. It could be broken.

She tried clawing at the finman, but without fingers she couldn't get a grip on his arms, and her small nails left only superficial wounds. It was all she could do to keep him from wrapping a limb about her throat as he dragged her over the sand and back toward the fissured rocks.

Her world began to go black at the edges. She had an indignant and wholly inappropriate thought that the sailors had all gotten it wrong; There was no anesthesia to ease the pain of the last moments. Drowning was not a pleasant death. It was not peaceful. There was plenty of time to think and feel as your skull and chest seemed to balloon with used air and began to spasm in pain. And she wasn't even to the point where her lungs exchanged cold seawater for depleted breath.

Ruairidh, she called again, beginning to despair. *I'm sorry, love.*

Regret was so strong that it pierced even her personal horror. That was what came at the end of life—regret! She could see it all in terrifying plainness. There would be war now. Her babies, the hope of the People, would die, too—and it was all her fault for being too stupid to realize that she was being lured by magic.

Sorry, Ruairidh . . .

If the finman's attack was sudden and vicious, then Ruairidh's was even more so. Hexy saw at once how selkies differed from seals. Ruairidh's arms were strangely elongated as they reached for the finman, and at the end of each flipper tip was some sort of retractable claw that jutted out into long, wicked hooks.

Selkies also had long teeth.

To her, no selkie could ever be as physically horrifying as a finman, and perhaps they were not as heavy and strong in the arms. But they were fast and, she now knew, they were ruthless. And these usually gentle seal people could kill efficiently.

The shocked finman tried to untangle his arms from around Hexy's body to meet the attack, but he was too slow. Claws slashed over his face, rendering him first blind and then hemorrhaging as his throat was cut in four places.

The dying creature spasmed, his convulsion so sharp that it forced most of the air from Hexy's lungs. Her world was fading, but Ruairidh circled his opponent, coming close enough to give her one quick breath. It was a small thing, no larger than a sigh, but it was sufficient to sustain her while her love tore the dying finman's arms away and pushed her toward the surface.

Once her head was above water and he saw that she could swim on her own, Ruairidh abandoned her, returning to the seabed to see that the job was finished and this time Sevin's minion died, too.

They did not talk on the way back to Avocamor. Their swim was slow, both of them being bruised and exhausted, and Hexy was too wracked with guilt for casual conversation.

When they finally reached the cave and climbed out onto the low ledge around the pool, Ruairidh assisted her out of her skin and then shed his own.

"Go rest." His voice was quiet, unemphatic, and Hexy did not like it at all. He almost didn't sound like Ruairidh.

Nor did he look like a conquering hero, aglow with the satisfaction of having vanquished an enemy. His face was white, nearly bloodless, and for the first time he showed no reaction to her naked body.

Hexy's guilt deepened. Once again she had caused Ruairidh to be wounded while he risked his life for her, and she had put him in a position where he had had to kill another being. He probably hated her now.

"Ruairidh—"

"Not now. I shall nae be long, *aroon*. I need tae tell the others what has happened. We were tae merciful. We maun be sure that all of Sevin's slaves are dead."

She tried to take comfort in the fact that he had called her *aroon*, but the thought of Ruairidh telling Cathair and Keir of her selfish foolishness only deepened her gloom. Keir especially would probably never believe that she had been lured out by the last vestiges of Sevin's will planted in the surviving finman.

If Ruairidh had thought before that she probably wouldn't be able to live among the selkies, he would be convinced of it now. Maybe he would send her into exile at that cottage he had mentioned.

Back in their bedroom, Hexy dropped her wet skin beside the bed and, ignoring the spreading bruises that blossomed over her body and the trickles of blood at her shoulder and hip, flung herself down on the sea grass bed and curled in on herself. Unable to hold back the accumulated fright of the last two weeks, she covered her face with her hands and began to cry.

Fear and a near drowning hadn't brought her any kind of anesthesia, and neither did guilt.

Chapter Eighteen

When Ruairidh returned to his sleeping den it was to find Hexy curled in a ball and weeping. He was exhausted, but all thought of rest fled when he saw her. Alarmed that she might have been hurt in some nonvisible way, he came immediately to her side and touched her on the nape, seeking to soothe her.

"Lass? What is wrong? Are ye hurt?"

"No, but you are."

Ruairidh's hand arrested in midstroke. "What?"

Hexy raised flooded eyes to his. In the blue glow, the expanded pupils looked like they had drowned in a deep well. He could now see purpling marks on her throat and ribs and two identical punctures at her hip and shoulder where the finman had set his barbs when he tried to latch onto her face.

Rage and delayed fear of what might have happened filled him in equal measure, but he was careful not to let it show. He felt no remorse at taking the bespelled finman's life, and a part of him feared that Hexy was shocked at the savagery of his attack and might grow alarmed if she sensed the anger in him.

"I am sorry, lass," he said gently, trying to soothe her by stroking down her neck and then touching her gently at the site of each wound. "I truly thought ye were safe, but I shouldnae have assumed that it was sae, not after ye told me of being called tae Wrathdrum. That wasnae the work of any chained soul, but of Sevin's wicked sorcery. Had I been more alert I would hae seen this."

Hexy shook her head. More tears welled up and spilled down her cheeks. Ruairidh didn't say anything about the effect the tears had on him, but her weeping drove him mad. He didn't know how this could be, since a summoning spell could only be cast once, but her tears still affected him, each one as potent as the last.

"It was *my* fault. I should have realized that someone else was in my head and not listened to the voice. But it was like having a sort of amnesia—I couldn't use my brain . . . And now your brother will truly hate me. Probably your father, too—and even you will."

Ruairidh shook his head at this display of remorse for something that was not her fault. Almost he smiled at the wildness of her fancy.

"Tosh! I'll hate ye the day the oceans run dry . . . or yer teeth turn green. Can't abide green teeth," he added. "Stop crying now, lass."

Hexy sniffed and then answered in a small voice: "You are just trying to make me feel better."

"Well, of course I am. What sort of a beast dae ye think me? Any road, there's nae real harm done," Ruairidh said, smoothing the maddening tears away with his thumbs. They made his skin sting and his heartbeat deepen. It was difficult, but he forced his voice to remain calm. "A lock of my hair shall hae yer skin sewed up in nae time, and these bruises are nothing. Pups get worse on their first swims all the time."

It was a lie, of course. Every mark on her body was a travesty. But they would heal, and soon. And someday, maybe, they would both be able to forget what had nearly happened.

Surprised, Hexy finally stopped weeping.

"My skin? You are going to sew up my fur?"

"Of course, as soon as we've rested." That

hadn't been his first thought, but he'd soon realized that he could not let his fear for her safety cripple her. He stroked a hand down his chest and then began rubbing gently at her wounds. She slumped against him at once.

" 'Tis best if ye gae out into the sea immediately, else ye may grow fearful. That would never dae."

"We'll go back out together?" she asked, her voice growing weaker.

"Of course. But we maun rest now." He lowered her onto the bed and then spooned in behind her.

"You drugged me again," she muttered. "Is that bad for the babies?"

"Nay, the babes enjoy it, and it helps them grow."

"Are you going to send me away to that cottage?" she asked, sleep clotting her voice as the tranquil painkiller flooded her system.

"I shall send us both away for a bittock," Ruairidh promised. "I've had enough of Avocamor for the time being. They can finish the debate wi'out me."

"The debate?" she murmured.

"On where the new boundaries should be. We'll not make war on all finmen for Sevin's evilness, but we shallnae be so trusting as we were before. Their place is tae the north away from the People and away from the humans, like mad John, whom they can sae easily control."

"The finwoman was very nice to me," Hexy said. "I want to be sure that she is better."

"We'll find her," Ruairidh promised. "And dinnae fear: The exile will nae be against the finwomen. Any who seek it shall have a place here."

"Thank you," Hexy breathed, sliding the rest of the way into slumber. "I pity them greatly."

"Aye, sae dae we all."

Ruairidh laid a hand on her belly, assuring himself that the babes slept, too. Once satisfied that they were also well, he allowed his own eyes to close and followed her into oblivion.

When Hexy awoke, it was to find Ruairidh dangling a trinket above her, swinging it back and forth like the pendulum in a clock.

"What is that?" she asked, smiling quickly before a yawn chased it away. "They look like pearls, but I've never seen any that color before."

"They are the seeds of midnight," Ruairidh answered, urging her to sit up so he could drop the smoke-colored pearls over Hexy's head. "These are very special pearls—both tae be appreciated and deplored."

"Why?" she asked, touching the pearls once and then snuggling against Ruairidh. The temptation to slide back into slumber was very strong.

"Because I delayed my return tae gather them for ye, and ye had time tae swim tae Wrathdrum."

"Oh." Hexy started to frown as bits of memory returned to her in unpleasant flickers that stung her brain. The salt offered a sort of amnesia, but it was short-lived.

"But it was also there that I spoke tae a skua who was wearing a fine lace bandage, and 'twas he that told me where ye were."

Hexy stiffened as full recollection flooded her. The vision of the finman's crazed, burned face filled her mind. "Ruairidh!"

"Dinnae fret, lass," Ruairidh said, closing his arms about her immediately. He sank a fist into her hair and urged her head back. " 'Tis over. Yer safe."

For a long moment, he stared into her forlorn eyes and then lowered his mouth to hers, determined to take the stain of unhappiness away.

He meant for the kiss to be chaste. But, as always, the act of touching sent breakers of desire rolling through his body. And he could feel her responding, giving in to the pleasure of the kiss and letting the wild tide take her.

Her fingers tangled in his hair, snagged midstroke when pleasure made them fist. She

317

moaned softly and then leaned over and tasted his neck. Pressed heart to heart, he could feel the change in her pulse and the moment when her body began calling to him.

He laid her back upon the bed and returned the favor, kiss for kiss, taste for taste, allowing the flavor of her to send him into divine madness. Down he kissed the median of her body, pausing to run a cheek against the gentle swell of her breasts.

She was fire—the only fire he had ever craved or wanted, for unlike land fire it was a blaze that did not consume. It was eternal. It could be banked for a time, but not entirely snuffed out, so there would always be heat and light between them.

Skin slid over skin, moving with ease. Breaths quickened. Pulses raced. Skin flushed as heat roared through them.

Though his body proclaimed the urgency of joining itself to hers, Ruairidh waited, taking the time to appreciate and savor all the wondrous things that made Hexy what she was.

Her eyes—no summer yet had known such green! The hollows of her cheekbones, the bow of her mouth—they were all miraculous, unique. He kissed, tasted.

Her delicate collarbone, the slender arms, her long fingers that made her hands so graceful and feminine. He kissed them, too, enjoying the different textures beneath his lips, noting the scars where once they had been joined by a web of skin, and finding them beautiful, too.

His pulse hammered at him, crying out its urgency, throbbing even to the tip of his fingers, but he did not hurry. He let his touch tell her in ways that no words could that he found her beautiful, sweet, soft, alluring, and the cause as well as cure for all the sensual hunger he had ever known.

Beneath him she twisted, a fine mist of perspiration sheening her skin in delicate silver. She urged him closer, whimpering when he didn't come to her, then muttering and finally biting his shoulder with only enough restraint to avoid breaking the skin.

"Ruairidh!"

He laughed softly at her complaint, though his blood hammered so hard that he could barely breath and steam rose from his skin into the cooler air and plainly announced his desire.

He curled his hand over her soft hair that guarded her feminine heart, feeling the heat of her desire lick at him. It was not the way of the People to be possessive of women—but he would be possessive. Hexy was his—now and forever more.

He caressed her once and felt her shudder. He recognized the small sunburst of pleasure that exploded within her. They were joined in

319

thought now, a part of her melded into him, and he could feel her wants and needs as though they were his own.

He realized then that she would likely feel the same way he did, that his sensations and desires were her own. He worried for an instant that they might frighten her, so direct and hungry were they. But if she had any fear of him, it did not show.

The sharing of sensation was exquisite, but it peeled away his control, chipping at it until hunger finally overcame restraint and he could wait no more.

Her hands were hot on his skin, but not as incendiary as the fire at the place that called him in. There waited cataclysms, pleasure that was just this side of agony. He pressed into her, giving himself to the fire. Then he rolled and settled her astride his hips.

"Dae as ye will," he urged her, his lips barely able to form words.

She rocked against him, sliding over his aroused flesh and sending ribbons of flame through his body. Her movements grew stronger; she leaned forward as she increased the tempo of their mating dance, driving them both toward conflagration.

A low moan of pleasure came from her lips, and he felt her tightening around him. The world went away in a flash of blinding fire.

* * *

"Are you certain that you forgive me?" she asked later, with a shyness that she knew suggested the lingering doubt she felt. It seemed a strange question to ask when the flush of rapture was still on her body and she gleamed with it in the blue light, but she needed to know.

"Aye. I shall tell ye just what I said tae Keir." Ruairidh's voice was low and serious. "There is nae part of what ye did that requires forgiveness. Whatever the cause, ye went tae Wrathdrum and tae face yer worst fears because ye thought tae save me. Ye were willing to risk yer life tae save mine. That is an act of devotion that nae selkie—and certainly nae finman—has seen in over four hundred seasons. I'd forgive ye anything for that alone."

Hexy blushed and looked down at her shoulder. There was only a small red mark remaining of the finman's wound.

"Look! I am healed!"

"Aye, of course." Ruairidh touched her hair, smoothing it from her face. "The exchange of salt has great healing properties. That is part of why selkies are hunted. I believe it is why Sevin tried tae take the pups and stole our dead. His evil magic was eating him alive. He needed something tae stop it, and he thought that the People were the answer. Of course, he was wrong."

"The salt only heals other selkies?"

"Or the women we love. 'Tis a gift we can give tae our lovers even when we cannae give of ourselves beyond the one year we are allowed at a summoning."

"And have you loved many women?" Hexy asked, eyes courageously steady as she gazed at Ruairidh. "Will there be one every year forever more? Or are there more than one?"

Ruairidh's lips curled into their odd smile, which she found so endearing. His dark eyes glowed softly. "Nay. Looking after the one is quite task enough for me. I doubt that I shall ever need another."

Ducking her head so Ruairidh would not see her disappointment in his reply, Hexy nodded. "That I can well believe. I've always thought the polygamists insane."

"Keir believes he can manage it, but that isnae the life for me. I have my woman. I need nae other."

"I see."

"Dae ye?" he asked, his voice a bit skeptical. "I think that sometimes ye listen but dinnae actually hear what I am saying."

"We'll see how you feel at the end of the year." Not wanting to spoil the moment, Hexy asked hurriedly, "You are certain that the salt is good for the babies?"

She watched as Ruairidh ran a hand over her

silvered skin, tickling her with his clever fingers until she giggled and pushed his hand away.

"Faithless one. Mayhap you'll be assured when the year has come and gone and I am still wi' ye."

"I'm sure I will," Hexy answered.

Archimedes probably hadn't figured out how to calculate pi right away either. She would just have to keep hunting for a solution to her worries.

"Aye, ye will, mistress of doubt. Now, about yer other worries . . . ye need nae be concerned about the salt. It is like mother's milk tae the babes."

"Only not exactly given the same way," she teased back, making every effort to keep the mood light.

"True. I am nae their mother, nor can they suckle from me."

"But I can." Hexy leaned over and inhaled the delicious, slightly sleepy scent of his skin, and then pressed her lips and tongue against his chest.

Ruairidh inhaled sharply. "Aye, you can. But is that wise?"

"Probably not. But being near you has done dreadful things to my brain. In fact, I believe it has gone missing."

"Och! Best we see about finding it again. We cannae hae ye walking about wi'out a brain."

"I suppose not—but let's look later."

Chapter Nineteen

Hexy was very relieved to find that it didn't hurt when Ruairidh sewed up her skin. She had feared that she might have caused him terrible pain with her own meticulous sewing. Mostly the skin seemed able to heal itself once the edges were rejoined, perhaps because the wounds were not magically inflicted. It might also be that it healed quickly because she finally had the right food to eat. The babes had certainly settled into quiet contentment once she consumed sea fruit.

She did not see Keir or Cathair again before the two left on their fishing trip, which suited Hexy. Ruairidh insisted that they understood what had happened with the finman, but Hexy was not so certain that their forgiveness was complete. She was not even certain if Ruairidh's was, because even in the throes of blinding passion when they were sharing senses, he had never spoken of love.

Perhaps, she thought, having no females—not wives or mothers or daughters—they did not know what the emotion could be. Some human cultures, like the Vikings, had no notion of romantic love. It would not be so surprising if the selkies had failed to develop one.

If this was the case, then there was hope that in time Ruairidh could be exposed to this new idea and perhaps embrace it. If that happened, then there was reason to believe his promise to be with her when the year of the summoning was over.

Time would provide answers.

And in the meantime, there was the sea, and joyous euphoria that being in it brought to her body and soul. Or so she prayed. The moment of actually donning her skin and again entering the ocean was more difficult that she had expected.

The cave was talking to them as they neared the great pool and prepared for the transformation. Ruairidh explained that normally this would be done at night, but that he wanted her first return visit to the ocean to be made during the day. And because they were in Avocamor, the change could be made from woman to seal even without the moon.

Hexy paused with her legs only half inside her skin. Her mind was clear this time because neither Ruairidh nor the finmen were influencing her.

She listened, felt and looked with her new rawer senses, taking in the details of the sea and cave that had previously eluded her.

Ruairidh watched her carefully as she sampled the air, neither urging nor discouraging her chosen slow pace.

Her heightened awareness told her many things, but the most important was that her fur was alive and well, and anxious to join itself to her body.

Unable to resist its pleading, she pulled it up slowly, aware of a brief stinging like the swarm of a thousand bees where it touched her skin. But the invisible insects seemed to come with anesthetizing darts, and the pain vanished almost before it was truly formed and the fur pulled in tight against her.

"Ruairidh?" She stopped with the skin gathered about her throat. "Why does it feel different this time?"

"It is because it is still day, Hexy lass, and ye are not pain deadened with salt. There isnae pain when you change on the ninth day or under a full moon." Ruairidh asked her, "Are ye ready, then?"

Hexy nodded and pulled the hood over her head, sinking down to the floor as her body transformed. Fur snugged down over her ears, but instead of muffling her hearing, it suddenly grew more keen.

"Remember, lass, ye willnae be able to talk until yer skin is away."

Hexy nodded again, but she was distracted. She was keenly aware of a distant and eerie ululation that might have been mistaken for the moaning of the damned lost at sea. The unearthly obbligato made her uneasy, and she wondered for the first time if she would be struck by panic—maybe even stricken with the feeling of suffocation that she had known on her last visit into the ocean.

Fur in place, and therefore unable to speak, she turned her eyes to Ruairidh. His own gaze seemed to have lightened to the color of honey, and Hexy wondered if her eyes had changed, too, or if she was a seal marked as unnatural by green eyes. She would have to ask later, or else find a mirror.

The cave gave one last moan and then the sepulchral threnody subsided.

Hexy turned and faced the glowing blue pool. The water seemed less opaque today, and she could see a bright spot where the light of the tunnel leaked in through the blue. It twirled slowly, a kaleidoscope of sunlight that beckoned.

Ruairidh was at her side, touching her gently. His presence was both an encouragement and a shield. She knew that he would understand if she pulled back from the expedition, but she didn't want to disappoint him again.

Taking a last breath, Hexy let herself fall into the deep. Liquid pressed against her eyes, nullifying earthly realities and making her body buoyant.

And all at once everything was as it should be. In an instant, Ruairidh was again at her side. Together they made for the open sea, tails pumping hard, racing through the cool blueness for the sheer joy of it.

Though Ruairidh was supposed to be teaching Hexy to catch fish, they ended up playing a game of tag, chasing in and out among the kelp and racing around the rock formations.

Hexy knew that Ruairidh was allowing her to elude him when it was his turn to give chase. She recalled the speed with which he had attacked the finman and knew that she would never surpass it with her strange seal body that had tufts of long red hair floating at the crown.

When she began to tire, Ruairidh slowed the pace and began leading her toward one of the islets. She wondered at first if they were returning to Wrathdrum, but he turned south before the fishermen's isle and began following a stony ridge that rose higher and higher out of the sloping seabed. They did not swim deep because Hexy needed to rise to the surface every few minutes and replenish her air, but finally Ruairidh reached some destination that required they descend into the murk that swallowed up the bottom of the cliff wall.

Hexy looked a question at him, frustrated that she didn't know how to speak in the selkie tongue, which was all that her mouth and vocal chords could manage while wrapped in fur.

Ruairidh smiled mysteriously, and gestured for her to descend.

Puzzled but intrigued, Hexy took a deep breath and dove for the bottom. Pressure pushed against her tiny ears and wrapped itself about her chest as she descended into the twilight.

The first thing she saw on the seafloor was the tip of an old jar protruding from the thick sedimentary sand. Near it were some half-buried plates and some columns shrouded in barnacles.

Understanding where they were, she slowed her pace, allowing Ruairidh to take the lead. She wondered if he was taking her to see one of the many German ships that had been sunk during the war. The HMS *Strathgarry* and *Hamp-*

shire had both perished in these same waters.

Ruairidh was showing her some of the sea's treasures that she had longed to visit as a child.

As anticipated, a large shape loomed suddenly in the eerie stillness, as big as a small mountain, though its uniform lines proclaimed it as the work of humankind. The perfect symmetry of the vessel was marred on one side where the wooden ribs were stoved in, doubtlessly battered against the undersea cliffs whose cruel pinnacles rose almost to the surface of the water.

Hexy swam closer to the ancient wreck, for some reason relieved that it was not one more recent.

The scar that marked the fatal blow was visible because the ship listed to port, settled on its side in the thick sediment with its damaged belly turned partially toward the sky. The hole had weathered, worn smooth by the ocean's cold hand, and did not seem so horrible now that the splinters were gone. It had about it a certain air of morbid grandeur, somehow managing dignity even in death.

The inside of the hole was filled with dark shadows. There could be treasure inside.

There could also be ghosts.

Hexy shivered at the thought. She had had enough contact with lost spirits. No amount of gold would lure her inside that watery tomb.

Giving Ruairidh a quick smile and a shake of her head, Hexy swam up over the ornamental railing and looked at the one cannon still protruding from the side of the ship. The cold water had kept it from rusting, so she was careful to keep her distance. Her skin might protect her from the effects of cold iron, but she wasn't willing to take the chance that it didn't.

She realized that while lost in timeless reverie, her body had been busy consuming air at its usual pace; it was time for her to head back for the surface. Still, there was one last thing she wanted to know before leaving the derelict to the sea.

Carefully, she traveled the ship's perimeter until she found what she was looking for.

She pointed the name out to Ruairidh, who nodded.

It was called *The Yarmouth*. She knew its history, too. It was one of the ships used by Oliver Cromwell when he attempted to subjugate the MacLeans of Duart back in the 1650s. *The Yarmouth*'s sometimes traveling companion had been *The Swan*, a ship that had been built by Charles I but whose captain had switched allegiance to Cromwell's commonwealth government when it offered better pay. *The Swan* had been lost in the Sound of Mull while transporting soldiers, ammunition and provisions to Duart Castle. It went down during a storm along with *The Margaret of Ipswich*, *The Marthe* and *The Speedwell of Lyn*. *The Yarmouth* had also disappeared en route during the fearsome squall. No one on land was certain where the ship rested; but she knew.

The wrecks had saved Clan MacLean and loosened Cromwell's grip in Scotland.

Ruairidh stayed close to her side until they broke the surface, when he drew her close and used his strong tail to keep them afloat, allowing her a moment to rest.

Grateful, she relaxed into his heat and allowed her tired muscles to go slack. The sea rocked them in its watery cradle.

Feeling more rested, Hexy lifted her head and forced her lips into the odd, curling smile of the seals. Ruairidh jerked his head toward land, asking if she was ready to return.

Hexy looked up at the sky. The sun had wheeled past high noon and was heading for the west. They had about four hours of daylight left.

She had agreed that she needed to go back to Fintry that evening and give some explanation for her sudden departure. Though part of her wanted simply to disappear, she knew that it would not be wise. The selkies did not need any more wild stories told about them. Instead, she would pack up her clothes and move them to the cottage that Ruairidh had arranged for her to live in until the autumn, when they would return to Avocamor.

And packing was a sound notion with strong appeal, because she was heartily sick of the one dress she was wearing when not wrapped inside her skin. Shoes and underclothes were a must as well, her others having been ruined by their long exposure to the sea.

Too, she was finding that she missed Jillian and wanted to say good-bye to her employer. Perhaps she would even agree to the kirk wedding that Ruairidh wanted. That would surely bring Jillian back from Italy, if for no other reason than to try and talk her out of marrying a local lad.

Resigned that their play was over, Hexy nodded and gave a small sigh.

Ruairidh laughed, apparently guessing her thoughts. Rolling her onto her stomach, he let go and started out toward the shore, threading his way between tiny upthrusts of stone.

Hexy followed with less enthusiasm until he suddenly veered off course for Fintry, and set out toward another islet. The gray smudge soon resolved itself into a small outcropping of sheer granite that rose up some thirty feet into the air. It was not an inhabited island. It had no beach at all, no place for a boat to dock. There was only a narrow stone stair cut in the ragged cliff face, which was all but invisible until you were right upon it.

Ruairidh pulled himself out onto the staircase and then tugged his skin down off his face. As soon as the hood was gone, he was able to speak.

Still awkward on land, Hexy joined him on the stone stair and also pulled her fur back from her head. It parted only very reluctantly, and the salt wind on her skin stung like a hornet's fury.

"What is this place?" she asked through gritted teeth.

"It is called Lilligarry and was built by monks of St. Ninian. They used it as a home for recluses. But is was tae inhospitable for most men, even holy ones, and was abandoned thousands of seasons ago. The People have used it since then when they had need of a place on shore. It shall be our home for a while, if ye like."

"Can we go see it?"

"Well . . ." Ruairidh's expression was doubtful. "Ye mayn't put off yer skin until darkfall, not when we are away from Avocamor. The pain would be tae great."

Hexy looked up the steep stairs. It was wide enough to accommodate her body. She wouldn't be graceful hauling herself up the narrow stairs, but it wasn't all that far to the top, and she was terribly curious about what her new home would be like.

"Let's try it."

"As ye wish." Ruairidh reached over and kissed her quickly, and then pulled her skin back in place. Only then did he see to his own fur.

Turning easily, he started up the stairs.

Hexy took note of his style of locomotion and did her best to copy him.

They soon arrived at the top of the islet, and Hexy could see the stony abode that waited there. It was tiny and square, and had a steep pitched roof with very small windows and a narrow door that sat above the plain balustraded stair that served as a porch. The architecture was what you would expect of a recluse's cell and was, in a word, bleak.

Yet there was loveliness here as well, for some time in the past, some lover of beauty had brought flowers to the island, lilies and orchids and one wild, climbing honeysuckle that had rampaged over the building and smothered it with gay garlands that perfumed the air.

There were also small statues in the garden, mermaids and a miniature Poseidon—or perhaps it was the Celtic sea god, Damnu.

The venerable monks would have fainted in distress at such frivolous paganism, but Hexy found it lovely beyond all expectation.

Hexy sighed, this time with happiness. She leaned over and touched noses with Ruairidh.

"Thank you," she tried to say, but the words wouldn't form.

Smiling, he tickled her with his whiskers, telling her that he understood and was glad that she liked her new home.

Chapter Twenty

Hexy looked back from the altar, prepared at last to say her vows, or receive blessings, or do whatever it was that Ruairidh and the People asked of her.

The chapel of the fishnets was still austere, even with the boards pulled off the windows, but that did not come as any great surprise. The building was not a normal church. It had no decorative belfry. It had no bell. There was no cross or statues, no communion tokens, or wafers, or chalice.

But somehow the square bulk was almost pretty today, a symbol of something eternal, though Hexy suspected that it would soon be a ruin if no one intervened to save it. Wood and sandstone did not weather well—not unless the stone was transformed into glass, as it had been at Avocamor.

She sighed. Avocamor would have been her first choice for such a ceremony, but of course their non-selkie guests could not have attended. And that would have been a shame, for the assemblage was one worth seeing. The colorful guests that filled the church more than compensated for the gray of the plain wood and nude stone that made up the building.

How it had been cleansed of the finman's presence Hexy did not know, but all traces of that evil taint were gone. In its place was an equally strong feeling, one of bubbling magic that fizzed like champagne as the various creatures' auras collided and refracted their special magics back into the room. So distracting was this rainbow of personalities that one hardly noticed the odd and sometimes ancient and ill-fitting human clothing that they had donned for the occasion.

The finwoman, Syr—one of the last to arrive—had introduced herself to the assembly and was warmly received by the younger selkie males, especially by Ruairidh's cousin, Domnach, who had finally healed from his fight with the finmen.

Jillian, minus Donny, was also in attendance,

and was—as ever—surrounded by handsome bodies, so thick in numbers that Hexy had had only one brief glimpse of the stunning Worth creation she was wearing before it was obscured by a wall of muscled flesh.

What had at first been most amusing to Hexy was that among Jillian's many admirers was a smitten Keir, who was wandering around with her mink stole, looking a bit as if he had been sandbagged. She hoped that he had been hit hard enough that a good deal of the native arrogance had been knocked out of him. It would make her brother-in-law a better, or at least more pleasant, person if he finally were humbled by love—or at least intense longing.

A truly unexpected but welcomed guest was Ruairidh's mother, Irial. The lovely fey, with her ankle-length golden hair and silvered eyes, had been sought out immediately on her arrival by her stunned sons and her very pleased one-time lover. Her presence was Cathair's gift to his son.

Ruairidh and Keir had soon been pulled away by other obligations and distractions, but Cathair had firmly remained at her side, not touching, but his posture protective when anyone neared her.

Yet caution seemed unnecessary. None of their guests were discomposed at having a faerie in their midst. The wonder of the occasion—of actually meeting a *NicnanRon*—was overwhelming. And perhaps some of the old prejudices had faded with the long peace among the *sidhe*.

Hexy was more nervous than anyone about meeting Irial. Though as a *NicnanRon* she was supposedly an object of wonder in her own right, it seemed a small thing next to seeing a real faerie. Surely no one had ever had such a lovely or mysterious mama-in-law—and this woman would be her babies' grandmother.

"Ready, *aroon?*" Ruairidh asked, touching her sleeve and recalling her to the practical present.

Hexy nodded, looking up at her husband-to-be and smiling at his serious face.

"Ye look beautiful," he whispered.

"Jillian brought me the dress," Hexy whispered, smoothing a hand down the almost nude chiffon confection made in a shade of blush and sewn over with icy crystals that captured and broke the sunlight into rainbow segments that shimmered around her.

Ruairidh shook his head. "It isnae the dress that makes ye bonny," Ruairidh answered, taking her hand in his and turning her to face the officiant. The man who was presiding over the ceremony was Aon, the eldest of the selkies in Ruairidh's clan. Aon did not look like Ruairidh or Cathair. He had the same ageless skin of all the selkies, but he had a complete absence of facial and cranial hair. His bald pate gleamed like the button of his double-breasted jacket, which also sported several rows of naval decorations, honors to which Hexy was fairly certain he was not legitimately entitled. She could only hope that, if the coat was recently purloined, none of the human guests would recognize it.

Aon hummed once, the sound having the timbre of a horn, and the assembly quieted. Ruairidh and Hexy turned to face each other and joined hands. Worry and frivolous thought fell momentarily away as she gazed into his eyes.

"Most blessed of my brothers from the sea of Domnu, and sisters of the dry lands and northern waters, draw near and witness the miracle. The *NicnanRon* is returned tae the People and conciliation with nature and with man may begin." Aon's voice was beautiful and clear.

From the corner of her eye, Hexy could see Jillian frown in puzzlement and turn to question Keir. Admittedly, this sermon was not standard Church of England fare. It wasn't even Scottish Free Kirk, but she didn't think there needed to be any long explanations that involved Keir cupping Jillian's dainty ear and stroking a finger down her neck. Most likely, Jillian wouldn't recall the ceremony at all.

Aon hummed again, and Hexy turned her

attention back to Ruairidh, listening to Aon's blessing.

"May grace pour over the union and amply warm our brother and his mate as they journey intae a new life, and may the joy they have given tae us be returned tae their bosom sevenfold." There was a soft murmuring hum in answer to this that sounded like a chorus of gentle reeds.

"We gather here tae acknowledge this act of divine kindness and tae give our own humble blessings tae this miracle—this revival of our flesh and blood, this revival of hope that the *NicnanRon* brings. The People shall live still."

Ruairidh's eyes glowed gently and Hexy could feel her own eyes fill with tears. The moment would have been perfect, if only there had been some mention of love.

"All health and blessing upon ye. May the seeds of this act of divine charity find fertile ground and bring prosperity to ye in abundance. This I wish for ye both. Gae now and receive the blessings of yer clan and kin, and may the strength of yer union shine forth as a beacon for the People."

Ruairidh leaned over and brushed his lips against Hexy's, drawing a cheer like a blast of horns from the assembly, which shook the little chapel. A tempest of strange atonal vowels filled the air. And at the windows there was a great fluttering of birds' wings, as though the avians who had come to witness the ceremony were also applauding.

Turning, with hands still linked, Hexy and Ruairidh faced their guests. In front was Jillian, wide-eyed but smiling, applauding enthusiastically. But something about her had changed. Hexy recognized the look she wore. It was the slightly unfocused gaze of one lost to some otherworldly attraction.

Keir had a hand resting on her neck, and he wore a smug expression on his face as he lounged beside her. The placement of his limb on Jillian's nape suggested to Hexy the classic selkie seduction maneuver.

Hexy scowled. The move might be a classic among selkies and their usual village prey, but Jillian had not read many erotic classics—and certainly none about mythical seducers from the sea. Under normal circumstances, Hexy would have backed Jillian to win against any marauding male. But she knew for herself how ineffectual one's best efforts could be when a selkie got serious about his wooing. They could be very sweet, but they were also ruthless.

"Ruairidh," she began.

"I see it. But there isnae harm in it. He is just amusing himself."

"Ha! He probably wants Fintry."

"Naebody wants Fintry. And Father shall watch out for her. Now come greet our guests."

Hexy had to admit that this was probably true, but she still planned on speaking to Jillian as soon as the opportunity presented itself. Not that she would have much hope of dispelling Jillian's attraction to Keir as long as he was luring her with salt. And Cathair seemed more than a little distracted from his duties as host by the shimmering presence that was Irial.

Perhaps some yew in Jillian's pocket would do the trick. Or a little yew tucked into Keir's cast-off skin. If he put it on without noticing, it would itch like poison ivy and distract him from his plans.

It was quite a while before they could get away from their guests and return to the peace of their island cottage, but the homecoming was a beautiful one.

Someone had been there before them, filling the house with flowers and candles—dozens of them that flickered in a small galaxy of hot stars. There were tall tapers stuck into bottles and candlestick holders, and shorter, fatter candles guttering in saucers and jars placed on the table and the small mantel above the unused fireplace.

"Ruairidh," she breathed, feeling the tiny points of flame reaching across the room to tickle her naked flesh. "It's beautiful."

"Aye." He drew in a breath and then said with

surprise, "It was Keir. 'Tis he who left this present for us."

"Truly? Then I shall have to thank him later." Hexy hung her skin on a peg near the door. Unlike Ruairidh's fur, which dried the instant he came on land, hers always had to drip-dry.

"I hope ye will, *aroon*. I believe that he is ready tae make peace wi' ye now."

Hexy thought about the way Keir had hovered over Jillian and balanced it against the beautiful gift of much-loathed fire he had left for them. "We'll see. In any event, I shall certainly thank him for arranging this."

Ruairidh sighed theatrically. "I should insist," he said, running a finger down her neck and causing her to shiver. "But I must admit that I hae other matters preying on my mind."

"On your mind?" she asked, turning to look at Ruairidh's gleaming flesh, which shone like honey in the candlelight. His body had begun to stir. Entranced by his beauty as she always was, Hexy reached for her husband. "I fear that your organs have been disarranged. Or is your anatomy so different from my own?"

Ruairidh's arms closed about her, pulling her tight against him. His tumescence was pressed between them. "I'm nae different than any other man. It is just that as a lassie, ye cannae understand."

"Oh, I understand," she answered, smiling up

at him. "It's really very simple—only one moving part."

"I think I'd best remind ye of the importance of that *part.*" Ruairidh scooped her up and headed for their bed.

"By all means, remind me," Hexy answered, then laughed into Ruairidh's beautiful eyes.

"Wi' pleasure, *aroon.*"

Epilogue

Before the first bad storm of late autumn Hexy and Ruairidh returned to Avocamor. On the last day in their cottage, Hexy burned a small branch of rowan, since it was supposed to keep away any evil from a home for the space of a year.

Ruairidh had been concerned about Hexy growing bored in Avocamor without female companionship, but his concerns proved groundless. Until the time of her confinement she was able to make visits to the village, and she also had two frequent female visitors: Syr and Irial. There was no teary tempest of argument about spending the winter there.

347

In the beginning Ruairidh and Keir found it very odd to face their mother, especially as she again shared Cathair's bed when she visited. But since she was not at all sentimental, and did not show any desire to be addressed by any title other than her name, they were soon able to put themselves at ease and enjoy her very non-maternal presence.

Syr was a stranger creature by far than Irial, her mood and expression somber. But she was slowly learning to laugh in Domnach's company, and all of Avocamor was hoping for another productive union.

A new treaty was made with the finmen, with their territory set to the extreme north of Hildaland, and there was celebrating in Avocamor because war had been avoided. And the People's joy was increased when three other finwomen asked to stay with them—and they were allowed to.

Though Hexy said nothing to Ruairidh about the passing of time and what the land calendar said of the date, he nevertheless knew when it was the season of Yule, and with the help of his brother, they were able to drag a small pine tree down to Avocamor.

What Cathair and Keir truly thought of this strange decoration, Hexy never knew. But they brought her strings of pearls and pretty shells to decorate it with. They also came in for each of the twelve days of Christmas to sing and play the clarsach for her. At first, the primitive harp had sounded odd, because it could play no sharps or flats, but gradually an appreciation for the beauty of selkie music grew in her and she came to love it passionately, and asked Cathair to teach her how to play.

Her lessons had to be delayed for a while, though, because it was on Twelfth Night that their children chose to enter the world. As she had known, almost from the beginning, the babes were two beautiful girls. They had their mother's red hair but their father's beautiful eyes.

Hexy's labor was an easy one, since Ruairidh was there with numbing salts and Irial was nearby in case she needed stronger healing magic.

The girls were called Catriona and Mairi, knowing that on land they would be Catherine and Mary.

Avocamor again rejoiced and there was another celebration, which involved consuming a great deal of a strange species of fish. Hexy passed up much of the mealtime offerings. Once she was no longer pregnant, the appeal of raw fish had left her.

The winter was a happy one, but as soon as the weather moderated, Hexy and Ruairidh took the children back to the island cottage, where they would not be visited daily by curious selkie and finfolk.

Not that they were permitted to go for many days in a row without visitors. Irial and Syr came regularly, and a week after they were settled, Jillian arrived at the cottage escorted by Keir.

Jillian's expression was dreamy and Keir's defiant, but Hexy did not say anything while they were all together.

Her former employer brought what she imagined to be appropriate baby gifts, though when the girls would have occasion to wear such delicate ruffled gowns Hexy could not imagine. Still, the gesture was well meant, and both Hexy and Ruairidh were sincere in their thanks.

It surprised Hexy to see how good Jillian was with the babies, for nothing in their former relationship had led her to suppose that Jillian had had any experience with infants. But whatever the reason, past experience or natural aptitude, Jillian had a knack for making the girls smile.

Hexy bided their time until there was a natural occasion to speak to Jillian alone. But once they had their privacy over the tea things, she broached the subject of Keir's attentions.

She was quite shocked when Jillian giggled at her warning. She had expected indignation, or perhaps fear, but she had never anticipated laughter.

"Of course he was out to seduce me, darling. He has been for months. Don't think that I didn't make him wait for a good long while—and bring some lovely gifts, too." Jillian touched the strand of pink pearls that hung from her neck and then went back to setting out cups and saucers.

"And you weren't surprised at the different—um—" Hexy tried to think of a way of asking about their making love without being crude.

"Yes, I was!" Her lovely eyes widened, but her mouth was mischievous. "But, darling, that is half the fun. What other man could actually drive you mad?"

"Well, frankly, Donny's talk of cars was enough to drive me mad," Hexy joked.

A dimple peeped in Jillian's cheek.

"Mad with *passion*, I meant."

"None that I know of," Hexy admitted, trying not to smile. "But Jillian, this is serious. Did he explain about—about children?"

Jillian gave a trill of laughter. "You are too precious. Darling, I've known for ages about how not to have children!" Jillian's expression suddenly grew sober. "Until now, I've never considered having any. I mean, the inconvenience is almost unimaginable."

Just then Ruairidh and Keir returned to the

cottage. Hexy gathered up the tea tray and led the way back to the front of the cottage, which functioned as the parlor. Setting the delicate pot down with care, she leaned toward her brother-in-law and whispered, "I want a word with you later."

Keir nodded, looking both rueful and resigned.

Hexy didn't have another opportunity to speak privately to Keir that day, but she did extract a promise of a return visit on the morrow. Ruairidh's unusually serious expression told Hexy that he had already either guessed or been told by Keir about his relationship with Jillian.

"We're alone," Ruairidh said, lifting a hand in farewell to the rowboat that bore their visitors away. "And the bairns are sleeping."

"Yes, they are," Hexy agreed, dropping her honeysuckle bouquet and slipping an arm about Ruairidh's waist. She turned to face him. "Jillian was just reminding me about a particular virtue of the selkie."

"Aye. She values her fresh fish, then, does she?" He wrapped his arms about his wife and held her loosely.

"Um . . . no."

"If it isnae his skills of fishery, then 'tis his knack for finding pearls, is it nae?"

"No—well, perhaps that is a bit of it," she

352

admitted. "But it isn't the main attraction."

"Nay?"

"No." Hexy's hands crept under Ruairidh's shirt. "What she likes best is being . . . driven mad with passion."

"That's what she likes best?" Ruairidh feigned surprise. "What a strange lass she is, tae be sure."

Hexy pinched him.

"I should not in the least mind being driven mad with passion," she added. "At least for a little while."

"Well, there shall be nae more passion for ye until ye've consulted yer calendar," Ruairidh answered firmly.

Hexy blinked.

"Why should I consult the calendar?" she asked, confused.

"Because I want ye tae make note of the fact that a year and two days has passed since we were joined and that I am still wi' ye."

"So you are," Hexy answered, a wonderful smile dawning. "But that is an excellent reason for a bit of madness."

"Aye, it is," Ruairidh agreed, bending at the knees and scooping her up in his arms. "I just wanted ye tae make note of it."

"It is duly noted."

"And also, for the record, I love ye, *aroon*."

Hexy blinked back sudden tears.

"And I love yôu, too, Ruairidh."

"Good. Then I am all for a bittock of madness myself," he answered happily, as they disappeared inside their cottage.

Author's Note

Unlike *Night Visitor*, whose faeries were comparatively easy to investigate, there is not a great deal of information available about the selkies of Scotland. To any of their descendents, I make apologies for deficiencies of fact about their culture, language, etc. I hope a vivid imagination has somewhat compensated for the lack of concrete information.

The Selkie is set at an odd time for romance novels. Not much has been written about Scotland in the 1920s, probably because it was a bleak era; people were recovering from the first World War. There were many exciting things about this era, though, which made it ideal for this story. Aside from having fun with the clothes and early MG roadsters, the time period also allowed for the introduction of the beginnings of technology and medical enlightenment—mainly a knowledge of allergies and the telephone, which were very useful plot devices.

In addition to the resources listed below, I had input from readers and friends. My finmen—Sevin, Turpin and Brodir—were all named by readers. And I want to thank Nikki from Horrorlit for being especially helpful with matters of traveling circuses in Great Britain.

While saying thanks, there are two other people I need to mention: my good friend Lynsay Sands and my long-suffering agent Helen. Writers—though happy with their solitary careers—sometimes need a cheering section, and these two have always generously supplied it. (NOTE: My editor is long-suffering, too, but he has been given his own dedication in another book. And besides, I already apologized for that joke about the heroine giving birth to a litter of seal pups.)

Welcome to my version of 1929 Scotland. The pleasure of your company on these adventures is always special. Hope you enjoyed the visit.

—Melanie Jackson

Resource List:

The Rites of Odin by Ed Fitch
A Dictionary of Ghost Lore by Peter Haining
The World Guide to Gnomes, Fairies, Elves and Other Little People by Thomas Keightly
Scottish Ghost Stories by Elliott O'Donnell
The Ghost Book by Alsadair Alpine MacGregor
Oicheanta Si (Faery Nights) by Michael mac Liammoir
Cornish Faeries by Robert Hunt
Ireland by Richard Lovett
And special thanks to Deborah Anne Mac-Gillivray of W.I.S.E.
http://mars.ark.com/~ramsay/selkies.htm

http://www.orkneyjar.com/folklore/finfolk/
index.html
http://www.fortunecity.com/rivendell/
chronos/254/merrow.html
http://www.legends.dm.net/fairy/sel-
chies.html
http://userpages.umbc.edu/~dgovar1/selk-
ies.html
http://www.contemplator.com/folk.html